Nine

Jane Blythe

Bear Spots Publications
Melbourne Australia

bearspotspublications@gmail.com

Paperback
ISBN: 0-6484033-6-X
ISBN-13: 978-0-6484033-6-4

Cover designed by QDesigns

I'd like to thank everyone who played a part in bringing this story to life. Particularly my mom who is always there to share her thoughts and opinions with me. My awesome cover designer, Amy, who whips up covers for me so quickly and who patiently makes every change I ask for, and there are usually lots of them! And my lovely editor Mitzi Carroll, and proofreader Marisa Nichols, for all their encouragement and for all the hard work they put into polishing my work.

MARCH 3RD

2:12 A.M.

Desperation to get a date to her senior prom was going to get her killed.

Literally.

Her ninety-nine hours were almost up.

Ally Brown tried to stretch her sore, cramped body, but there wasn't really much room for that. The plastic zip tie that circled her left wrist kept it secured to a pipe. The pipe ran along one of the basement walls and was attached with several metal brackets spaced about a foot apart. When they had restrained her, they'd left her sitting down, meaning the only way she could stand up was to bend over. As uncomfortable as standing hunched over was, she tried to do it every couple of hours just to stretch out, her bottom was sore from so many days spent sitting on the cold concrete floor and any break was welcome.

She hadn't realized plastic was so durable.

At first, she'd spent hours trying to break it, using her ring— her grandmother's engagement ring that her nana had given her on her deathbed because she was the only granddaughter—to try to saw through it. When that failed, she'd tried to break the zip tie by pulling it as hard as she could—the only thing that achieved was making the sharp plastic cut into her flesh. After that, she'd tried rubbing the zip tie up and down against the pipe, but that had done no good either. In the end, all she had to show for her hours and hours of work was a bloody wrist and several missing layers of skin.

Now, she didn't bother trying to get free.

1

She had accepted that she wasn't going anywhere.

Even if she could somehow manage to get out of the zip tie, she doubted she would get far. You didn't kidnap someone and tell them you were going to kill them in ninety-nine hours and then not make sure they were safely locked away.

Ally contemplated screaming again, but she already knew it would do no good.

There was no one to hear her screams.

She had the raw throat to prove it.

No one could hear her.

No one was coming.

No one would save her.

According to the timer on the wall, she had exactly three minutes and forty-one seconds left.

Sitting here for the last four days watching the hours and minutes and seconds tick down toward her death had been odd.

A weird choice of words, perhaps, but it was the only word that completely summed it up.

It had been terrifying, of course, and it had filled her with hopelessness. She'd felt powerless and angry and sad, and yet, having a solid understanding of the outcome had also been comforting, in some way.

Her fate was sealed.

From the second she'd been thrown into the back of the van, this was always going to be how things would end.

There was nothing she could do to change it.

The timer counting steadily down was proof of that.

Knowing what was coming took away some of her fear. She didn't have to worry about what was going to happen to her.

That brought about a measure of acceptance.

Just because she had accepted her fate didn't mean she wasn't terrified about how she was going to die. Would she be tortured? Would her death be fast or slow? Were they going to rape her before they killed her?

So far, other than locking her up here, no one had laid a finger on her. He brought her meals twice a day and made sure she had plenty of water to drink. She'd even been given a blanket, so she didn't get too cold.

She was an eighteen-year-old girl, and okay, she wasn't the most beautiful girl around, but she wasn't horrid, either. If she wasn't here so they could rape her, then why was she here?

If it wasn't to do anything to her before they killed her, then it had to be for the kill itself.

Ally was trying not to think about it too much, but sometimes, she couldn't help it—those thoughts just crept in.

Shot?

Stabbed?

Strangled?

Why were there so many ways to kill someone that all started with S?

Maybe there was something jinxed about that letter?

It made sense. There had been an S in the message.

Was that why she was here?

Ally sighed.

She was losing her mind. If she was contemplating the possibility that she was here just because of a letter of the alphabet, then she had to be. Maybe she wouldn't have to worry about how she was going to be murdered; perhaps she would lose her mind first.

Two minutes and eleven seconds left.

Although she knew it wouldn't help, she tugged again on the zip tie. If she could just get free, she at least stood a chance. Sure, she suspected the door at the top of the stairs would be locked, but maybe it wasn't. Maybe her abductor was confident enough in the plastic tie that they didn't think she could get free so hadn't bothered to lock the door.

Really, she didn't care. Even the chance that she could get away was worth it.

Ally yanked as hard as she could, but the thing wouldn't budge.

"Aarrggghhh," she screeched at the top of her lungs as she flung her hand back and forth as hard and fast as she could.

For a moment, she lost her mind.

All she did was scream and thrash and yank on the pipe.

In the end, exhaustion had her falling silent. Even with the bread, water, and fruit she'd eaten over the last four days, just sitting here seemed to have sapped away her strength. Like it had seeped out of her and into the concrete she had been sitting on.

Her wrist was bleeding.

Blood.

It was so red.

One minute.

She heard the sound of a key sliding into a lock.

Footsteps.

Someone was coming.

Ally couldn't take her eyes off the blood.

She liked the color red.

Her prom dress was red.

In a way, that seemed fitting since it was the reason she was here. If she hadn't been so desperate to find a date, she'd be home safe and sound, asleep in her own bed in her own room in her own home, instead of tied up in a basement about to be murdered.

"It's time, Ally."

She heard the voice, but she didn't look away from her bloody wrist.

Death was blood.

Blood was red.

Red was death.

She liked red.

If she liked red and red was death, then how bad could death really be?

It had really happened.

She'd lost her mind.

Was she really thinking that death couldn't be all that bad just because her favorite color was red?

Ally had expected that when the time came, he would cut the zip tie and remove her from the basement to take her to wherever he planned on killing her.

At the back of her mind, it had been her last chance. When he took her out of here, she would run or scream or fight or do whatever she could to get away.

Maybe she *hadn't* really accepted her fate.

Maybe, instead, she had just been biding her time waiting for this very opportunity.

Only, it seemed like this opportunity was never going to eventuate.

Slowly, she turned her head and lifted her eyes to look up at him.

He was big and tall, and in his hands, he held a bucket.

He was going to kill her with a bucket?

That made no sense.

He bent down to kneel beside her, and water sloshed over the sides of the bucket.

Her gaze fixed on the puddle.

A puddle.

Water.

She didn't need to be a genius to figure out what was going to happen next.

Ally looked up, her eyes met his, something passed between them. Knowledge of what was happening, anger and disbelief on her part, determined indifference on his.

He didn't care that he was about to take her life. Perhaps he had taken others before hers; she was sure he would take more after. He wasn't going to feel remorse for this. Whatever his reasons, he was happy and confident in his decisions.

Beep, beep, beep, beep, beep.

The alarm went off.

It was time.

Ally briefly debated begging for her life, but she sensed it wasn't going to do any good. She didn't know what purpose her death would serve in this man's life, but he was obviously doing this for a reason.

He didn't speak, just roughly grabbed hold of her and dragged her onto her knees. His hand was large and tangled in her waist-length brown hair as he clamped it around the back of her head and shoved her downwards and into the water.

Instinct had her lips pressing together, preventing water from flooding her lungs.

She fought, she thrashed, but it did no good.

She held her breath for as long as she could, but eventually, her lungs forced her to try to take a breath.

Instead of air, all they got was water.

Ally fought against it. She tried to close her mouth again; she tried to fight the inevitable; she tried to find oxygen where there was none; she tried to fight her attacker.

Death came slowly.

She hadn't realized that it took so long to drown someone.

Her struggles grew weaker, the world grew dimmer, scenes from her life floated lazily through her mind.

Then she was floating too.

In a haze of fluffy white.

She floated away.

* * * * *

6:43 A.M.

Detective Ryan Xander hated these cold winter mornings.

Oppressive gray clouds unrelentingly filled the sky, blocking the sun for so many days on end that it was beginning to make him forget what it looked like. Day after day of icy winds, sleet, and snow, made climbing out of bed each morning harder and harder.

He was ready for spring.

It had been a long and unpleasant winter, and he was hoping that when the warmer weather came, things would start to improve.

There was one thing he hated more than cold mornings.

His eyes fell on Ally Brown's body.

The girl had been dumped on her own front doorstep, where she had been found by her mother about an hour ago.

"I know Ally," his partner, Detective Paige Hood, said quietly, also staring at the dead teenager. "Hayley was tutoring her in biology."

Paige's daughter was only fifteen, but Hayley was brilliant, and he wasn't surprised to hear that she had been tutoring a senior even though she was just a sophomore.

"What do you know about Ally?" he asked. Although his daughter Sophie was the same age as Hayley and the girls had gone to the same school as Ally, he hadn't ever met or heard of her before.

"She was a quiet girl who struggled to fit in. She didn't have many friends, and although she worked hard and studied a lot, she didn't make good grades. I spoke with her parents about a month ago about Hayley tutoring her in a couple of other subjects because her mother was worrying that she wasn't going to get accepted to any colleges with her current grades. I guess it doesn't matter now, though."

"No, it doesn't," he agreed. Just a week ago, Ally's biggest problem had been college admissions; now, she was dead. Life could change in a second. Something he knew all too well from his own experience. This time last year, he would never have expected his family to have become what it was now.

"I can't imagine what it was like for her mother to find her like this." Paige's brown eyes were stricken. He knew his own must be too. They were both parents, and they were both imagining themselves in Hilary Brown's position.

Ally was dressed in a slinky black dress and stilettos. Her long brown hair, which reached her waist, was tucked under her body, and she looked like she'd been posed. Her arms were spread wide, and her legs were together and bent at the knees. She was arranged on her back, facing the front door. When Hilary Brown opened the door, the first thing she would have seen was her daughter's lifeless face.

For a moment, hope may have had her believing that Ally was still alive. That she was just drunk or drugged and had passed out. But as soon as she looked closer, she would have seen the empty, glassy look of death in her daughter's eyes, and her skin's complete lack of color.

Still, Hilary had probably clung to hope as she ran to her child, touched her, felt her icy cold skin, searched for a pulse, checked to see if she was breathing. Although she would have fought against it, eventually, reality would have sunk in, and she would have realized that her daughter was dead.

A horrible ending to a horrific four-day ordeal.

Any hope that her daughter had merely become a runaway like thousands of teens across the country had evaporated.

Ally hadn't just run away because she didn't like her parents' rules or because of some boy or because she had done something she regretted. She had been kidnapped and murdered.

"You think she has one?" Paige asked.

He knew what his partner was asking about without her having to go into details, and unfortunately, yes, he did think that Ally had one. "We won't know for sure until Jenny gets here and checks the body." Jenny Buckley was the new medical examiner, and she was working this case with them. Once she got here and photographs of the body had been taken, she'd be able to move Ally and confirm that she had the tattoo, but Ryan already knew that she did.

"How did the killer dump her body without anyone seeing anything?" Paige asked, her eyes still fixed on Ally's body.

"Dumped her early while everyone was still in bed asleep. It's winter, less likely that anyone would be out jogging or walking their dogs."

"It's still pretty cocky," she said, finally tearing her gaze away from the teenager to survey the neighborhood. "This is a residential neighborhood. I can see five front doors just from this spot, not including the houses on either side of the Browns', or the one behind it. That's a lot of people. Any one of them could have been up for any number of reasons; it was pretty risky to come and leave the body here. Especially *right* here. For all he knew, Ally's parents were awake inside, yet he probably parked in their driveway and spent at least a couple of minutes getting the body out and onto the porch and arranged the way he wanted it."

His partner was right; this killer was brimming with confidence. *Over*confidence. He didn't believe that he was going to get caught, so he was happy to take as many risks as he needed to so long as he achieved his intended goal.

And one of his goals appeared to be inflicting as much pain as possible to Ally's family.

"Leaving Ally here was cold," Ryan said. "He could have dumped her body anywhere. A park, the side of a road, an alley, he could have buried her in a shallow grave, or he could have burned her. And yet, he didn't do any of those things. He brought her here—to her house—and left her on the doorstep. He wanted her to be found, and he wanted her family to be the ones to find her."

"Maybe this isn't just about Ally; maybe it's about the whole family."

"Maybe," he agreed. Right now, he didn't really see any clear motive. "We need to talk to Ally's parents, see what they can tell us."

"No coat," Paige said.

"What?"

"She's dressed up like she's out on a date, but it's March. It was snowing yesterday, and she isn't wearing a coat."

"Maybe the killer chose this outfit."

"We can ask Hilary if the dress and shoes are Ally's or not."

Both of them lingered on the porch for a moment longer, neither really wanting to enter the house and speak with the mother who had just lost her only daughter.

With a loud sigh, Paige turned and stepped over Ally's body and through the front door. With a sigh of his own, Ryan followed.

They found Hilary and her husband Yul in the lounge room. With the front door open, the house was cold, and Hilary was wrapped in a blanket as she sat huddled in the corner of the couch. Yul stood over by the window looking out, but he immediately turned to face them when they entered the room. Yul was Hilary's third husband; the first had been Ally's father, and they had divorced when Ally was three. Hilary married again just after her daughter's fifth birthday, but her second husband died six years later. Two years later she married Yul, and the couple had been together for the last five years.

He and Paige would look into both Ally's biological father, who hadn't been in her life since he left, and her stepfather. It was the nature of murder. The people closest to the victim were always the first to be investigated.

"I'm so sorry, Hilary." Paige went to Hilary and hugged her.

"I ... this ... it doesn't ... doesn't feel real," Hilary mumbled as she returned Paige's hug with one arm and blotted at her teary eyes with her other hand.

"I'm sorry. Ally was a good kid, and I can't imagine what you're going through right now, but we need to ask you a few questions." Paige sat beside Hilary on the couch. Ryan took a seat on the couch opposite, and Yul remained by the window.

"Mrs. Brown, the dress Ally was wearing, do you know if it was hers?" he asked.

"It was. She bought it when she started high school, to wear on dates, only she never got a chance to wear it," Hilary replied.

Ally was eighteen—that she had never been out on a date seemed odd. His daughter had gone on her first date when she was thirteen, and over the last two years, they'd slowly increased her dating privileges. From hanging out at the house with her boyfriend, or at his home with his parents, to afternoon dates at the mall, to dinners and movies, his little girl was growing up way too fast.

"How did Ally feel about not being asked out?" he asked, although he could guess. He'd been a teenager once, but he wanted to get her mother's take on it and any specifics she knew.

"It made her feel that she wasn't beautiful, that she wasn't popular, that she wasn't worthy. She was determined to find a date to her senior prom, it was all she talked about since last summer."

That Ally had been found in the dress she had bought specifically for dating—as well as being obsessed with getting a date to the prom—seemed to be connected to her death somehow.

"Ally snuck out of the house the night she disappeared. Do you have any idea who she was meeting?" Paige asked.

"No," Hilary cried.

Ryan looked at Yul, and he also shook his head.

"Could it have been a boy?" he asked.

"I guess, but I have no idea who it would be. We were close, but not close like that. We didn't talk about her love life."

"Do you remember anyone hanging around the house or your daughter's school? Did Ally receive any messages, emails, phone calls that seemed unusual? Was there any unusual activity on any of her social media?" Ryan asked.

"I don't remember seeing anyone around here who shouldn't

have been, but I don't really pay any attention to her social media. She's eighteen, I trusted her to make good decisions. She doesn't have a lot of friends, and I thought she was too smart to fall for any of those men who tried to lure kids. We talked to her about it when we first got her a cell phone. I told her that she should only ever talk to people she knew in real life. I made a mistake, didn't I? I should have paid closer attention to what she was doing online."

Although he wouldn't say it out loud, the answer was *yes*.

It had been a mistake on Hilary's part not to pay closer attention to her daughter's social media. He monitored Sophie and Ned's daily.

Ally might have been smart enough to know not to talk with any men she didn't know, but she was also desperate.

That desperation made her vulnerable.

And someone had taken advantage of her vulnerability.

* * * * *

8:51 A.M.

This was the best day of her life.

In her fourteen years, she'd never been this excited. Christmases, birthdays, family vacations, none of them even came close to today.

Brianna Lester did her best to contain her excitement; she didn't want to draw any undue attention to herself.

She had never done anything like this before. If her parents caught wind of it, they were going to be mad. *Really* mad. More like off the charts furious.

But only if she got caught.

And she had no intention of getting caught.

She couldn't deny she was a little apprehensive though. She was a good kid, she worked hard in school, and she had never,

ever cut class for anything. Even as a high school freshman, she took her studies seriously. She wanted to keep her grades up so she could go to college on a basketball scholarship. She wanted to play professional basketball when she grew up, and then, when she got too old to play, she wanted to work in sports medicine. To do that, she had to work hard, and she did, every day, but today was different.

Today was special.

Today was the last day of her childhood and the first day of her life as a woman.

She had never been on a date before. Her parents thought she was too young, and always told her to focus on basketball and her schoolwork. There would be time to date when she was older; that's what her dad always said. Her mom always said that fourteen was just a child and that children shouldn't date other children, that dating was for grown-ups, and once she was grown up, she could start looking for love.

Brianna disagreed.

Yes, she was only fourteen. She wasn't experienced in love, but she'd had crushes, and she'd felt attraction; she was ready to take the next step.

And she *had* taken the next step.

Which was why she wasn't going to school this morning. It had been so hard during breakfast not to let it show that she was up to something. Her parents were usually pretty perceptive, but her mom was in the middle of trying a big case and had been too wrapped up in that. Her dad was working on some big advertising campaign, so he had been focused on that. Her big brother was always wrapped up in himself, so that hadn't been a problem.

After breakfast, she'd left for the bus stop just like she did every morning. Then halfway there, she'd told her brother she had forgotten a book she needed for school that day and that she needed to go back to get it. She had pretended to head back home, but as soon as she was around the corner, she'd headed off in the opposite direction.

Away from home.

Away from school.

Now she was almost there, just a couple of blocks to go.

She wasn't sure why he wanted to meet her in the park, but that was what he had said on the phone. She would have thought that he would have wanted her to meet at school—that seemed like the more logical place—but if he wanted to meet at the park, she was happy to do it.

This could be the start of something.

Something real.

Something big.

The start of the love story of the century.

Maybe one day she would be sitting, surrounded by her grandchildren, telling them the story of this day.

Brianna knew there was a huge grin on her face, but she was powerless to wipe it off.

She was so excited.

This could be the first day of the rest of her life.

Despite what her mother thought, she wasn't too young to fall in love. Anyone could fall in love—young or old. Love had no boundaries. Love was love, it was for everyone; it didn't discriminate. And she could be about to find love.

She really could.

Love.

Real love.

The kind of love that books and movies were all about.

There it was.

The park.

It was winter and cold out. It was supposed to snow later today, but despite the bad weather, there were quite a few people about. Joggers, people walking their dogs, moms with their toddlers playing in the playground, and kids who were going to be late to school but didn't seem to care.

Brianna carefully scanned what she could see of the park. She didn't want anyone she knew to spot her. She planned to head straight to school after this, hopefully making it there by lunchtime, where she would tell her friends every little detail of what happened here. She had forged a note from her mom to say that she'd been at the orthodontist, and hopefully, the school would buy that and not call her parents. If her mom and dad found that she had skipped school to meet a boy in the park, she would be grounded for the rest of her life.

She didn't see anyone that she knew who might tell on her, so she headed for the parking lot at the other side of the park. He had said to meet there so they could go for a walk through the park together, talk, get to know each other. Only she was hoping they were going to do more than just talk.

She wasn't ready for sex or anything like that, but she wanted to be kissed. Really kissed. Her first kiss had been at a make-out party when she was twelve. Her parents had freaked when they'd heard about it.

With that kiss, she'd been caught in the act right as her lips touched the lips of her seventh-grade crush. This time, that wasn't going to happen. This time, no one was going to interrupt.

Brianna hurried across the park, walking under archways of leafless trees, past the playground, the lake, and the large open field where she and her brother used to play soccer and fly kites when they were younger. She was too old for games like that now; she was growing up whether her parents liked it or not.

She could see the parking lot from here and the white van that he said he'd be driving. He had apologized for having to drive his mom's florist van and added that his convertible was getting a gear change. She wasn't really sure what that was—she wasn't old enough to drive yet, but she didn't care what car he was driving. She just wanted to meet him.

She didn't see him; he must be waiting inside the van because of the cold morning. Was he going to want to hang out in the van instead of the park? If he was, did that mean he had more planned for this meeting than talking and maybe a little kissing? If he did want more from her, would she give it to him? Brianna knew she wasn't ready for sex, but she wasn't sure she was strong enough to say no if he asked.

After all, that was what becoming a woman was all about, right?

It was about doing grown-up things.

And sex was definitely a grown-up thing to do.

Although she was still excited, her steps slowed a little as she approached the van. Something suddenly felt wrong, but she wasn't sure what. It was probably just being afraid that she was going to get caught lying and skipping school to meet boys.

Yes.

That was it.

With a little of her confidence returning, Brianna walked up to the van, and when she saw that there was no one sitting in the driver's seat, she knocked on the side. There was no logo on the van; that seemed a little odd. Didn't he say it belonged to his mother and that it was the van she used to transport flowers for her business? Most businesses had logos on their vans, right? Or maybe not. She had never really paid attention before.

That feeling in her stomach intensified.

Something *was* wrong.

Brianna was just turning to leave the virtually empty parking lot and head to school when the van door was suddenly flung open and strong arms wrapped around her, yanking her inside and clamping a hand over her mouth before she could even process what was happening and scream for help.

By the time her common sense had kicked in, and she started to struggle, he was already covering her mouth with tape and binding her wrists with plastic zip ties.

Kidnapped.

She was being kidnapped.

She should have listened to her gut when it told her something was wrong.

It looked like she was growing up, after all.

She was developing intuition. She just hadn't learned to listen to it yet.

Brianna prayed she wasn't going to die before she got the chance to learn what being a grown-up was really all about.

* * * * *

12:22 P.M.

"No one cared that Ally was missing. No one was looking for her," Paige said. She hated that. Ally was a good kid. She shouldn't have spent four days in the hands of a killer while no one was bothering to try to find her or was even worried that she was gone.

"Ally was eighteen, not a minor, and there were no indications that there was anything suspicious about her disappearance," Ryan reminded her. "She snuck out of her bedroom in the middle of the night. We didn't know that she was in danger."

"We should have known," she contradicted. There was no way she was going to feel good about this whole situation. If it were her daughter who had disappeared, she'd want the police to take it seriously, not just tell her that sometimes teenagers ran away because they were throwing the equivalent of a toddler tantrum.

Hayley was fifteen now, a teenager, and although they didn't always agree about everything, she knew her daughter, and she knew that Hayley would never run away. She was sure Hilary and Yul knew their daughter too. If they said that Ally would never have run away, they should have been believed. It didn't matter if the majority of missing teens left on purpose; Ally was Ally and not anyone else. And obviously, her parents had been right. Ally hadn't just run away—she'd been kidnapped and murdered.

"We did what we could. You know there was no way that we could have known the two cases were related."

Why did her partner have to be so logical?

She didn't want to be logical right now.

She was feeling guilty. She should have done more for Ally. She should have looked into the case. But it hadn't been a case until her body turned up on the doorstep of her family's home. It wasn't a crime for an adult to disappear.

"We wasted four days looking in the wrong places trying to find Talia Canuck," she said. That was two teenage girls dead because they hadn't known what was really going on.

"We looked into everything we could when Talia disappeared," Ryan reminded her.

That was true.

She knew that.

But they had been so far off base.

"Everything we did on that case we did because it was logical," her partner continued. "Her parents were in the middle of a bitter custody battle fighting over her and her two younger siblings. We looked into both of them because the most likely scenario was that one of them had done something. We also looked into the possibility that it was Talia's ex-boyfriend, given that the two had recently had a bad breakup, and the whole school knew he was furious about it."

Talia Canuck had been abducted a month ago. She had disappeared one afternoon sometime between leaving school after her last class and when her father arrived home in the early evening. Both her younger siblings had made it back, but there was no sign of Talia.

Her father had called the cops around nine when he still hadn't heard from her, and unlike when Ally's parents had reported her missing, there was a reason to believe that Talia might not have left of her own accord. She and Ryan had worked the case nonstop trying to find who might have abducted the sixteen-year-old.

Then Talia's body turned up on the doorstep of her father's house.

Just like Ally.

"Even after Talia's body was found, we kept looking into her parents and her ex, trying to find which of them had killed her so no one else could have her," Ryan said. "We didn't give up on her, and we worked her case the best we could with the information we had at the time."

"Yeah, you're right," she reluctantly agreed.

"We did everything we could to find Talia's killer, and now that we know the same person who killed her abducted and killed Ally Brown, we have a new direction to move in."

"Maybe," she said slowly, her mind ticking over.

"You think not?" Ryan arched a blond brow.

"I don't know. It could still be one of Talia's parents or her ex. What better way to throw suspicion off yourself than to make it look like a serial killer killed your daughter? And Talia and Ally went to the same school, so it's possible that her ex killed them both. Either he had a grudge against both of them, or he just wanted to make it look like a serial killer."

She and Ryan had worked together for a long time. A *very* long time, over fifteen years, and she could usually tell what he was thinking by the look on his face. Right now, he looked like he considered the theory she had suggested wasn't likely, but he hadn't ruled it out as a possibility.

"Okay," Ryan agreed, "let's say for now, that it isn't one of Talia's relatives or her ex. Let's say this wasn't personal to either girl, or it was personal to both girls. How would we profile our killer?"

"He doesn't seem to have any particular preference in appearance," Paige said, willing to play this game because she wanted to pursue every single avenue so they could catch this killer before another teenage girl wound up dead on her doorstep.

"No, he doesn't. Talia was blonde with blue eyes, and Ally was a brunette with brown eyes."

"Different ages too, Talia was sixteen, and Ally was eighteen, although they were both in high school."

"The girls also had very different personalities," Ryan said. "Talia was outgoing, confident, popular; she was a cheerleader. Ally was the opposite—quiet, shy, and didn't have many friends. Both struggled with their grades, though Talia more than Ally, but that could be something to look into. I know Hayley was tutoring Ally; was she getting tutoring from anyone else?"

"Not that I'm aware of, but we should ask Talia and Ally's parents to see if they might have been getting academic assistance from the same person or place. The girls didn't run in the same social circles, they lived in different neighborhoods, they didn't have any hobbies or interests in common. So far the only common denominator was the school they attended. We'll have to look into every other aspect of their lives, dentists, doctors, orthodontists, grocery stores, gyms, every place they might go that overlaps where the killer might have come into contact with them, but for now—"

"For now, it's the school," Ryan finished. "The school where a killer could be roaming about searching for his next victim as we speak. The school our fifteen-year-old daughters attend."

That thought almost paralyzed her.

She and her husband Elias had adopted Hayley and her younger sister Arianna ten years ago. The girls had a very rough start in life and progress had been slow but steady for Hayley, who, while still quiet and reserved, was otherwise thriving. She had a best friend in Ryan's daughter, Sophie. She was very bright and was going to be able to go to any college she wanted on a full scholarship. Because Hayley struggled to make friends, Paige and Elias had suggested she play a team sport. Hayley had been dancing since they first adopted her and had taken up volleyball when she started middle school—and loved both.

Hayley was going to go far in life, and she was sure Arianna would follow in her big sister's footsteps. Arianna was much more outgoing than her sister; she was bright and bubbly and full of energy. She did well in school, but she spent more time talking with her friends than she did listening to her teachers. She was also a dancer, a very talented one, who'd already won several national titles.

Her kids were her life.

Her heart.

Her light in the dark.

If anything ever happened to either of them, she didn't know what she'd do.

"We have to find this killer, whoever he is, before another girl goes missing." She looked desperately at her partner.

"There's one thing that makes it look like these killings weren't committed by any of Talia's relatives," Ryan said.

She didn't have to ask to know what he was talking about. "The tattoos."

"Why would Talia's mother or father put a number nine tattoo on both girls?"

"Why would anyone?" she retorted.

"I don't know." Ryan looked thoughtful. "But it has to mean something."

"It doesn't seem like anything you would do just to do it," Paige agreed. "But *why* do it?"

"If we figure that out, I think we'll know who our killer is."

Something just occurred to her. "Ryan, Talia was missing for about four days, right?"

"Right."

"And Ally was too."

"Right."

"Four days is ninety-six hours. We don't know exactly what time either girl was kidnapped, but I think it's safe to assume they could have been missing around ninety-*nine* hours."

Ryan's blue eyes lit up. "Ninety-nine hours and a number nine tattoo, that is too big a coincidence to ignore."

"Now we just have to figure out who at the school has a link to something with the number nine that would lead them to kill two innocent teenage girls." Paige had no idea what that could be, but she and Ryan *would* figure it out.

They had to.

If they didn't, every single one of the four hundred girls who attended the high school was in danger.

Ryan's daughter was in danger.

Her daughter was in danger.

And she would do whatever it took to eliminate anything or anyone who was a threat to her child.

* * * * *

6:53 P.M.

"Mo-om, I'm starving, when's dinner?"

Sofia Xander looked up to see her twelve-year-old son Ned standing in the kitchen doorway.

Her little boy was really growing up. He was taller than her now, and he was starting to look like the teenager he would be in just a few short months and not the child she sometimes still wished he was.

Her kids were growing up so quickly.

Too quickly.

Some days she wished she could turn back the clock a couple of years, back to when her kids were small and sweet and innocent. Back to when they still got along.

"Mom," Ned snapped. "I'm hungry."

"Watch your attitude," she reminded her son. They were all tense these days, but she wasn't going to repeat the mistakes with Ned that she and her husband had made with their daughter.

There was going to be no letting him off the hook, no letting bad behavior slide just because excuses could be made for it.

"Sorry," Ned said immediately. "Are we eating soon?"

"When Dad and Sophie get home."

"So possibly never," Ned sighed dramatically.

"What did I just say about attitude," she reminded him. Although, to be honest, he wasn't entirely wrong.

"Sophie comes and goes as she pleases," Ned said. "Why do we have to wait for her?"

"Because she's your sister and a member of this family," Ryan said as he came up behind their son.

"She doesn't act like a member of the family. She's hardly ever here, and when she is here, all she does is yell at all of us," Ned contradicted.

This time Sofia didn't bother to reprimand her son.

He was right.

Sophie's behavior was getting more and more out of control with each passing day, and she had no idea how to get her once-caring-and-compassionate daughter back on track.

Apparently, Ryan felt the same way because he didn't say anything to Ned either. He just entered the kitchen, set a stack of paper folders on the counter, and gave her a quick kiss.

"How was your day?" she asked her husband, wanting to force some normalcy into their lives. Their lives and their family had been so out of control lately that all the little things she'd taken for granted, they never did anymore.

"It was busy," Ryan answered vaguely. That was always his answer when he didn't want to tell her about a case he was working. "How was yours?"

"It was busy too. We had one of the kids who came to the center about a year ago participate in her first debate at school. She was the quietest, most timid, shy girl, and seeing how much she's come out of her shell since we encouraged her to join the debate team is such a joy." It was one of the things she loved the most about the center that she'd started a decade ago, seeing what finally living in a safe environment did for the women and children who came seeking help as they fled from abusive partners or parents.

"That's great." Ryan smiled as he stirred the pasta sauce on the stove. He knew how much it meant to her that she had taken the money she had inherited—when her family had been annihilated—and done something good with it. Other than her children, the Matilda Rose Women's and Children's Center was the best thing she had ever done.

"Can we please eat? I'm starving," Ned begged.

"Have you finished your homework?" Ryan asked.

"Yes."

"Then sure, let's have dinner."

Sofia shot her husband a surprised glance. They usually waited to eat dinner as a family. With Ryan's sometimes erratic hours there had been plenty of times they hadn't eaten together, but with everything going on with Sophie she and Ryan had decided they were going to make family time a priority.

"Do we even know where she is?" Ryan said quietly so Ned wouldn't overhear.

"I can guess."

"So can I. She knows it's straight home after school. She knows until she pulls her grades up and her attitude improves that there is no hanging out with friends. If she keeps deliberately disobeying, then we're going to have to start having someone drop her off and pick her up every day."

She hated to admit that it might have come down to that.

Treating their fifteen-year-old like the five-year-old she kept behaving like.

Although when Sophie had been five, she'd been a lot more mature.

"Okay, let's eat," she agreed, draining the pasta. Ned set the table, and Ryan was pouring drinks when the front door suddenly slammed closed.

"She's ba-aack," Ned said, all *Poltergeist* like.

Footsteps thundered up the stairs, and Sofia and Ryan exchanged glances then headed up to their daughter's room together. It was crucial that Sophie realized they were a team and that everything they did was as a team and that trying to play one of them off the other wasn't going to work.

"Where were you?" Ryan asked as he threw open Sophie's bedroom door.

"Get out of my room," Sophie glared at them.

"Where were you?" Sofia repeated her husband's question. Sophie might think she was in charge here, but she was mistaken. This was Ryan's and her house, and Sophie was a minor. Respect was not negotiable.

"I was with Hayley," Sophie said sullenly.

"No, Hayley was already home before Paige and I left for the day," Ryan said.

Sophie just rolled her eyes.

If she wasn't with her best friend, then there was only one other person Sophie would have ignored the rules to spend time with, instead of coming home.

"Were you with Dominick Tremaine?" Sofia demanded.

Sophie shrugged.

"You are not allowed to see him." Ryan was almost vibrating with anger. They'd had this conversation with Sophie a dozen times. She was a fifteen-year-old sophomore, Dominick was an eighteen-year-old senior. They had forbidden Sophie to date Dominick partly because of the age difference and partly because of Sophie's recent behavior.

"You are not the boss of me!" Sophie screamed back.

"We are your parents, and you are a minor." Ryan's voice was also rising.

"You are not my parents!" she screeched, then shoved past them and ran into the bathroom, slamming the door behind her.

There was nothing her daughter could have said that would have hurt her more than those words.

She may not have given birth to Sophie, but she had loved her like her own ever since the day Ryan had entered her hospital room and placed baby Sophie in her arms.

She had been there for Sophie every day since.

Through fevers, nightmares, and tears, she had been there for Sophie's first steps and the first day of school. She'd helped her learn fractions when Sophie had been convinced she would never conquer the skill and make it out of the third grade.

Sofia knew she was Sophie's mother in every way that mattered, but what her daughter had just said was true. She wasn't Sophie's biological mother.

And learning that she was adopted and who her biological parents were had ruined Sophie's life.

"We shouldn't have told her," she murmured under her breath.

"You know we had to," Ryan said.

"It ruined everything."

"We'll get through this." Ryan sounded so confident.

Sofia had no idea why.

How could they get through this?

Sophie hated them and was punishing them by making sure she made as much of a mess of her life as she could.

It had only been a few months since they'd sat Sophie down and explained to her that she wasn't their biological daughter, and in that short time, Sophie had started dating a legal adult. She was failing all of her classes, and she was doing her best to destroy their family.

"Sofia." Ryan hooked his finger under her chin and gently nudged, so she was looking up at him. "Have faith. This has been a shock for Sophie. That doesn't mean it gives her free reign to behave like she has been, it's not a get-out-of-jail-free card, but she's acting out. She knows that we love her; she knows that nothing is ever going to change that, and she still loves us too.

She's angry and she's hurt, and you know from experience that what she's just had to take on is a lot, especially for a kid."

Just like her daughter, she knew what it was like to find out that your entire life was a lie.

That *you* were a lie.

That you weren't the you you'd always thought you were.

She wished there had been a way to protect her daughter from experiencing that pain, but she and Ryan had agreed that Sophie deserved to know the truth.

Sofia just wished that truth wasn't destroying her.

"She loves us, Sofia. Don't ever forget that." Ryan drew her close and held her tight. This was a nightmare for both of them but at least they had each other.

She rested her head on her husband's muscular chest and wrapped her arms around his waist. They had been together for fifteen years now, and they had the life she had always dreamed of. She had to believe that they could get that back. She and Ryan loved each other, they loved their children, and their children loved them. She just had to hold on to that.

MARCH 4TH

Ryan was struggling to concentrate this morning.

He kept replaying last night's argument with Sophie—as well as the last several months—over and over in his mind.

They'd thought that things would get better over time. They hoped Sophie would learn that just because they weren't her biological parents, it didn't make them any less her parents. That she would remember that they were the people who loved her and who had raised her and who would never turn their backs on her, no matter how hard she seemed to be trying to get them to do so.

But things weren't getting any better.

They were only getting worse.

And he had no idea how to make them better.

He had never felt this helpless before.

Then, again, his life had never been this out of control before.

His family meant everything to him, and there was nothing that he wouldn't do for them, but he had no idea how to fix this. How did he convince his daughter that they loved her? He had never thought he'd have to do that; he'd felt that she knew, but if he didn't figure out how to get through to Sophie, she was going to spin completely out of control.

Lying, sneaking out, ditching school, failing classes she used to get straight As in. If she kept this up, he feared she was going to wind up like Brianna Lester, and it would be two other cops knocking on their door to talk to him and Sofia like he and his partner were doing to the Lester family.

"I wonder what they're doing in there," Paige said as she

29

knocked again.

Ryan could only imagine.

Suffering, he knew that much.

The fear, the pain, the guilt.

Always guilt.

Before he had kids, he'd never realized that a huge part of parenting was doubting yourself and every single decision that you made.

"Think it's related?" Paige asked.

It had been twenty-four hours since Brianna Lester was last seen. She attended the same school as Talia Canuck and Ally Brown, so they weren't taking any chances. "I hope not. If she's just a teenage runaway, she's probably safer than if she's this killer's next victim."

"We have no leads."

His partner was right. Two dead girls, possibly another being held right at this moment, and they had no idea who the killer was.

They needed more information.

Talia's death had them focused on her family and ex-boyfriend. Ally's death hinted at a serial killer, and another missing teen from the same victim pool told them more girls were likely to die. The killer had to be somehow related to the school, but whom? A student? A teacher? A parent? Someone from the office or a janitor? There were too many people associated with the school; they needed a direction to start searching in.

The only way to get that was to better understand their victims and their final days.

Ryan hammered on the door, louder and more forcefully this time. They needed to talk to Brianna's parents if they were going to have any hope of bringing her home alive. If she was the next victim and assuming the killer stuck with the same schedule he had used before, then Brianna only had around three days left to live. Every second counted right now.

"Finally," he muttered when he heard footsteps.

A moment later the door was opened by a harried looking middle-aged woman with dirty, straggly shoulder length brown hair, and hazel eyes that were shimmery with tears making them appear more green than brown. "Sorry, I was on the phone. I'm supposed to be in court today, and I've been trying to get someone who can fill in for me. You're the detectives, right?"

"Detective Xander and Detective Hood." Ryan made the introductions.

"I'm Marie Lester, come in."

They followed Mrs. Lester through a large entrance foyer and into a very formal lounge room that looked like it was hardly ever used.

"I'll just get my husband. Please sit, can I get you anything to drink?" Mrs. Lester asked.

"Whatever you're having," Ryan replied, assuming it would be coffee. Brianna's mother looked like she needed coffee. *Lots* of coffee.

While they waited for Mrs. Lester to return with her husband, Ryan surveyed the room. The three-piece lounge suite was dark brown leather. There was a huge fireplace taking up most of one wall with a framed family portrait hanging above it. In the picture, the family was all smiling at the camera, but none of them looked particularly close. Over the years, he'd had lots of family portraits taken, and usually, he had his arms around his wife or one of his kids, but in his picture of the Lesters, they looked like four people who had gathered for a photo, not a family. Ryan wondered if that was an indication of the kind of family they were. If it was, he didn't hold out much hope that either of Brianna's parents knew anything about what might have led to her disappearance.

"This is my husband, Jeff," Marie Lester said as she entered the lounge room with a tray of coffee cups.

Jeff Lester was a tall, slightly overweight, middle-aged man, who was already completely gray but still had a full head of hair.

He looked irritated by this whole fiasco, and he glared at them, then said to his wife, "I really need to be getting off to work. Can't you handle this?"

"Our daughter is missing, Jeff. *Missing.*"

"You think Brianna is the kind of kid who would just take off for a few days?" Paige asked.

Jeff Lester shrugged.

"She's not," Marie said as she set the tray down and handed out cups before sinking down into the adjacent couch. "Brianna is a good kid. A *really* good kid. We've never had any trouble with her. She makes good grades, and she works hard in school. She spends most of her free time playing basketball. She already knows what she wants to do with her life. We had some trouble with her older brother a couple of years ago, but she was so good through it all. She started helping out around the house and said she understood when we couldn't spend as much time with her because we were busy with her brother. She wouldn't just leave. She wouldn't. Something has happened to her."

"Brianna never made it to school yesterday. Who would she have gone to see?" Ryan asked.

Marie bristled. "Whoever took her must have grabbed her before she made it to the bus stop. Brianna would never skip school."

"She did."

They all turned to see Brianna's older brother Luke standing in the lounge room doorway.

"What do you know, Luke?" Ryan asked the seventeen-year-old. They knew that Luke had gotten into a little trouble with the law almost two years ago. He'd gotten mixed up with the wrong kids, started smoking marijuana, gotten busted, been given probation, and gotten interested in writing. Now he was doing well in school, had kept out of trouble, and had even won a couple of competitions for his short stories.

"We were almost to the bus stop when she said she forgot a

book and had to go back for it," Luke said.

"Well, that's it then. She forgot a book, came home to get it, and someone grabbed her on the way," Marie said stubbornly. She clearly wasn't ready to entertain the possibility that her perfect little princess was just a regular kid who lied and sometimes made bad choices.

What Marie Lester had said was definitely a possibility. They didn't know who had taken Brianna or even if she had been abducted. And it was indeed plausible that she had forgotten a book and been kidnapped while returning home to get it. But they knew Ally Brown had snuck out of the house the night she was taken, so it was just as strong a possibility that Brianna had been sneaking off to meet her attacker.

"That's certainly what could have happened," Paige said tactfully. They both understood that no one wanted to believe their kid could do wrong, although, unfortunately for him, that notion was becoming harder and harder to cling to. "But if Brianna was sneaking off to meet someone, do you have any idea who that might be?"

Marie looked like she still wanted to argue the point that her daughter would never break a rule, but she bit her tongue and shook her head. "We monitor Brianna's internet access. She has her own phone, but I check it every day, go through her messages, look through her browser history, check all her social media. I haven't noticed anything out of the ordinary, and there was nothing on there that I was concerned about."

Ryan had to admire Marie Lester's dedication to making sure her daughter's online life was as safe as it could be. He and Sofia had always monitored Sophie and Ned's internet activities, but when Sophie had found out about her biological parents, they had backed off a bit, wanting to give her some space to vent to her friends in privacy. That had been a mistake. One he was worried was already too late to rectify.

"Are there any boys she likes?" Ryan asked. Brianna was a

fourteen-year-old girl, and boys were pretty much the center of a teenage girl's life.

"Brianna is too young to date," Marie said haughtily.

"Mr. Lester?" Paige asked.

"None that I know of," he replied, looking bored like he still believed they were all creating drama where there wasn't any.

"Luke, do you know of anyone who Brianna was interested in?" Ryan asked. Luke attended the same school as Brianna and Talia and Ally, and if anyone could point them in the right direction, it would be him.

"I'm a senior, and she's a freshman, we don't really run in the same circles," Luke replied.

"If there was a boy she had a crush on, who would know?" Paige asked.

"If there was a boy—and I don't believe there was, Brianna was too young to date, we both agreed on that—then one of her two best friends would know."

Ryan didn't buy that at all.

Brianna was a teenager. She was interested in boys, and he doubted she had agreed with her mother's assessment that she was too young to date.

"We're going to need the names of her friends."

* * * * *

9:50 A.M.

This one was a crier.

The first one had been angry, the second one quiet and accepting, but this one hadn't stopped crying since he'd tied her up in his van.

It was starting to get a little annoying.

If she kept it up much longer, he admitted, he was going to take great pleasure in forcefully shutting her up. He hadn't quite decided how yet, but he needed to teach her a lesson. They still had seventy-four hours left to spend together, and he wasn't going to listen to this racket for another three days.

He watched the girl through the window in the door at the top of the basement steps. She hadn't realized yet that he could see her. He liked to watch her, to try to figure out what she was thinking. He wanted to memorialize every single second of the ninety-nine hours they would spend together. That was why he had hidden a camera in the corner of the basement.

This was a journey of many parts.

Revenge was a large piece of it. He wanted to punish those responsible for his pain. He wanted them to suffer like he had. Maybe then, he would be able to find some peace.

Understanding also played a large part in why he had decided to do this. He wanted to know what it was like to be trapped, held against your will, locked away without any hope of getting free. That was why he was recording everything. He wanted to be able to go through it all and examine every single emotion and feeling and thought and fear that went through his victims' heads.

Lastly, he also just kind of wanted to do it.

He was intrigued by the idea of kidnapping someone, keeping them prisoner, and then killing them.

Plus, it was kind of fun to see if he could get away with it.

So far, he had.

No one knew that he had killed Talia and Ally, and no one knew that he currently had Brianna Lester safely tucked away.

He wondered how far he could push things, how long he could keep this up before anyone caught on to him. He was careful. As careful as it was possible to be when you were plucking girls straight off the street and then dumping them on the doorsteps of their family homes.

He chuckled.

That was a stroke of genius.

It wasn't something he had initially planned, but after he'd killed Talia and he was deciding what he was going to do with her body, the idea had occurred to him. He had to put her body someplace. At first, he'd thought he would try to hide it. Maybe bury it in a shallow grave or throw her in a river or lake weighted down with rocks, or toss her in a dumpster so she'd be taken to the dump and buried in so many tons of garbage she'd never be found.

But where was the fun in that?

He liked the thrill of trying to leave a body on the doorstep of a house where he knew people were inside and where he knew anyone in any of the other homes or driving or walking by could spot him. It was an adrenalin rush, unlike anything he'd ever experienced. Who knew murder could actually be fun?

Before he left the bodies, he gave them a very thorough clean inside and out. Not that they really needed to be cleaned inside; he wasn't into that kind of thing. He didn't need to force a woman to have sex with him. He was good-looking, smart, and charming; he already had them falling all over themselves to get him into bed. But he liked to be thorough, so he cleaned every single nook and cranny until he was sure that there was nothing left behind that would lead the cops to his doorstep.

It wasn't that he didn't want them to know who he was forever. Sooner or later they would. He wanted the world to understand why he was doing this. He wanted the whole world to know the injustices he'd suffered. He wanted the world to know that what had happened to him was not okay. He wanted the world to know that someone had to be held accountable.

The justice system hadn't given him any justice, so he'd had to find his own.

And he had.

In the form of pretty teenage girls.

If he was going to do this, he could at least do it first class with pretty girls.

Brianna Lester was a pretty girl, or she would be if she stopped crying long enough to get rid of the red splotches all over her face and the puffiness in her eyes. Although he *did* like the way the tears made her hazel eyes appear greener. He was a sucker for a pair of shimmering green eyes. Not that her eyes were going to save Brianna from the punishment she was about to get.

He'd had enough of the crying.

Twenty-five hours of it was more than he could take.

If he'd known that Brianna was going to do nothing but whine and sob and shudder convulsively, then he would have never answered her phone call.

Hysterics weren't his thing. He'd never been good at dealing with anyone deep in the throes of hysteria, and he had no intention of learning to be more accommodating. He didn't care if Brianna was only fourteen and had just been abducted and tied up in a basement. Sure, that was probably a fair reason for someone to be crying, but all he cared about was how much it was annoying him. The girl was just going to have to learn to control herself. If she didn't, they weren't going to make it through the ninety-nine hours, and it was imperative that he stuck with the plan.

Unlocking the door, he stalked down the steps.

Brianna looked up at him and shrank away, pressing against the basement wall as though it was going to offer her some sort of salvation.

"Enough is enough; quiet the crying," he ordered.

The girl just shuddered, tears continuing to stream down her cheeks.

"Brianna, stop." He raised his voice to just below chainsaw level.

She sucked in a breath and tried to quell her sobs by covering her mouth with her free hand, but they burst through anyway. "P-please," she wept, apparently giving up on trying to use her hand to force herself to keep quiet. "Please let me go home. Whatever I did to make you angry, I'm sorry. I won't tell anyone what you did. I won't tell them about you … I won't … I promise. Please, just let me go home."

Begging was almost as annoying as crying.

He wasn't putting up with this.

She could be angry with him. She could yell and scream and rage, threatening to beat him to a bloody pulp like Talia had. Or she could just sit there and watch his every move with those probing brown eyes like Ally had done. But he wasn't spending another second with this blubbering mess.

He had been patient for over a day now, but he'd reached the end of his rope.

"Shut your mouth, Brianna, now." He raised his hand and took a threatening step toward her. He hadn't laid a hand on the other girls, only when it came time to drown them, but he wasn't adverse to the idea of beating Brianna Lester into submission.

Brianna shrieked and shrank farther away from him.

His threat only seemed to have the opposite effect than he had desired. She didn't stop crying; her tears started coming faster, and she was sobbing so hard that she was almost hyperventilating.

He wondered what it would be like to hit her.

To deliberately inflict pain on another human being.

Sure, he had killed two people, but that was different, that was just to prove his point, get his revenge. But this wasn't a necessity unless he counted saving his sanity. This would be hurting her just because he could.

Would he feel bad about it?

There was only one way to find out.

"Last chance," he warned.

"P-please, please don't hurt me," Brianna wept.

He had been fair. He had asked nicely. He had given her plenty of warnings. What happened next was Brianna's fault, not his.

His fist swung through the air and connected with Brianna's jaw with a crunch. She squawked with pain, and then began to cough and splutter. Blood dribbled out her mouth and down her chin, and when she lifted her free hand to press to it, he saw that one of her teeth had been knocked out.

He'd done it.

He'd hit her.

Made her bleed and knocked out a tooth.

She was shaking, but the tears had stopped.

It had worked.

He'd hit her to make her stop crying, and he didn't feel the least little bit bad about it.

* * * * *

12:34 P.M.

"Principal Barone said the girls are waiting for us in her office," Paige announced as she pocketed her phone.

"Good," Ryan murmured distractedly. This case was hitting too close to home for him. Girls going missing and being murdered from the same school his daughter attended. Sophie's recent rebellious behavior that he knew was going to lead her down a path where she was going to get hurt. He hated the idea of his child being hurt, and he hated that his child's behavior was hurting his wife. He and Sofia were going to have to put a stop to Sophie's behavior—whatever it took.

"Things not getting any better with Sophie?" his partner asked as they weaved their way through the hordes of teenagers on their way to the office.

"They're getting worse."

"Hayley's worried about her."

"She is?" If Sophie's best friend was worried about her, he knew things had to be pretty bad.

"She said she's tried to talk to Sophie, get her to ease up on you and Sofia, tried to convince her that being adopted doesn't make her any less your daughter. She's distraught that she hasn't been able to get through to her."

Hayley Hood was a good kid—sweet, thoughtful, kind, caring. She was a good influence for Sophie, and he was glad the two were friends. He knew how important it was to a teenage girl to have a best friend, and he couldn't have asked for a better one than Hayley. If anyone could get through to Sophie, make her see reason, then it was Hayley.

"Tell Hayley how much we appreciate her trying," he told Paige.

"I will. Hayley won't give up on Sophie, none of us will. You can't give up on her either, she needs you and Sofia now more than ever. Elias and I won't ever forget what Sophie did for Hayley when we first adopted her. Anything you need, all you have to do it ask. If you want her to come and stay with us for a while, that would be fine."

Sophie had asked to go and stay with Hayley right after she found out that she was adopted, but he and Sofia had thought it would be counterproductive and would feed into her idea that they weren't her real parents if they allowed her to move out— even temporarily. But now, nearly six months later, he was ready to try just about anything. Maybe some distance would help Sophie settle down, get back to focusing on school, to stop dating that eighteen-year-old senior. Get herself back on track so she could calm down and realize how much they loved her, and that nothing, not even biology, could stop them from being a family.

"I'll talk to Sofia about it. Thanks, Paige."

"Of course." She smiled up at him. "You'd do the same for me and my family if we needed it."

"Hi, detectives." Principal Barone met them at the office doorway. Ryan had met with the principal a few times since Sophie started here last school year. Most recently because of her slipping grades and disruptive and rude behavior in class.

"Are the girls ready?" Paige asked.

"They are. Do I need to call their parents to come and sit in with them while you interview them?"

"No, the girls aren't suspects. We just want to know what they know about Brianna Lester and whether she might have known her attacker," he explained.

"Should I sit in with them?" the principal asked.

"No, I think they'll feel freer to open up without their principal in the room," he said. Getting teenagers to talk was hard enough as it was without having the school principal there.

"Okay, then." Principal Barone looked nervous like she was afraid of backlash, but there wouldn't be any—neither Debra York or Susanne Rollins were suspects. "I'll be right out here if you need me."

When they stepped into the principal's office, two sets of frightened eyes latched on to them. Brianna and her friends were freshmen, and his daughter was a sophomore, so he didn't know Brianna, Debra, or Susanne, but what he'd heard about them, they were all good kids.

"Hi girls." He smiled at them as he and Paige took their seats.

"Is Brianna really missing?" Debra asked.

"She is."

"Someone killed Talia Canuck and Ally Brown," Susanne said. "Is it the same person who took Brianna?"

"What do you think?" he asked. They weren't here to give the girls information; they were here to get information out of the girls. Hopefully, something that would lead them to Brianna. They didn't know exactly what time she'd been abducted, but she had been gone around twenty-four hours now; her time was running out.

The teenagers exchanged looks and wriggled in their seats, but neither said anything.

"We know that Brianna told her brother that she'd forgotten a book and left him to go back to the house yesterday morning. Then she never turned up at school. Was she going to meet someone?" Paige asked.

Again, the girls exchanged glances, but this time Susanne gave a small nod.

"Susanne," Debra quickly admonished.

"They already know. We may as well tell them. What if we don't and Brianna dies because of it?" Susanne stated.

Debra seemed to internally debate that but eventually gave a conceding nod. "Okay," she agreed.

"Brianna was going to meet someone?" he asked.

"Yeah, her mom thought she was too young to date, she was really strict with Brianna, checked her phone every day. Brianna hated it. Since her mom checked all of her social media stuff, Brianna created new Snapchat and Twitter and Instagram accounts that her mom didn't know about. Debra and I would let her log in on our phones so her mom couldn't find out about them," Susanne explained.

Typical teenagers. They were always finding a way to work around parents' rules. "Did Brianna meet someone on her social media?" he asked.

"Not on there, here, at school," Debra answered.

"She was dating someone here?"

"Not dating. She called him. There was a note in one of the girls' bathrooms. On the mirror. It said, 'Girls, if you're looking for a hot date, call S,' and there was a number. We talked about it, and Brianna wanted to do it. She was sick of her mother always telling her that she was too young to date. She's fourteen, almost fifteen, and in a few months, we'll be sophomores. She wanted to start dating. She called S, and she was going to meet him. She wanted to get to know him, and then once they'd been dating for a few months, she was going to tell her mom," Debra said in a rush like she needed to get the whole story out before she lost her nerve.

"She called from one of your phones so her mother wouldn't know and see it in the call list when she checked?" Paige asked.

"From mine," Susanne said in a small voice.

"That's who she was going to meet yesterday morning?" Ryan asked.

"She was going to go and meet S at the park and then get back to school by lunch time and tell them she'd been at the orthodontist," Debra said.

"Do you know where at the park?" If they could get an exact location, they'd send CSU down there and see if they could find anything.

"The parking lot. The one over by the lake," Debra told them.

"Do you know who S is?" Paige asked.

"No," Susanne replied.

"Can you show us the message in the bathroom?" Paige asked.

"It's not there anymore. It was gone yesterday morning," Susanne answered.

"Do you still have the phone number?" Ryan asked.

Susanne reached into her bag and pulled out her phone. She scrolled through it, then turned it around and handed it over. "There's the number."

Ryan jotted it down. They'd call the number as soon as they got back to the precinct. Hopefully, it would lead them directly to the person who had kidnapped Brianna and murdered Talia and Ally.

"We didn't know it was dangerous. We offered to go with her, but we thought it was just a kid at school, and everything would be okay. We were happy for her, excited for her. We thought she was going to meet this awesome guy and fall in love," Susanne said.

The girls would blame themselves, but they had no reason to expect that anything should be wrong. The only person to blame if Brianna died was the killer. "It's not your fault," he told Debra and Susanne. "And what you've told us could help us to find her. You can head back to your classes."

Susanne and Debra hurried out of the room, and Ryan turned to Paige. "This could be what we needed to end this."

Anxious now to get back to the precinct and call the number and find out who was on the other end, he and Paige said goodbye to the principal and headed for their car. They were walking through the halls when they bumped into Sophie and Hayley.

"Dad?" Sophie looked angry to see him. "What are you doing here? Did you come to my school to check up on me?"

What had happened to his daughter?

The child who used to be so intuitive and empathetic, who used to always be looking for people who needed help and support and giving it to them, who cared more about others than she did about herself.

Now the *only* person she cared about was herself.

"This wasn't about you, Sophie. Not everything is about you. Girls who go to this school are being kidnapped and murdered. It's time for you to start growing up and acting more responsibly. You can't keep going around thinking the whole world revolves around you."

Ryan knew he shouldn't have snapped at her, but he was getting tired of Sophie's attitude. So she was adopted. So she had learned that her birth parents weren't good people. It wasn't the end of the world. She had a good life, she had parents who loved her, a brother who looked up to her, an extended family who were always there for her. She had so much more than so many other kids her age, and it was time she started realizing it.

Sophie just glowered at him.

Then burst into tears and ran off.

"I better go after her." Hayley shot him an apologetic smile. "See you tonight, Mom." Hayley gave her mother a kiss on the cheek then went running off after Sophie.

"It'll get better, Ryan," Paige assured him.

It better.

It had to.

It certainly couldn't get worse.

* * * * *

1:11 P.M.

"I hate my parents," Sophie sighed dramatically as she and Hayley stood in the school's parking lot.

"This is hard for them too," Hayley reminded her.

"Pfft." She shrugged and made a dismissive motion with her hand. "They're the ones who started this by lying to me my whole life."

"They were waiting for the right time to tell you."

"Fifteen years later? I think there've been plenty of times for them to sit me down and tell me the truth, but they chose not to." It didn't matter what her best friend said. Her parents had done the wrong thing, and she hated them for it.

Hated them.

Actually hated them.

She had never hated anyone before, hadn't even thought she was capable of such a strong emotion, but she was. Her parents, who weren't really her parents at all—but her niece and her niece's husband—had ruined her life. Why should she forgive them for that?

"They were probably afraid." Hayley's blue eyes were serious and sad. Her friend was quiet but extremely empathetic. She hurt when someone she loved was hurting. "I know my mom has always been afraid that something will happen, and someone will take my sister and I away from her."

"But the only one who would possibly have taken you and Ari away from your parents is Eliza. And she's happy that she let Paige and Elias be your parents. She knows it was the right thing to do, and she doesn't regret it."

"Love isn't always logical." Why did Hayley always have to be so smart and sensible? Sometimes she wished she had a best

45

friend who just raged with her and hated her parents just because she did, instead of a best friend who was always so grown up. "In her head, my mom knows that my biological parents are dead and that Eliza is happily married to George and raising their two kids together. That she would never try to take Ari away from the only home and parents she's ever known. But in her heart, my mom always has that lingering fear that maybe one day Ari will get angry with her over something and want to go and live with her biological mother."

"But Ari loves your mom. She knows Eliza gave birth to her, and she knows that her biological father was a bad man who did terrible things. She loves Eliza, but she's not her mom, and nothing will ever change that. Paige and Elias are her parents and your parents, and if Ari ever said differently, it would only be out of anger because she didn't know how else to deal with her feelings."

Hayley gave one of those smiles that looked like the same kind her mom would give her when she saw the potential for a life lesson. "You're right. Ari and I love our parents even though we're not biologically related to them. Just like *you* love your parents regardless of the fact that you aren't their biological daughter. You're angry at them for lying to you, and I get that. I was five when I was adopted. I always knew what happened, and we all sat down—Mom, Dad, Eliza, and I—with Ari when she was about five and told her the truth about who her parents were. I can't imagine finding that out now. But, Sophie, you know that your parents love you, and you're lying if you say otherwise."

Sophie couldn't come up with a good comeback for that, so she just kept her mouth shut.

"You love them, you're just angry with them, but over time that anger will fade."

Right now, she couldn't see her anger ever fading.

How did you forgive the people you had looked up to your whole life for lying to you?

How did you get over finding out that you weren't who you thought you were?

How did you move on with your life when you had no idea who you were?

Her whole identity had been ripped away from her in that one second.

She had gone from being the fun, bubbly, smart, empathetic daughter of a cop and a woman who ran a center for abused women and children, to a ... a ... a ... she didn't even know.

"Soph." Hayley reached for her hand and squeezed it tightly. "Stop being angry, please. At least give them a chance to explain why they didn't tell you until a few months ago. I'm sure they had their reasons."

"I don't care about their reasons. All I cared about is that they lied to me. Every single minute of every single day of every single year of my life. Even if I did listen to them, I wouldn't believe a word they said. They're nothing but liars."

"Sophie," Hayley sounded exasperated. "Are you planning on being mad at them forever? Being adopted isn't the worst thing in the world. I'm adopted, and I don't care. I'm just so thrilled that I got the most amazing parents in the world as mine."

"It's not the same." Sophie was getting annoyed now. She and Hayley had had this conversation before.

Several times.

Well, at least part of the conversation.

She always backed out before she admitted exactly what hurt her the most about this whole situation.

"What's different?" Hayley asked.

Sophie drew in a deep, steadying breath. Maybe she should just do it, admit what scared her the most, and perhaps, that would make things better. That was what her parents had always told her. Talking about things helped. She wasn't sure she believed it, but maybe it was worth a shot.

Couldn't make things worse.

"It is different." She met Hayley's gaze squarely. "Your parents were normal people. There was nothing wrong with them. They just died. But my parents … they're the complete opposite. My mother only got pregnant with me to blackmail my father. She didn't even know who my father was. She just knew she could use me to get rich quick. And my father was some judge who manipulated the law when it suited him. Who tried to kill his wife's illegitimate son, who allowed his own son to kill women, who lied and ran his family with an iron fist, so they were all too scared to speak out against him. *That* is where I come from." Tears welled up in her eyes, but she fought them back. She didn't want to cry in the school's parking lot where anyone and everyone could see her.

"Oh, Sophie." Hayley threw her arms around her. "Is that why you've been so angry? So hurt? Because you're worried about bad genes?"

"What if that's how I'm going to turn out? What if my parents' DNA is too strong to overcome?"

"Nature and nurture both play a part in who we are. I was raised in a home with a psychopath for the first five years of my life, and I've turned out fine."

"Yeah, but you had good biological parents and good adoptive parents. They kind of cancelled out those five years."

"You were raised in a loving home by two loving parents, that cancels out any potentially bad DNA."

"What if nature is stronger that nurture?"

"What if it's not? You were raised by two of the most wonderful people on the planet, one of whom is your biological niece. She has the same genes that you have, and she was raised in that house. Nature and nurture both suck for Sofia, and yet, look at how she turned out."

That was true, Sophie reluctantly admitted to herself. She and her mother did share the same genes, and her mother had grown up in that house of horrors, and yet, her mom was a good mother.

Well, aside from lying to her, her whole life.

"Sophie, you can't be angry forever. If you're scared about turning out like the people who created you, then tell your parents. They'll be able to help you. That's what parents are there for."

Was her friend right?

She really wasn't sure.

She was too angry right now. Angry about being lied to. Angry about being adopted. Angry that her parents thought they could tell her what to do when they weren't even really her parents. Angry about them trying to decide who she could and couldn't date. Angry—just so angry.

She wasn't a little girl anymore.

Her parents couldn't just kiss her booboos and make them all better.

Sometimes she wished she was still that innocent little girl who thought her parents were so powerful that they could fix all the problems in the world.

"Hey, babe." Arms suddenly wrapped around her waist and spun her around; a kiss was planted on her lips.

"Dom." She grinned up at him. Her boyfriend was the only good thing she had going on in her life right now.

"Everything okay?" he asked.

She quickly brushed at her eyes, wiping away any last trace of tears. "Fine. Just saw my dad." Dominick knew all about the problems she'd been having with her family.

"Want to go hang out for a while?" he asked.

"We have class," Hayley reminded them.

Go to class or go and hang out with her boyfriend? Yeah, that wasn't even a choice

"You go to class. I'm going to spend some time with Dom, I couldn't concentrate on anything after what my dad said." His words had hurt her, mostly because, in a way, they were kind of true. She probably was being a little immature, and she had changed a lot in the last few months, but none of it was her fault. She was just reacting to the situation she'd been thrown into.

"Are you sure?" Hayley asked.

"Sure."

"Okay, call me later," Hayley said as she headed back into the school.

Sophie allowed Dom to take her hand and lead her to his car. Once inside it, she let him drag her down onto his lap and kiss her senseless.

This was what she needed

As Dom's tongue entered her mouth, Sophie felt all her problems float away.

* * * * *

8:47 P.M.

"You want to just give up on her?" Sofia couldn't believe what she was hearing.

"No, I'm not giving up on our daughter. I would *never* give up on our daughter. I'm trying to do whatever it takes to get her back on track," Ryan said.

"But sending her away is so extreme." It was almost nine o'clock, and there was no sign of Sophie. She hadn't come home after school like she was supposed to, and she hadn't called to let them know where she was. She wasn't with Hayley Hood, which meant she was almost definitely with her boyfriend. Ned was staying with Ryan's brother Jack and his family tonight because he'd asked to spend some time with his cousin who was only six months younger, and they'd decided their son deserved a night off.

Sofia wished she could take a night off.

Just one night where she didn't have to worry about her daughter ruining her life. Sophie was so young, and she was smart and talented and could do whatever she wanted when she graduated from high school. But if she kept letting her grades slip and trading time with her boyfriend—who she had already been forbidden to see—rather than her family, and held on to this anger, she was going to destroy her life before it ever even started.

Why couldn't Sophie see that telling her that she was adopted was the hardest thing they'd ever had to do?

Was she asking too much of a fifteen-year-old to accept that? To accept that the reason they had waited to tell her was because learning the truth about her biological parents was a lot for a teenager to handle?

Ryan was right.

They had to do whatever they could to get Sophie back on track.

She just wasn't sure this was the way to do it.

"Is it fair to Paige and Elias to ask them to take on Sophie? They already have Hayley and Ari and both of them have full-on jobs. It doesn't seem right to hand over Sophie and let them deal with her problems," she said.

"What if being away from us for a bit helps Sophie?"

How could being away from her family help Sophie?

Had it really come to this?

That the only solution was to send Sophie away?

That felt like giving up.

And if they gave up on Sophie, how could she ever believe that they loved her?

That was what the whole problem was about. Sophie was angry because she thought they didn't love her. And if they let her go and stay with the Hoods for a while—even if it was what Sophie said she wanted—then surely, they were only reinforcing that belief.

"I don't think we should do it." She swiveled on the sofa, so she was facing her husband. "I think it's only going to make things worse."

"Then what *should* we do?" Ryan looked as helpless as she felt.

Sofia hated when her husband looked helpless. That always shook her. He was her rock—always had been—ever since they'd met fifteen years ago. Their marriage hadn't been perfect; they were both human, and they both made mistakes, but they were happy together. They supported one another, they lifted each other up, they were always there for one another.

She wanted to do the same thing for her daughter.

She remembered the day they'd met Sophie for the first time. She had been in the hospital after nearly being killed, and Ryan had come walking into the room with Sophie in his arms. Sofia had loved her immediately. From that moment onward, she had been Sophie's mother.

She wouldn't give up on her daughter.

She couldn't.

"Don't cry, sweetheart," Ryan said, touching his fingertips to her cheeks, catching the tears that were rolling down them. "If you don't want to send Sophie to Paige and Elias's, then we won't. But what *do* you want to do? We have to do something. We can't just keep letting all of this slide because we feel guilty about telling her the truth. We have *nothing* to feel guilty about. Nothing. You know that, right?"

She knew it, but sometimes it was hard to believe it. "You know it, too, right?"

Ryan gave her a half smile. "I think we both need to be reminded of it. We haven't done anything wrong, except for letting Sophie get away with this behavior. A year ago, we would have never tolerated this. We've given her time to adjust to the news. We've given her time to come to terms with it. Now, she's out of time."

"I agree." She nodded, probably a little bit more forcefully than was necessary, but she was starting to feel better about things. They just needed a plan.

"We take her to school and pick her up each day. I think we

should talk to the school, make sure they let us know if she doesn't attend all of her classes."

"And no more phone. Having a phone is a privilege, not a right, and I don't think she's earned that privilege with her current behavior."

"No more dating. We've told her we don't approve of this relationship, that she's too young and immature to date an eighteen-year-old. She's ignored us. No more. It's over. When she's got her attitude under control and her grades up, then we can talk about her starting to date again. Boys her own age," Ryan added.

"I think she needs a job," Sofia announced. "Something to occupy her time and keep her busy, and hopefully, it will teach her some responsibility."

"We should keep in contact with her teachers and all homework assignments they hand out, as well as any tests or quizzes or anything that's happening at school. That way we can make sure she completes everything. There's only a couple of months left until the end of the school year, and if she doesn't get her grades up, she's in danger of failing her finals."

"Okay," She allowed herself a small smile. "We have a plan. I also think we should consider sending her to see someone."

"You mean a shrink?"

"Yes. But not Laura." Their sister-in-law was a psychiatrist and an amazing one, but Sophie was angry with the whole family right now because none of them had told her the truth.

"We can ask Laura for some recommendations."

"Actually, I have someone in mind. From what I've heard, he's terrific. I have a friend who's been seeing him for years, and he's helped her a lot."

"Sounds perfect. I don't quite like the idea of our daughter talking to a stranger rather than us, but I'm prepared to do anything. We need to do something before she starts to spin further out of control. She's on the edge, we have to get her before she falls because if she falls, it's likely to be into drugs and alcohol, and once she starts down that path, she might never get back."

Before Sofia could reply, the front door swung open.

Sophie was home.

"You ready to do this?" Ryan asked her.

"Ready as I'll ever be."

Together they stood and went to confront their daughter. She needed to know that they were in this together.

"We need to talk," Sofia told Sophie, as Ryan blocked the stairs so she couldn't flee up them and hide in her room. There was no more hiding.

"I'm not talking to you," Sophie said sullenly.

"Oh, yes, you are." Ryan grabbed Sophie's arm and led her into the living room. "Things are about to change around here."

"Don't touch me." Sophie tried to shrug out of her father's grip.

"Sit down, Sophie. Now," Sofia ordered. She hated seeing her daughter behave like this. It was hard to believe she'd been such a mature child, wise well beyond her years, and now as she was approaching adulthood, she had regressed into a sulky, whiney, self-centered, spoiled brat.

Sofia hated, even more, knowing that she and Ryan were partially responsible for letting things get this bad.

"We are sorry that we let you down," Sofia said once they were all seated.

"What?" Sophie looked confused.

"Your father and I shouldn't have cut you this much slack. The second you started acting out, we should have put a stop to it. We're sorry for that, but we're putting a stop to it now. You can expect changes around here. You have demonstrated that you can't take care of yourself right now and make good choices so your father and I will be making your choices for you. No more dating, no more phone, no more making your own way to and from school. From now on, we will be monitoring all of your schoolwork and homework assignments. And you will be getting a job. From now on, your life is going to consist of school, work, and family. When you've shown us that you can be more responsible, we can talk about you spending time with your friends. If that goes well, we can discuss dating. Until then, you can kiss your social life goodbye."

"You can't do that!" Sophie raged.

"We can, and we did. Now get to bed. We'll be taking you to school early tomorrow morning so we can talk with your teachers," Ryan informed her.

"Goodnight, Sophie. We love you, and whether you believe it or not, I know exactly what you're going through. When you decide you're ready to talk, I'm here. I'm always here. Your father too. You may hate us right now, but one day you'll understand that we held off telling you about your parentage because we love you and we were trying to protect you. We love you more than we can ever express with just words, and we're hurting too. Being angry isn't the answer. Talk about it, cry about it, deal with it."

Sofia kissed her daughter's cheek, then she and Ryan headed upstairs to bed, leaving Sophie to think about what they'd said. She prayed that this new tough stance would work. She didn't want to lose her daughter.

MARCH 5TH

9:49 A.M.

"Hey, Ryan." Paige looked up as her partner dropped down into his desk chair. "How did things go at the school?"

"Okay. I hope," he added, rubbing wearily at his eyes.

"Do you think you got through to Sophie?" Ryan had texted her this morning to let her know he was going to be a little late for their morning meeting because he and Sofia were going to take Sophie to school and then meet with some of her teachers. It seemed that last night he and Sofia had sat down and worked out a plan to deal with their daughter, and they weren't going to hesitate to start implementing it.

"Maybe. She didn't say much this morning, but she didn't fight us on anything. We took her phone. We had her up early, ate breakfast together and then drove her to school. She was sullen, but at least that's a typical teenager. She knows we're going to be monitoring everything she does, and we've talked to her about her getting a job to keep her occupied."

"Sounds like a plan." Paige was so grateful that Hayley was such an easy kid. She was quiet and very serious for a teenage girl. She wasn't into dating, and she wasn't really into partying or hanging out with large groups of kids. Paige didn't think that Hayley was ever going to give them any trouble. Arianna, on the other hand, was a different story. She was loud and outgoing, and even at ten, was starting to show an interest in the opposite sex. Paige suspected that Ari's teenage years were going to be a lot more work than Hayley's were.

"We have to do something. I feel like we're at the turning

57

point. Either we get a handle on things now, or they spiral out of control."

"But you *are* getting a handle on things, and Sophie seems to be responding. I know you and Sofia blamed yourselves for waiting so long to tell her about her parents and giving her so much space lately, but maybe this approach will work better."

"I hope so." Ryan picked up the framed family photo he kept on his desk and stared at it for a moment. Then he set it down and looked over at her. "Stephanie and Jenny coming soon?"

"Should be here any minute, meeting is at ten," she replied. Usually, they met at nine, but they had rearranged things to reschedule for ten so Ryan could take care of things with his daughter.

"Once we finish up, we need to see if we can track down the phone number."

Yesterday, when they'd finished up at the school interviewing Debra and Susanne, they had called the number the girls had given them. The number had been disconnected. Since that number was the only link they had to Brianna Lester, and her abductor and the man they believed had killed Talia Canuck and Ally Brown, they had to do whatever they could to try to track down who the number had belonged to. Brianna had been gone for around forty-eight hours now. That meant she only had a little over forty-eight hours left until she was murdered.

"We should also talk to Talia and Ally's friends," Ryan continued. "See if they also called a phone number from a message in the bathrooms. So far, it's the only solid link we have, other than the school, and this certainly fits in with the school being where the killer is choosing his victims."

"It does," she agreed. Which terrified her. She had always been scared of losing her daughters to Arianna's biological mother. Ever since she adopted her girls, that fear had been there. That one day, Eliza would feel more settled and decide she wanted her daughter and the girl she had raised for five years back. Those fears had intensified when Eliza had gotten married and given birth to her first son. But every time they caught up, Eliza maintained that she was so happy she'd made the choice she had about Ari and Hayley's futures and that she didn't regret it at all.

Despite the dangers of her job and the fears all parents had that something would happen to their children, she'd never seriously thought that her girls could wind up kidnap and murder victims. Now, that was a genuine possibility. A killer was using the school her daughter attended as his hunting ground. It wasn't likely that Hayley would ever call some number on a bathroom mirror, but the killer could stop choosing victims that way and just start randomly grabbing girls.

"That's Steph and Jenny," she said as she caught sight of the two women heading toward their desks.

"Hey guys," Stephanie Cantini, a fifty-four-year-old crime scene tech, greeted them.

"Hey, Steph, Jenny." Paige gathered her files and stood. "Why don't we go talk in one of the conference rooms, it'll be quieter in there."

The four of them headed into the nearest room and took seats at the table, each arranging their files. Hopefully, between what they knew, whatever forensics Stephanie could give them, and whatever Jenny got from the autopsy, they would be closer to finding their killer.

"Do you want to start, Jenny?" Ryan said.

"Sure." Jenny beamed at them. She was new to the medical examiner's office and was still full of that youthful enthusiasm Paige remembered from when she first joined the force. Although she still loved her job, she was forty-five now, a mother to a fifteen-year-old and a ten-year-old, the job was less about her enthusiasm and more about making the world a safer place for her girls.

"Did you get anything from Ally's body?" Paige asked.

"She was drowned," Jenny replied.

"Just like Talia Canuck," Ryan said.

That was another link between the two girls. They attended the same school, they had both been killed in the same way, they had both been posed and left on their doorsteps.

"She wasn't drowned in tap water though," Stephanie inserted.

"Salt water again?" Paige asked. She'd forgotten that Talia had been drowned in salt water.

"Yes, but not seawater," Stephanie clarified.

"So, why the salt?" Paige mused aloud. "Is it because they had salt water laying around or does the salt water hold some sort of special meaning? Like the number nine."

"Did Ally have the tattoo, Jenny?" Ryan asked.

"Yes, she did."

"Same place as Talia's?" Paige asked. When Talia's body had been examined, they had found a small number nine tattoo on the cheek of her left buttock. It was an unlikely tattoo for a teenage girl to choose, and an unusual location to put it, and no one in Talia's family or circle of friends knew of her ever getting a tattoo.

"Same place," Jenny confirmed.

Another link between the girls.

"Ally's body was scrubbed clean," Jenny continued. "With bleach. He cleaned everywhere. Everywhere. Under her eyelids, up her nostrils, inside her ears and her belly button, in between every toe, he was extremely thorough."

"Did he clean her inside her vagina as well?" Paige asked tightly. She hoped that Ally Brown hadn't been sexually assaulted. It was a sensitive topic for her and one that hit very close to home. Ally was a good, sweet kid. She didn't deserve this; she didn't deserve any of this.

"He did," Jenny said, her cheeks turning pink. "But there were no signs of sexual assault. From what I could see, the girl was still a virgin."

Relief washed over her.

At least that was something.

"Were there any other injuries?" Ryan asked.

"Her left wrist was badly cut. It looked like she had been restrained, probably with a plastic zip tie. Her nails were torn as well, probably from trying to get free," Jenny explained.

"Nothing else?" Paige asked. If the killer hadn't raped Ally and he hadn't physically assaulted her, then what had he done with her for four days? Just put a tattoo on her and then left her alone until her ninety-nine hours were up and then killed her?

"Nothing else," Jenny replied.

"Stephanie, did you find anything?" Ryan asked the crime scene tech.

"I went over her clothes with a fine-tooth comb and all I found were a couple of gray fibers that looked like they came from a blanket. He probably used it to transport her. Other than that, I didn't get anything. He was thorough, not just with the body but with the clothes too. He doesn't want you to find him."

That was not what Paige wanted to hear.

This killer was methodical. He had a secure location to hold his victims, and he didn't physically or sexually abuse them other than to tattoo them. He was charming enough to lure the girls in, and as far as they knew, all three girls went to him of their own accord.

How did you catch a killer playing things this smart?

* * * * *

11:19 A.M.

"Do you want to sit this one out?"

"No," Ryan entered firmly.

His partner shot him a doubtful glance. "Are you sure?"

"Yes."

"You know we're not here to discuss Sophie," Paige warned.

"I know," Ryan assured her. They were back at the school, not to check up on his daughter—although he couldn't deny he was probably going to check in on her before they left—but to start interviewing the kids. There were around eight hundred kids who attended the high school. There was no way they were going to be able to interview them all quickly, so they were starting with anyone who'd had anything to do with any of their victims.

The teachers had also been asked to ask their classes if there were any girls who'd called a phone number they'd gotten from a note left on the bathroom mirrors. Those girls were all potential victims, and they needed to make sure that they were warned and knew not to go sneaking off to meet up with anyone—not even someone they thought they knew. So far, their killer wasn't plucking girls off the street. He was getting them to come to him. If they could make sure that all potential victims made no plans to meet up with anyone alone, maybe this guy would just lay low for a while, give them time to find him.

Next on their list were Victor and Dominick Tremaine.

The Dominick Tremaine.

Sophie's eighteen-year-old boyfriend.

He could interview the kid though.

He could pretend for the next fifteen minutes or so that this kid was nothing more than a teenager who attended the same school as the victims.

He could.

He really could.

He hoped.

"Okay, then." Paige still didn't sound convinced, but she didn't offer any more protests. "Let's call them in."

The school had set them up in one of the classrooms as they'd be here for the rest of the day. And probably tomorrow and the next day, and as long as it took to get a solid lead on their killer. Forensics and the autopsy hadn't given them anything concrete, so they were counting on a statement from one of the students to break this case.

Ryan stood and stretched. Although they'd only been interviewing kids for the last thirty minutes, he'd been under such stress lately with the drama at home that his body was constantly in a state of tension.

"Come in, boys," he said when he opened the door. In the interest of getting through the interviews as quickly as they could, they were interviewing siblings or friendship groups together. So Dominick Tremaine and his twin brother Victor were going to be interviewed together.

"Hello, Mr. Xander," Dominick said as the boys followed him into the room and over to the area they'd set up to conduct their interviews.

"*Detective* Xander," he corrected. Usually, he only called himself Detective Xander when he was working, and while he was working right now, that had nothing to do with why he wanted the teenager to address him as detective. Right now, he just wanted to remind the young man who was dating his daughter that he was a cop and that he was watching every move he made and would make sure that his relationship with Sophie was over and done with.

"Detective Xander," Dominick nodded. "This isn't about Sophie, is it?"

"No, this isn't about Sophie. This is about what happened to some of the students here."

"Talia and Ally," Victor said.

"Did you know Talia or Ally?" Paige asked.

"I didn't know Ally, never heard her name until the rumors started going around school about her," Victor replied.

"Dominick?" Paige asked.

"Never heard of her, until the rumors." He echoed his twin's words.

"What kind of rumors have been going around the school?" he asked, interested in finding out what the kids were talking about. Sometimes you could learn a lot from rumors. Although they generally contained a lot of false information, they were usually based in fact. If the killer had participated in starting any rumors, maybe they could find out something they didn't know yet.

"We heard that Ally was found strung up in a tree in her front yard, naked, with over a hundred stab wounds," Victor replied.

Other than that she was found on her own property, nothing in that was even remotely true.

"We heard," Victor continued, almost gleefully, "that she was secretly a whore and that her pimp made her spend the night with a dozen men and that they were all high and after they shared her around, they each took turns stabbing her."

He wondered how many times that story had passed around, no doubt each person adding their own little details until the story had grown into something ridiculously over-the-top. He also wondered what the story would have become by the end of the school day.

"Is-is that what happened?" Dominick asked. He was quieter than his brother and seemed content to let his twin do most of the talking.

"Not exactly," he answered, "but Ally was killed, and we believe it was by someone at the school."

"You think it was one of us?" Victor's brown eyes darkened at the idea.

"We think that it's someone at the school," he repeated. Did he really think his daughter's boyfriend was a killer? No. He knew Sophie would be devastated if Dominick was a killer, but right now, they didn't know who the killer was, and he couldn't discount the possibility it was one of the Tremaine twins.

"You said you didn't know Ally Brown," Paige said, "but what about Talia Canuck?" They already knew the answer to that question, but they wanted to see what the boys were going to volunteer.

"I dated her for a while last year," Victor reluctantly told them. "She was a cheerleader, and I play football. We met at a party, made out, then dated for a couple of months. We broke up over a year ago. She was dating Ted Landry after that."

They knew all about Ted Landry.

He had been questioned extensively after Talia's disappearance and again after her death.

Ted was the ex-boyfriend who'd had the bad breakup with Talia only a couple of weeks before she went missing, then turned up dead.

While it didn't seem likely that Victor Tremaine had killed Talia because they had dated briefly before she'd been with Ted, he had undoubtedly seen stranger things than that happen.

"Who ended things, you or Talia?" Paige asked.

"It was mutual." Victor shrugged.

"Were you angry about it?" Ryan asked.

"Not really." Victor looked disinterested and borderline bored. "I'm not really interested in a serious relationship. I like to keep things casual."

From the smug look on Victor's face, it was clear he meant he liked to sleep around with no strings attached. What did girls see in guys like that? What did his daughter see in guys like that? If that was Victor's attitude, it was probably Dominick's as well.

"What about you, Dominick, did you know Ally?" Paige asked.

"Only through Victor," Dominick replied.

"Did either of you know Brianna Lester?" Ryan asked.

Both boys shook their heads. That made sense. They were eighteen-year-old seniors, and Brianna was a fourteen-year-old freshman.

"Victor, are you involved with anyone at the moment?" he asked, deliberately phrasing it as involved rather than dating since he didn't really think Victor Tremaine dated.

"They are a couple of girls I've been spending a bit of time with." Victor winked.

There was no point in asking Dominick the same question. Unfortunately, he already knew the answer to whom he was involved with. Or at least had been up until last night. But there was no way he was allowing his fifteen-year-old daughter to date a senior.

Especially *this* senior, with his perfectly white teeth, his thick hair, his tanned skin, his perfect physique, and his charming smile.

Dominick was off limits.

"Is there anyone you can think of who might want to hurt Talia, Ally, or Brianna?" Paige asked.

"There are plenty of guys here who are angry enough to kill, and plenty of girls who would rip each other's eyes out over a guy, but no one that stands out," Victor replied.

"Where were you boys the day before yesterday? Early in the morning, before six?" Ryan asked. They were focusing on the time Ally's body had been discovered when they spoke with everyone. Since Brianna was not officially a victim of their killer, there was no point in finding out where everyone was when she'd gone missing.

"Home. Bed," Victor answered, and Dominick nodded, indicating the same answer.

"Anyone who can verify that?"

The boys looked at each other. "Just each other. Mom goes to work early; Dad is dead," Victor said.

"All right, boys, thanks for your time." Ryan was done being in the same room as Sophie's boyfriend. The longer they were together, the more he wanted to tell the boy to stay away from his little girl, and today was about work, not his personal life.

Victor stood, but Dominick remained where he was. "Mr.-Detective Xander, I know you don't like me dating Sophie—"

"No, I don't," he said.

"I love her; I wouldn't do anything to hurt her." Dominick looked so sincere, but Ryan had been a teenage boy. He knew how they thought. In high school, he'd thought he was in love plenty of times, and while he knew it was possible for kids to fall in love—his brother Jack had loved his wife Laura since they were

66

both kids—he didn't believe it happened often.

"But you *are* hurting her. You're coming between her and her family and taking advantage of the fact that she's vulnerable right now." After learning who her biological parents were, Sophie's sense of self had been decimated. She needed someone who could make her feel loved, special, whole. Who made her feel like she fit in someplace. And since she was angry with him and Sofia, they couldn't make her feel that. Dominick was taking advantage of that and using it to get close to Sophie. Ryan was sure he knew why. Sex. That was what motivated most teenage boys.

"I don't want to hurt her," Dominick said.

"Then leave her alone. Focus on yourself and school. You'll be off to college in just a few months." Assuming the kid was smart enough to go to college; he didn't really know much about Dominick Tremaine other than he was eighteen and Sophie was fifteen. "How are you going to continue a relationship with a high school kid after that? You can't give Sophie what she needs right now. She needs stability, and you can't give her that. We can. Her mother and I have told her that this little relationship is over. If you love Sophie like you say you do, then honor our wishes."

Dominick didn't say anything, but Ryan could see he'd gotten to the boy. Who knows, maybe the kid really did have feelings for Sophie beyond wanting to sleep with her.

"I don't know what Sophie sees in him," he muttered as the Tremaine boys left the room.

"He's cute," Paige said with a grin. "If I were fifteen, I'd have a crush on him. And he seems like a good kid. He makes good grades, and he hasn't been in any trouble. I don't think it's a good time for him to be dating Sophie, but Hayley says he's always respectful of her."

Ryan just grunted.

He wasn't ready for there to be any other man in his daughter's life.

He knew he would have to let her go eventually.

He knew she would grow up and fall in love and get married.

But not yet.

For now, she was still his little girl, and she needed him whether she realized it or not.

* * * * *

6:23 P.M.

Forty-one hours, twenty-nine minutes, and sixteen seconds.

That was all the time there was until her life ended.

Brianna hated that clock.

She hated the way the numbers glowed so brightly like they were all cheerful about counting down the remaining minutes of her life.

She hated that she had to watch the countdown like they were waiting for the New Year's fireworks.

Countdowns were supposed to be for fun things. She always counted down the days until summer vacation and to Christmas and her birthday and when her family went on holidays, but no one should have to countdown to their death.

He was just doing it to torture her.

She'd learned her lesson earlier though.

She wasn't going to risk doing anything to antagonize him again. She was just going to sit here quietly, not making a sound, not saying anything, doing exactly as she was told until …

She guessed until she died.

She was too young to die.

Fourteen years old.

Her life had barely started, and yet, she was sitting here staring her death in the face.

How stupid was she?

She had offered herself up to him as a sacrificial lamb.

She hadn't even made it hard. He'd told her when and where

to meet him, and she'd come. The thought that she was walking into a trap had never even occurred to her. She had believed that she was going to meet the man of her dreams, her prince charming, her soul mate; instead, she was going to meet her dragon, her bogeyman, her killer.

It turned out her mother was right.

She was too young to know anything about love.

If she were smarter, older, more mature, then she wouldn't have agreed to meet someone she didn't even know in a secluded location on her own.

If she weren't so young, she'd have made sure someone knew where she was going. She'd have made sure that she met in a public place, and she'd have made sure that she had talked to him a few times, that they had exchanged pictures, that she actually knew who she was meeting.

If she weren't just a child, she never would have rung a phone number she found on the mirror in the school bathroom and made a date with a stranger.

She should have known it was a setup.

Why would anyone want to arrange a date with a fourteen-year-old?

There was only one reason.

To hurt them.

This was all her fault.

Brianna hated that she was going to die, and she had no one to blame but herself.

It was too bad that there were no do-overs in life. That even though you realized you'd made a mistake and learned a lesson, it didn't mean that everything was fixed. That whatever bad thing had happened was righted. That you got a chance to put into practice what you'd learned. She had learned so many things in the last forty-eight hours, and it didn't do her any good. She was still going to die.

She wished she had a chance to make things right. To tell her mom that she was sorry for not listening to her and believing her, for tricking her brother and sneaking off on her own, for ditching school to meet a boy. She wished that she could just give her mom and her dad one more kiss, one more hug, tell them she loved them one last time.

Brianna hated knowing that her death was going to cause her family pain. Would they ever get over it? Would it ruin their lives? Or worse, would they be able to go on as though nothing had happened—like her death didn't really bother them?

She loved her parents, and she knew they loved her, but they weren't really close. They were too controlling. They micromanaged every single aspect of her life, and when they weren't doing that, they were busy with their own lives.

But they loved her, and she loved them.

And now, she was never going to see them again.

The minutes kept ticking down, and it didn't matter how much she wanted to grab that stupid clock and smash it into a million pieces, her death was careening toward her, and no one could stop it.

Another sob wanted to burst out, but she pressed her hand to her mouth and held it in.

All that did was remind her of the throbbing pain in her mouth, and a small sob burst out anyway.

That was her fault too.

He had warned her what would happen if she didn't stop crying, but she hadn't been able to make herself stop.

Her tongue moved in her mouth to probe the gap where her tooth had been. She'd been so shocked when his fist connected with her face that she'd gagged and almost swallowed the tooth.

It had bled a lot.

A *lot*.

Brianna hated blood.

She hated the sight of it, the smell of it, the feel of it and the taste of it.

It was disgusting, and she was trying to make sure that she didn't look down and see where blood had dribbled down her chin and onto her clothes.

She supposed that was one good thing about him hitting her in the cheek, it seemed to have broken her cheekbone and made her eye swell so much she could no longer see through it. Between the blood, the black eye, and the possibly broken jaw, she didn't have any appetite. She wasn't sure she could eat even if she wanted to—the pain in her mouth was too severe. Brianna was worried that her lack of appetite was going to make her abductor angry, but so far, he didn't seem to care that she hadn't eaten the sandwiches he'd brought for her.

Brianna wished she knew what to do.

She didn't want to cry and make him angry again, but she also didn't just want to sit back and wait for him to kill her.

She should fight back.

Right?

That was what she was supposed to.

Wasn't it?

She was so confused.

She wanted to do the right thing. She just didn't know what it was. How could she fight back when he had bound her wrist to a pipe on the wall with a plastic zip tie that had painfully gouged its way into her flesh?

Maybe she could wait until he cut the tie and then make a run for it?

But surely, he wouldn't let her do that. The door would probably be locked.

Brianna scanned the room with her good eye in search of a weapon, but there was nothing. Other than herself, the sandwich he'd brought her earlier that sat untouched on a plate beside her, and that mocking clock, the room was empty.

She had no options.

She was trapped.

Soon, she would be dead.

There was nothing she could do to stop it from happening.

When tears welled up in her eyes, she didn't bother trying to stop them from falling out.

The worst that was going to happen if he found her crying was that he would hit her again. Other than that, it wasn't going to change anything. He was still going to kill her.

Barely a minute after tears started to stream down her cheeks, she heard the door to the basement open and footsteps thunder down the steps.

"Was I not clear earlier? Because I thought I made my position on crying quite clear. Do you need another lesson?"

That was a rhetorical question, so she offered no answer.

The first time he'd hit her, he had seemed unsure, like he'd never hit anyone before and wasn't sure how he was going to feel about it.

This time he looked positively ecstatic about the prospect of striking her.

Brianna sucked in a breath and held it, hoping that would stop the tears. Now that he was standing in front of her with that smile on his face, any bravado she had felt before he came down the stairs, vanished.

"Don't try and hide it. You were crying. There are tears all over your face. You obviously didn't learn anything from our little talk earlier. Seems like you need another lesson."

His fist connected with the side of her head.

A ringing started in her head.

It was worse than the pain.

Almost, anyway.

The second blow got her in the nose, and suddenly, the ringing in her ears was forgotten.

Pain bloomed out from her nose across her face.

Blood gushed out and down her chin.

She started to cry in earnest.

Fear and pain mingled together, growing exponentially with each passing second until it overwhelmed her to the point of crushing her.

For the first time, she wished the clock would hurry up and get to zero already.

MARCH 6TH

7:19 A.M.

"We'll be leaving for school in ten minutes," her mom called up the stairs.

"Okay," Hayley called back.

"I'm so glad your parents convinced my parents to let me come over here this morning." Sophie flopped dramatically onto the bed.

Her best friend was always dramatic.

Sometimes she wondered how they had remained best friends for ten years now. Maybe it had to do with how great and supportive Sophie had been when she'd first come to live here.

Hayley's start in life had been far from normal. Abducted from her crib when she was just a few months old by a man who had intended to keep her as his prisoner until her death or his. By the time she was rescued, her biological parents were deceased, and the only relative she had left was an elderly grandmother who couldn't care for her.

She would forever be grateful that Paige and Elias had adopted her. She couldn't have asked for better parents, and as far as she was concerned, they *were* her parents.

Between her parents and Sophie, she had adjusted to normal life, although she knew she would never really be completely normal. But she was happy. Really and truly happy, and a big part of that was because of Sophie.

"They're really sticking to the new rules?" she asked as she dropped down onto the bed beside her friend.

"Yeah," Sophie pouted.

"So, no more staying out at night until you feel like going home?"

"Nope. If one of them can't pick me up, then they're sending my grandparents."

Sophie's grandparents weren't like regular grandparents. They were nice, but they didn't believe in spoiling kids. They would probably be tougher than Sophie's parents would be. "What about Dom? You're not allowed to see him, right? Did you tell him at school yesterday?"

"I'm not going to stop seeing Dom." Sophie got that determined look on her face that Hayley had seen so many times before.

"Aren't you going to get in trouble if you keep seeing him?" She liked Dom. He was nice and often seemed to be in the shadow of his twin brother which reminded her of her relationship with her sister. Although they could pass for biological siblings, she and Arianna weren't related, and they weren't alike at all. She was quiet and serious; her little sister was bright and bubbly and full of spunk. Hayley loved and adored Ari, but she was often overshadowed by her sister in social situations.

"I don't care." Sophie sat up and crossed her arms across her chest. "I love Dom, and he loves me. My parents have no right to tell us that we can't be together."

"Are you going to hide it from them then?" She was sure that this was going to wind up blowing up in her friend's face. But they were best friends, and she would support her however she had to, even if it meant lying to Sophie's parents, or hers.

"No."

"No?"

"I'm not going to lie to them. I want them to know that they aren't the boss of me. I'll go to school and try to do better with my classes, but that's it. I'm going to keep seeing Dom, and I don't care if they know it."

"Are you sure?"

"Positive. How could I stop seeing him anyway?" A dreamy smile curved Sophie's lips up, and she got that faraway look she always did when she thought about her boyfriend. "I love him so much. I've never felt this way about any other boy before. When he touches me, I get this feeling in my stomach … I don't know how to explain it, but it's love. True love. And when he kisses me, it's like for those seconds, the whole world stops spinning and becomes just us."

Hayley's eyes grew wide. "Have you two done *it*?"

Sophie's grin grew mischievous. "Not yet, but we're close."

"Has he asked?"

"Not in so many words, but he wants to and I want to and I don't see any reason why we should wait."

"You're not just going to have sex to make your parents angry, are you?" She didn't think her friend would do something that big just to get back at her parents, but Hayley had never seen Sophie this angry before. She was really shaken up by learning she was adopted, and after Sophie had admitted it was because she was afraid she was going to turn out like her biological parents, she finally understood why. Since Sophie was so angry, Hayley wouldn't put anything past her right now.

"No. I want to do it, *really* want to do it, but not to make them angry, just because I want to." Sophie released a semi-awkward giggle. Neither of them had ever had sex before, and Hayley knew what a big step it was to take—one she knew she wasn't ready for.

"I'm glad you found someone that you love." She didn't know if Dom and Sophie's relationship would ever survive, not many teenage romances did, although Sophie's uncle Jack and aunt Laura were an example of one that had. She was glad her friend was so happy. Young love was still real love.

"What about you?" Hayley got that glint in her silvery gray eyes that meant she was up to something, or that she wanted to be up to something.

"What about me?" she asked. She was much more comfortable

discussing her friend's love life than her own.

"Dom's brother Victor likes you, you know; he thinks you're hot."

Her?

Hot?

Hayley had been told that she was pretty with her long dark hair, milky white skin, and large blue eyes, but she didn't really think of herself as attractive. It wasn't that she was self-conscious about her appearance. She liked wearing makeup and trying out new hair styles, and she liked to go shopping and keep up with the latest trends, but she liked to blend into the background, not stand out.

"Why don't you go out with him?" Sophie asked. "It doesn't have to be serious. You two could just hang out with Dom and me. And Victor is cute and smart and funny, and his body is almost as good as Dom's." She giggled.

She could feel her cheeks heat with embarrassment. She couldn't deny that Victor Tremaine was good-looking, and she was a little attracted to him. And although she didn't know him as well as she did Dom, if he was even half as charming as his brother, then he would no doubt be a good date.

Hayley cleared her throat. "He's not really my type."

"Then, who is your type?" Sophie asked with a teasing smile. "If it isn't a sexy football player with a body to die for, then who is it?"

"Victor is too confident; I like quieter guys."

"Any quiet guy in particular?"

"Umm ..."

"There is." Sophie squealed delightedly. "Who is it? Who? You have to tell me. We're best friends, and best friends don't keep secrets from each other."

She groaned. She knew there was no way to avoid telling Hayley who she had a crush on. If she tried, Sophie would just pester her until she gave in and gave up a name. "It's Zane

Bishop," she said as her cheeks went from embarrassed pink to fire engine bright red.

"The piano prodigy?" Sophie's eyes grew as round as saucers. "He's cute. I mean, he's no Dom, but for a musician, he has a great body, and the way he wears his hair, so it hangs into his eyes a little is very sexy. I bet he's a good kisser. And romantic too. That is one area Dom lacks in ... he's never romantic, but I bet Zane would be. Candles, flowers, music ... I bet he'd make your first date like a movie, and your first kiss—"

"Sophie ..." She groaned. Why did her friend have to torture her like this? Sophie knew that she wasn't entirely comfortable when it came to boys. It was because she knew what men were capable of. She knew what her abductor had done to his other victims and what he would have done to her if she hadn't been rescued. She also knew that not all men were like that. Most weren't, and she wanted to fall in love and get married and have kids of her own one day.

One day.

And that day wasn't today.

For now, she was comfortable taking things slow.

Very slow.

"Girls, let's go," her mom yelled up the stairs.

Perfect timing.

She and Sophie both stood up and grabbed their coats and backpacks, then Hayley straightened her bed. She hated going out for the day without her room being perfectly tidy and organized.

"What?" she asked when she looked up to see Sophie watching her with a bemused smile.

"You're weird." Her friend laughed.

Hayley shrugged. She was confident in herself and wasn't concerned if other people thought she was odd. She was. She wasn't like most teenagers, and she was okay with that.

"Just so you know, I'm talking to Zane today," Sophie announced, then took off down the stairs.

"You wouldn't dare," she called after her.

Sophie just laughed.

She was glad to hear that sound again.

After how stressful and dark the last few months had been, it was nice just to hang out with her friend—her old friend—the friend Sophie used to be.

Maybe Ryan and Sofia implementing some rules were exactly what Sophie needed to get back on track.

* * * * *

2:46 P.M.

"Brianna Lester will die in less than twenty-four hours, and we have nothing." Paige stood so quickly her chair teetered and almost toppled over.

Ryan watched as his partner paced the classroom. He understood her frustration. They were no closer to solving this case, and Brianna's impending death looming over them made them both extremely conscious of every passing second. All kidnap cases were time sensitive, every second counted, but in this particular case, they knew the killer's timeline, which made the pressure so much worse.

"We don't have anything," Paige ranted. "We know he drowns them in salt water. We know that he probably wrapped them in a gray blanket when he moved them. We know he didn't rape or physically assault them while he held them captive. We know he cleans their bodies. We know he's obsessed with the number nine, and none of those things help."

His partner was right.

None of what they knew so far was going to lead them to the killer.

They might help to prove that they had the right guy *after* they already had a suspect, but that was it.

So far, they had interviewed dozens of students from the school, but no one had given them anything useful. They had found another eight girls who'd also called the number from the bathroom, but it had quickly become clear that the number was a dead end. Each girl had called a different phone number, and all of those numbers seemed to belong to disposable cell phones.

The girls said when they called the number, they spoke to a male who sounded like a kid their age, who was charming and sweet, and who talked about looking for someone to share the high school experience with and maybe even their lives. None of the girls had recognized the voice but had just assumed that it was someone from their school.

All the girls who had called were either quieter girls who didn't have a lot of friends or boyfriends, or girls who had recently broken up with long-term boyfriends. They had all been searching for the same thing—love. And they had all been sure that making that phone call had been the first step in finding it.

"Do you think we did enough to keep the girls safe?" Paige stopped her near frenetic pacing.

"The others who called?"

"Yes. I know we warned them that they could be in danger, but you know what teenagers are like. They'll think that we're just exaggerating, that they're indestructible, that nothing is going to happen to them."

"We've done all we can," he assured Paige, although he had the same concerns she did. She was right; teenagers were prone to thinking that they were unbreakable and they were immune to the bad things that happened in the world.

"Have we?"

"What else can we do? We've warned them; we've informed their parents that there is a chance they could be this killer's next victims. And we've made sure that all the kids at the school know not to go out on their own and not to make plans to meet anyone alone in a secluded location. There's nothing more we can do."

"Well, that's not good enough." Paige resumed pacing, "We should be able to do something. Isn't that our job? To keep people safe? Why do I feel like we keep failing at it?"

"Because we're only human, and there's a limit to what we can do," he reminded her, and himself. After how rough the last six months had been, he needed the occasional reminder that he and Sofia were doing the best they could with their kids.

Had they made mistakes?

Yes.

But they loved Sophie and Ned, and everything they did was because they thought it was in their children's best interests.

"I'm sorry, Ryan." Paige came and sank down into the chair beside him. "I know you guys are going through a rough time with Sophie; it's just, this killer is here. At our girls' school. What if they get mixed up in this? What if this guy starts devolving? He could easily go off script and just start killing any of the girls here."

He was just as afraid of that happening as his partner was.

But they were already doing everything they could to find this guy.

They were still working through interviewing the students at the school, and that was about all they could do right now. Forensics weren't going to solve this case for them; at least, not yet, and there was nothing in the autopsy that had given them a lead. So they were going to have to focus their efforts on interviews and hope that someone knew something that would point them in the right direction.

Paige's phone beeped, and she picked it up from the desk and looked at it. "Elias just picked up the girls. Apparently, Sophie was there waiting with Hayley and didn't give him any problems."

That was a relief.

He couldn't help but expect the worst when it came to his daughter. She had been going out of her way for the last few months to cause as many problems as she could and to be as difficult as she could be that it was hard to believe she was just going to do as she was told without a fuss.

"She was good this morning, Ryan. Really. She and Hayley just hung out, talked, came right down when I called them. She and Hayley were giggling and whispering the whole drive to school. Sophie was even teasing Ari and having fun with her. Everything is going to work out with her. She just needs time. And I think being stricter with her is going to help. I think it makes her feel loved that you care enough to set boundaries with her even though she may not like them."

"Yeah, I think you're right. I wish we'd done it earlier." Maybe if they'd been tough on her from the beginning instead of coddling her, they could have avoided all this mess.

"You did what you thought was best at the time. You aren't clairvoyant. You couldn't have known that trying to give her space to deal with what she learned was going to wind up being counterproductive. She knows you and Sofia love her. She just has to learn how to let go of the anger."

"Thanks for helping out with her."

"Of course." Paige smiled. "You'd do the same if we were having trouble with Hayley or Arianna."

He would.

That was what family did. And while he and Paige may not actually be family, they'd been friends for so long that he considered her part of his family.

Paige picked up the photos of Talia, Ally, and Brianna from the file on the desk. She stared at them so long that he started to wonder if something had occurred to her.

"What are you thinking?" he asked.

"He didn't choose his victims," Paige said thoughtfully. "I mean, he left the note, but he had no way of knowing which girls were going to end up calling him."

"Which means this isn't about Talia, Ally, or Brianna. They were inconsequential to him. They aren't his real target."

"So, who is?" Paige looked up at him.

"Someone related to the number nine. So far, that's the most distinctive thing about his MO. Drowning people isn't a particularly common way to murder someone, but holding them for ninety-nine hours and going to the trouble of tattooing a number nine on them, that is so specific. The number nine seems too important to him that it can't mean nothing. But is it just ritualistic, or does it mean something deeper?"

"Something deeper," Paige said immediately. "But what?"

"We won't know that until we find him. If the girls aren't his real target, then it's not likely that we're going to find who he is by interviewing the kids. The only way we're going to find him is ..."

"Is if he slips up when he kills Brianna Lester and either leaves behind some forensics, or someone witnesses him leaving the body," Paige finished for him.

That was what he hated most about his job. When the only way to stop a killer was to wait until he killed another victim, and then maybe another and another and gave them enough information to lead them to him.

Eventually, this killer would slip up. He would do something that would reveal his true motives and his true target, and then they would find out who he was. But how many more girls would die before they learned enough?

"If this isn't about the girls specifically," Paige said. "Then it's not likely it's a student, but it *is* someone related to the school because he wrote the notes in the bathroom."

"So it's probably not a parent."

"It's probably a teacher."

* * * * *

7:35 P.M.

Only fifteen hours, forty-eight minutes, and thirty-two seconds to go.

He couldn't wait.

He stretched out his hand, examining his knuckles. They were a little bluish. Not enough to be noticeable if you weren't really looking, but if you looked closely, you could see it. There was also a small cut on one knuckle from where it must have connected with one of Brianna's teeth.

This was pretty cool.

He giggled like a schoolgirl. This was so much fun. For the first time, he was almost dreading the clock hitting zero. It was all going to be over too soon.

The cops were on to him.

Well, not *him,* per se, but they seemed to have figured out that the killer they were looking for was associated with the high school. It was a logical assumption—and a correct one—and he had known that they would get there eventually.

To be honest, he'd thought they would have figured it out after Ally Brown went missing, but perhaps that had been overestimating their abilities. They were cops, after all. And cops weren't really the brightest bulbs around.

He should know.

Dealing with cops wasn't new to him.

It was why he was doing this.

He didn't care about Talia, Ally, or Brianna. Well, he cared a little more about Brianna since the two of them had had such fun together. But beyond that, those girls were only here to serve one purpose. A purpose they'd already served. They were to bring the cops in, to draw their attention to him, so that when he was ready, he could move on to what he really wanted to do.

It was almost time.

The cops had linked the cases. He was sure they were baffled about the number nine tattoos, and he wondered if they had realized that each victim was killed exactly ninety-nine hours after they'd been abducted. A small smirk settled on his lips as he thought about them trying to come up with explanations for what it might mean. He wondered what they were thinking. It seemed odd if you didn't know the significance of the number nine. He had never really been one for superstitions, but this had just seemed to fit.

Now that the cops knew the girls had all been killed by the same person, and by someone who attended the school, it was time to get to what he really wanted to do.

It was time to show them that what had happened was unacceptable.

Not just unacceptable, but criminal.

Criminal and cruel.

The cops thought they could do what they wanted, that it didn't matter who they hurt so long as they didn't get caught.

Well, this time, they had been caught.

And they weren't going to get away with it.

Would he get away with what he was doing?

Probably not.

Definitely not.

That wasn't the plan.

The plan was to move on to the next stage and then the next until he reached his fiery finale. Not literally fiery, although he guessed that could be fun, but what was going to be even more fun was what he had already planned.

He had always known he was different than other people. That there was something inside him that didn't work correctly. He just hadn't known what it was. He had always wondered about it, ever since he was a small child. He had tried to figure it out. He'd tried to be like the other boys, but he could never do it. He could pretend, but that was it. It wasn't real. He felt unreal.

But now he knew why.

When he hit Brianna Lester that first time, it suddenly all became clear.

Now he knew what it was that was different.

He had no conscience.

He had enjoyed hitting Brianna. He had enjoyed watching the fear and pain coat her face and fill her eyes. He had enjoyed her screams; they were like music to his ears.

He was a psychopath. Or was it sociopath? He wasn't quite sure, but either way, it was kind of exhilarating to finally know who he was.

Now his whole world made sense.

Now *he* finally made sense.

Life was good.

Soon he would finally get the revenge he wanted, and then whatever happened after that, happened.

He stretched his hand, flexing his bruised knuckles. They hurt, but not so much that he couldn't take one last go at Brianna before he had to kill her. There were a few logistics still to be planned out since dumping her body on her doorstep wasn't going to work. The cops would, no doubt, be watching the house, waiting for him to turn up. He had an idea what he would do with her, but there were still a few kinks to iron out.

That could wait.

The next stage of the plan would be different than this one, so he had to enjoy this while he could.

He had worked hard; he deserved a little fun before he got back to it.

Unlocking the door to the basement, he sang out, "Brianna, time to play."

MARCH 7TH

7:14 A.M.

"Fifteen minutes, Sophie," her mom called up the stairs.

She took a deep breath.

It was time. She couldn't put it off any longer. They were going to find out soon enough.

Her parents were going to go ballistic.

Not that it would be anything out of the ordinary. It seemed like overreacting about everything was all they did these days. They never used to be so uptight.

Or maybe, she was the one who had changed.

She wasn't the sweet, compliant little girl they thought she was. She was growing up. She was fifteen, she was in love, and for the first time in her life, she actually knew who she really was.

Learning the truth had been painful, but it was for the best. At least now she knew. She was her mother's aunt. Growing up, her mom had thought that her parents were Judge Logan Everett II and some random woman he'd paid to get pregnant and give up her baby. Then, fifteen years ago, her mother had learned that the man she had thought of as her father was, in fact, actually her grandfather, and that her oldest brother, Logan Everett IV, was really her father, who had raped his stepmother, and the stepmother she had believed had never loved her was really her biological mother.

If that wasn't insane enough, then her mother had a younger half sister—they shared a father—who had had a mother who had blackmailed the Everett family. That same woman had taken a second go at getting money out of the Everett family by

89

producing another child, this time with the head of the family.

Her.

She was that child.

Her biological mother had been slaughtered before she was born. She'd been ripped out of her mother's stomach in the process, and her father had been killed not long after, along with the rest of the Everett family, except Sofia. Which was how Sophie had come to be raised by her niece and her husband.

How did Sofia and Ryan think she was going to react to finding all of that out?

How would anyone react to finding all of that out?

Did they really think she was going to say, *Okay, so I come from the most incestuous and insane family on the planet, but that's fine, thanks for taking me in?*

They were crazy if they had believed that.

She was the child of a manipulative, money-hungry blackmailer, and a man who had allowed his own son to rape his wife. That was whose DNA and blood ran through her veins. As far as she was concerned, it was only a matter of time until she turned bad too.

Nurture could only take you so far in life.

Despite what Hayley said, Sophie believed that nature played a huge part in who you were. Some people were just born bad, right? That was probably the excuse her biological parents had used for their behavior. They couldn't help it; it was just who they were.

Well, bad was who she was, and if she was bad on the inside, then she may as well stop pretending she was any better on the outside.

She didn't want to pretend anymore.

She didn't want to be someone she wasn't.

That sweet little girl who was bubbly and full of energy, who wanted to help everyone she came into contact with, was gone.

For good.

She was never going to be that girl again.

She didn't want to work hard in school, make good grades, go to college, then go to help run the center for abused women and children her mother had started with what she inherited from their evil family.

Now, she just wanted to …

Well, to be honest, she didn't really know.

Maybe, for right now, all she wanted was to not feel.

And the only place right now where she was truly happy and at peace, where she didn't have to focus on all the emotions swirling around inside her, was with Dom.

There was no way she was giving him up.

Her parents couldn't make her. They weren't the boss of her. They weren't really her parents, so they had no right to try to tell her who she could and couldn't spend time with. If her biological mother could have a baby with a son and his father, and if her biological father could sleep around and pay women to have kids for him, then surely, she could date a nice, sweet guy.

She loved Dom.

And he loved her.

Sophie didn't care whether her parents liked it or not. She wasn't going to break up with the man she loved just because they told her to.

"Soph—"

"I'm coming," she cut her mother off as she grabbed her backpack and left her room.

"Ten minutes till we leave for school," her mother said.

As she trotted down the stairs, she couldn't help but catch her mother's eye. She and her adoptive mother looked so similar that it had been so easy for them to pass her off as their child. The Everette genes must have been strong ones. They both had the same thick, red hair and the same gray eyes. Right now, her mother's eyes were so full of pain that Sophie almost stopped and gave her a hug to cheer her up, out of habit.

Deliberately, she stopped herself.

They had brought this on themselves.

They didn't have to lie to her, her whole life. They could have told her the truth, and they had decided not to.

Instead of throwing her arms around the woman who'd always been her mom and telling her she was sorry and that she understood, and that somehow, they could get back to where they used to be, Sophie brushed passed her and headed toward the front door.

"Don't you want to grab some breakfast?" her mom asked.

"I'll get something on the way to school."

"No, we don't have time to stop. I have to drop Ned off at Uncle Mark and Aunt Daisy's house after I drop you off at school, then I have to get straight to work. A new family came in last night, and I need to help them settle in."

There would have been a time where she would have anxiously peppered her mom with questions about the family. Who were they? What had happened to them? Were there any children she could try to help?

But that was in the past. Now, she just rolled her eyes at her mother. "I'm not going with you."

The sadness left her mother's eyes, annoyance taking its place. "We talked about this, Sophie. You know the rules. Your father or I or someone we know takes you to school and picks you up. This morning it's me, and we will be leaving in exactly eight minutes."

A horn honked outside.

"Actually, I'm leaving now."

She didn't wait for a response, just headed for the door.

"Where do you think you're going, young lady?" Her mother followed her.

"I told you, I'm not going to school with you. Dom is taking me."

"He is not."

"Is too." Okay, that was kind of a childish comeback, but her parents just made her so mad. Why did they think they got to boss her around after what they'd done? Paige and Elias had told their girls the truth about who they were and where they'd come from. Her parents could have—should have—done the same thing. They were only reaping what they'd sown.

"Sophie, I forbid you to get into a car with that boy," Sofia threatened.

"Ha," she barked a laugh and threw open the front door. "And how exactly are you going to stop me?" It was good luck her dad had already left for work, or he probably would have picked her up, thrown her over his shoulder, and locked her in her room before he let her get into a car with Dom. Thankfully, her mom was the same size as her and couldn't do anything to stop her.

"I mean it, Sophie. You are not dating that boy anymore, and you are certainly not driving to school with him." Her mother followed close on her heels as she ran down the front path.

Ignoring her mother, Sophie threw open the passenger door and slid into the car, climbing straight into Dom's lap and plastering herself all over him as she kissed him.

As soon as their lips touched, she felt it.

The change inside her.

Her anger started to die down, and that twirling ball of peace and giddy happiness took up residence in her stomach.

This was her happy place.

No one was going to take that away from her.

"Is everything okay?" Dom asked as he glanced behind her to the open door where her mother was standing, pulling her cell phone from her pocket to no doubt call her dad.

"Fine," she said, sliding off his lap and slamming the door closed. "Let's go."

"Are you sure? I don't want to make things worse between you and your parents."

All this time, her parents were worried about Dom being a bad influence on her, and he was the one who was always telling her to cut them some slack. That her parents loved her and that she should make up with them because one day they could be gone.

Well, that was just fine with her.

In fact, she wished that day was today.

The sooner they were out of her life, the better.

"Drive," she ordered.

As Dom complied, she felt satisfied as she glanced in the rearview mirror and saw the look of anger and betrayal on her mother's face.

Good.

Now she knew what it felt like.

* * * * *

12:06 P.M.

"He was expecting us to be at the house," Ryan said as he stared down at Brianna Lester's lifeless body.

They hadn't been able to save her.

They had been staking out the Lester house, anticipating—or more like hoping, since he didn't think the killer could be stupid enough to believe they wouldn't be watching the house waiting for him—when they'd gotten the call.

Brianna was officially the third victim of the Number Nine Killer.

She had been discovered by Davis Hilliard, a teacher at the same high school their victims all attended. He had been going out to his car to retrieve something he'd left behind when he'd spotted the body.

The killer they were hunting was apparently smart enough to know that the third time wasn't going to be the charm and that trying to leave Brianna's body on the Lester family front doorstep was virtual suicide. So, he'd picked a new location.

If there had been any doubt before that the school was the

link, that was gone now. All three girls attended the school, and now the killer had chosen it as his new dumping ground.

"Think he's going to take another victim today?" Paige asked.

"Yes." Ryan didn't have any doubts about that. Ally had been abducted the same day that Talia's body had been found, and Brianna had been kidnapped the same day Ally's body had been found. It only made sense that the killer would continue with the same pattern.

Which meant the next girl could already be gone, or she would be by the end of the day.

This day was just going to continue to get worse and worse.

When he'd climbed out of bed this morning, he'd thought things were finally getting better. Sophie hadn't given them any trouble yesterday. She'd been quiet and a little sullen, but she'd done her homework and eaten dinner at the table with them before retreating to her room.

Apparently, that was just an act to lull them into a false sense of security, because this morning she had ignored her mother and gotten into a car with Dominick Tremaine.

They hadn't turned up at school.

If they hadn't been expecting Brianna's dead body to turn up today, he would have just driven around until he found his daughter, dragged her home, and locked her in her room until he and Sofia could figure out what they were going to do with her.

His rebellious daughter was getting more out of control by the day. And the more out of control she became, the more out of control he felt.

Didn't Sophie understand that if she kept up like this, she could very well end up like Brianna Lester? Brianna had been a good kid, but one misguided mistake had cost her her life. It was that simple. Life could change in an instant, and sometimes there wasn't anything you could do to fix it.

"Look at her face," Paige said as she crouched down next to Brianna's body.

"It's a mess."

"It's the first time he's physically assaulted them, aside from the tattoo."

"Looks like he lost control," Ryan said quietly. One of Brianna's eyes was swollen closed, her lips were split in three places, and her entire face was a mottled mix of black and blue and purple.

"Jenny, do the bruises look like they're at different stages of healing?" Paige asked the medical examiner.

"Yep," Jenny confirmed.

"So, he went after her more than once. Why do I get the feeling he enjoyed that?" Paige shuddered as she stood and pulled her gray coat tighter around herself.

Ryan got the same feeling.

He was getting an awful feeling about this case in general. They were no closer to having a suspect than they'd been this morning. How many other teenage girls were going to have to die before they got enough evidence to find and arrest this man?

"Hey, guys, look." Jenny grinned up at them excitedly.

"What?" Ryan asked.

"She's missing some teeth." Jenny beamed.

Not catching the significance of that, he prompted her. "And?"

"He probably knocked some out when he was hitting her," Jenny elaborated.

"Oh." Paige's eyes widened when she apparently got where Jenny was going. "She might have swallowed some."

"Exactly," Jenny was almost vibrating with excitement. "If she did, then we might be able to get DNA. If he cut himself when he punched her, then hopefully, he left some of himself behind. I'll check to see if there are any teeth in her stomach as soon as I get her back to the morgue."

At least, one thing was going their way.

Hopefully.

"How could no one see anything? There are eight hundred

students, plus teachers and support staff. How could someone drive up, dump and pose a body, but no one saw?" Paige sounded as frustrated as he felt. This case was wearing on both of them, and they were both feeling the pressure, not just because they wanted to find this killer before another girl was killed, but because they were both worried that their daughters could be that next girl.

"The dress looks like the one Brianna's friends said she bought to wear when she met her mystery man for the first time," he said. Brianna wasn't wearing the jeans and pink sweater her parents said she'd been dressed in when she left for school the day she disappeared. She must have had the little black dress in her bag and changed into it before she got to the park. According to her friends, that had been the plan.

"Do you think it means anything that they all dressed up in black dresses when they went to meet this mystery man?" Paige asked.

"Maybe. There's no way to know for sure until we find him. But since all three girls were found in little black dresses, then it makes sense that it does. Black dresses and the number nine; that's all we have to go on for now."

"Not *all*." Paige's brown eyes travelled to something behind him.

Davis Hilliard was standing in the middle of the parking lot right where he'd been when they arrived here. The teacher hadn't taken his eyes off Brianna's body. "You think he could be involved?"

"We were looking for someone associated with the school who would have had access to the bathrooms. And since he couldn't leave the body at Brianna's house for fear of getting caught, maybe he thought this was a good alternative. It was also a good way for him to insert himself into our investigation."

"There's one way to find out," Ryan said. Right now, he was happy to have a direction—any direction—to move in, anything to not feel completely and utterly useless.

"Mr. Hilliard," Paige said as they approached the man.

"She was murdered," Davis said softly, his eyes still fixated on the body.

"What exactly did you see?" Ryan asked. Even if this man wasn't the killer, he might have seen something useful. So far, they didn't have any witnesses. If they could get something to go on, even just an approximate age, it would help them narrow down their suspect pool.

"Just the body. I left my cell in the car. I only realized when I needed it to make a call. I went back to get it, and when I was heading back into the school to go to my fourth period math class, I just saw something fluttering in the wind. I think it was her hair."

"Mr. Hilliard. Mr. Hilliard," Ryan repeated, trying to draw the man's attention away from Brianna, so they had at least a hope of getting something useful out of him. According to their ninety-nine-hour window, Davis Hilliard must have found the body only just after it was dumped. There was a chance he'd actually seen something but just didn't realize it. "Were there any vehicles just leaving the parking lot while you were getting your phone?"

The man finally tore his gaze away from the crime scene and looked at them. "I don't think—wait, there was something. A van. A white van."

A white van.

The vehicle of choice by serial killers across the globe.

"Did you get a look at who was driving?" Paige asked.

"No, the van was already pulling out into the street." The teacher gestured at the parking lot exit over by the gymnasium.

"Did the van have any distinguishing marks? Any company logos or anything?" Ryan asked.

"There might have been something; I'm not really sure. There could have been something blue. Maybe. I wasn't paying attention. I didn't know it was important," the man said a little defensively.

"What speed was the van driving?" he asked. Right now, they didn't even know if this white van, with possibly a blue something on it, was related to the case. If it was tearing out of here, it was, at least, something to suggest it was, indeed, related. Then, they could get security footage from the surrounding businesses and use the time frame they had to try to find the van. Then they could hopefully get the plates and track it down, find out if it did belong to their killer.

"I'm sorry. I really don't know. It was cold out, and I forgot to grab my jacket. I just wanted to get to and from my car as quickly as possible," Davis replied.

So, once again, they had nothing.

A van that may or may not have been used to dump Brianna Lester's body.

That was it.

Nothing substantive.

And another girl's time was quickly running out.

* * * * *

3:47 P.M.

"I really should take you home. You're going to get in trouble when your parents find out you skipped school today."

"I don't care," Sophie shrugged.

"Sophie—"

"Dom," she cut him off, "I really don't care. I've wasted enough time being angry and hurt about what they did to me. I'm done. I'm finished with them. I'm not going to worry about them or think about them or obsess about them anymore. From now on, it's just you and me."

"I love you, Soph." Dom reached out and ran a hand through her hair, then curled it around the back of her neck and drew her closer, touching his lips to hers.

This was what she needed.

This was what she wanted.

She didn't want to be Sophie Xander anymore. She wanted to be Sophie Tremaine.

Sophie Xander's life was full of grief and anger and fear about what her future held. She was struggling with her sense of identity and was so hurt by the life of lies she'd lived that she didn't think she would ever get over it. That was a life doomed to unhappiness and uncertainty.

But Sophie Tremaine's life could be anything she wanted it to be.

"Thank you." She caught hold of Dom's hand and squeezed it tightly. She didn't know what she would do without him.

"For marrying you? You don't need to thank me for that. I should be thanking you, for wanting to be my wife."

She had really lucked out with Dom.

At first, she'd merely wanted to date him because she knew the age gap between them would drive her parents crazy, and she wanted to punish them for lying to her. Sure, she had been attracted to him—Dom was hot, had dreamy brown eyes, scruffy brown hair, and a footballer's body. He was everything a teenage girl dreamed of.

The more she got to know him, the more she developed real feelings for him.

She was in love.

She wanted to spend the rest of her life with him.

He made her happy. He made her forget her pain. He made her feel loved and wanted.

She couldn't wait to marry him.

Sophie wasn't really sure how they were going to make it happen since she was only fifteen—not old enough to legally marry anyone. Dom had a friend who would perform a ceremony, and he'd said he thought his mother would let them live with her until he graduated in a few months and got a job so he could support them. Then, when she turned eighteen, they could make it official.

She was ready to make something else official.

"So …" She gave Dom a sly smile. "Since we're about to be married, do you want to …" She trailed off, a little embarrassed to say it out loud. She was a virgin. She and Dom had been dating for months now, but they'd never gone any further than kissing.

Until now.

Now she was ready to take that next step.

"Are you sure?"

"I've never been surer of anything in my life."

"Don't you want to wait until we can be somewhere a little more … romantic?"

Sure, sitting in Dom's car, in an alley close to her house, wasn't the most romantic setting for their first time, but she didn't care about that. Making love wasn't about the location. It was about the emotions, the love, and they had that.

"All I want is you," she said, moving so she was straddling Dom's lap.

She was nervous and excited all mixed into one. She was sure this was what she wanted to do, but it was still her first time, and she didn't really know what to expect.

Dom's hands spanned her waist, his fingertips brushing up under the hem of her sweater, tickling the skin on her stomach as he moved them higher.

Tap, tap.

They both started, their heads jolting up.

Victor stood at the driver's side window, smiling in at them. "Sorry to interrupt." He grinned, not sounding sorry in the least. "Hayley's here too." He stepped to the side, and there was her best friend. They'd asked Victor and Hayley to stand up for them at their wedding. Even if it wasn't an official wedding, she wanted her best friend there.

It looked like making love for the first time was going to have to wait. Sophie didn't really mind. Maybe it would be more romantic if they waited until after they were married.

Sophie climbed back off Dom's lap. "Come in," she called to Dom's twin and her best friend. It was freezing out, and it didn't look like Victor was wearing a jacket.

"Don't stop on our account," Victor teased as he and Hayley slid into the back seat. "Hayley and I can always make out a little, so you're not self-conscious. Right, Hales?"

Hayley rolled her eyes at him. Dom's twin brother was always hitting on her. It was apparent to everyone—other than Hayley who hadn't seemed to know since they'd talked about it the other day—that Victor had a major crush on her. But Hayley had her own crush, on Zane, the pianist, and she wasn't going to give in to Victor's advances, no matter how many times he tried.

"So, what did you and Dom need us to come running over for?" Hayley asked. "I was supposed to be watching Ari and Rosie, and if I'm not back before my mom gets home, I'm going to be in trouble."

"Oh," she said. She didn't think they were going to be done in time for Hayley to beat her mom home. "Sorry, Hayley, I don't think you're going to make it. Dom and I are getting married," she announced.

"Married?" Victor echoed, slapping his brother on the back.

"Married?" Hayley echoed, her blue eyes widening to an almost unnatural size. "Really?"

"Really." She nodded.

"Sophie, your parents will freak."

"I don't care," she said stubbornly.

"Yes, you do," Hayley contradicted. "You love them, Soph. I don't think you should do this. I think you should find a way to let go of the anger you have toward your parents. I know you and Dom love each other, but you don't have to rush into marriage to prove it."

She couldn't deny her feelings were hurt.

She had expected her best friend to support her, not try to talk her out of marrying the man she loved.

"I thought you'd be happy for me," she said, blinking back tears. Hayley had been the one constant through the whole ordeal. She needed her friend. She loved Dom, and she wanted to marry him, but he could never take the place of a best friend.

"I am, Sophie. I love you, and I'll support you any way I can. I just worry about you. I don't want you to make a mistake because you're angry and hurt. It doesn't have to be an either or. You can still have Dom and work things out with your parents."

Hayley could be right, but at the moment, she was too tired to think things through. She didn't want to think anymore. She just wanted to feel.

"If you two really want to get married," Hayley continued, "then I will support you one hundred percent. But not like this. Let's go shopping tomorrow, find you a beautiful dress to wear. Get your makeup and hair done. Buy some flowers. If you are really committed to each other, and if you're going to spend the rest of your lives together, don't you want your wedding to be perfect? If you don't want the rest of your family there, then let's at least make you look like a bride. You shouldn't be getting married in jeans and a sweater."

Okay, Hayley was definitely right this time.

What was one more day?

She believed that marriage was for life, so this was going to be the only wedding she would have, and it should be special.

"Dom?" Sophie looked at her fiancé. "What do you think? Could we do this tomorrow?"

The smile he gave her was warm and understanding. "I would wait for you forever. I want you to be happy. If getting all dressed up makes you happy, then do it."

How could she be so unlucky in one part of her life and yet so lucky in another?

"Maybe Hayley and I can also go shopping for something for tomorrow night." She waggled her brows suggestively at him. Shopping for lingerie would be so grown up.

"Come on, we better go. I left Ari and Rosie alone, and I really want to get back to them. You should come home with me. We can plan what we want to get tomorrow, and maybe my mom will let you spend the night."

"Okay." Now that Hayley had suggested getting dressed up like a bride tomorrow, she was excited by the idea. Not that a wedding was about the dress and hair and stuff, but it was her special day, and she should feel special. "I'll see you tomorrow, husband-to-be." She giggled.

"I can't wait, wife-to-be." Dom kissed her.

This was really happening.

Tomorrow she was getting married.

Married.

She was going to be someone's wife.

Getting married at fifteen was not how she had expected her life to turn out, but she couldn't be happier.

Who cared about her stupid family. Ryan, Sofia, the Xander family. They were nothing to her now.

Now, she had a new family.

* * * * *

3:59 P.M.

"We're gonna get in trouble," Rosie Xander said. "We're not supposed to go out on our own."

"Technically we're not on our own," Arianna Hood contradicted. "We're with my sister."

"Hayley told us to stay at your house and wait for her to get back."

Ari shrugged. She liked to live life on the wild side, and she liked to take risks and have fun. "You know my sister; she wouldn't have left us alone unless she had a really good reason to." Her big sister Hayley always did the right thing. She was sensible to a fault, and when she was asked to do something, you could guarantee she would do it. So, for Hayley, who was supposed to be babysitting them, to leave them home alone could only mean one thing.

Something big was going down.

And she was tired of missing out on all the fun stuff.

She was ten years old now—old enough to be included in life and not sheltered from all the bad stuff.

Ari knew that evil people existed in the world. And she knew that her biological father had been one of them. She knew that he had gotten her biological mother pregnant against her will and that if they hadn't been rescued, she would be trapped in that house. She liked her biological mother Eliza, and they always had fun when she and Hayley spent the day with her and her husband and their two little boys, but she loved her parents.

Paige and Elias were her mom and dad, and she wanted to be just like them when she grew up. She wanted to follow in her mom's footsteps and become a cop. She liked to help people, and she wasn't scared by gory stuff. Her mom said she had good instincts, and right now, her instincts were telling her that her sister was up to something big, and she intended to find out what.

"Aren't you tired of being treated like a little kid? Don't you want to find out what the big girls are doing? Aren't you curious about where Hayley is going?" she asked her best friend Rosie. Rosie was also ten. Ari's mom's work partner was Ryan. Ryan had a brother named Jack, and he was Rosie's dad. They had known each other since they were babies and had been best friends since they could talk. They liked to pretend that they were really sisters, and since they both had long dark hair, they could almost pass as such. They were similar in personality, too, only Rosie wasn't into gory things, and she always got nervous when they did something she knew they were going to get into trouble for. To Ari, the risk of getting into trouble was usually outweighed by the fun of having fun.

"I guess," Rosie agreed. "I just don't want to get grounded for life."

Ari giggled. Rosie was right. If they got caught, they were both going to get grounded for life. "It's only four, my mom won't be home until at least six, and my dad is on shift, so he won't be home until tomorrow. We have plenty of time to see what Hayley is up to and get back to my house before anyone even knows we were gone." It was Friday and Rosie was spending the night. Her mom had promised to pick up pizzas on the way home so she'd probably be even later. They weren't going to get caught.

"It probably has something to do with Sophie," Rosie said as they carefully trailed Hayley down the sidewalk, making sure to keep well back so she wouldn't see them if she happened to turn around.

"I agree." Rosie's cousin Sophie had been having problems lately. Big problems. "Sophie was at my house the other morning, and she and Hayley were talking about how Sophie wants to have sex with her boyfriend," she whispered conspiratorially. Arianna loved snooping around Hayley's bedroom when her sister had friends over; she always learned the best secrets.

"I heard my parents talking about how Uncle Ryan and Aunt Sofia don't want Sophie dating that Dominick boy."

Arianna didn't think she would let anybody tell her who she could date. But then, again, she wasn't allowed to date. Not until she was at least thirteen her parents had said, although if it was up to her dad, she thought he would never let her date.

"Look." Rosie pointed to Hayley who had turned into an alley.

"I wonder what she's doing in there." They both hurried to catch up, neither of them wanted to miss out on finding out what was going on.

When they got to the entrance of the alley, they saw Hayley

and a teenage boy standing next to a car.

"Can you see who's in there?" Rosie whispered.

Squinting, she tried to make out the faces of the people in the car. "I think it's Sophie and her boyfriend," she said.

"So, we were right," Rosie said triumphantly.

"What do you think they're talking about?" Ari wanted to try to sneak closer so they could hear, but there was no way to do that without being seen.

"We could wait till they leave and then follow them back," Rosie suggested.

"Think we can keep close enough to hear?"

"Us? Of course," Rosie said confidently.

Ari laughed. Sometimes Rosie was worried about doing something that would get them in trouble, but once she started, she always got into it.

"They're coming," Rosie announced as Hayley and Sophie climbed out of the car.

"Quick, hide over there," she squealed in excitement. She loved this kind of thing. She felt just like a private detective following a suspect. She was born to be a cop.

She and Rosie were just crouching down behind a dumpster when Hayley and Sophie came out of the alley, chattering away.

"Maybe we should just let them know we're here. Hayley was supposed to watch us, and she didn't. Maybe we can use that to get them to let us in on whatever they're up to."

"You'd blackmail your sister?"

"To find out what's so big she'd lie to Mom and leave us home alone? You bet."

Hayley and Sophie were just about to turn the corner when a white van pulled up right beside them.

Arianna wasn't really paying it any mind until a man dressed all in black jumped out.

He had a gun in his hand, and he grabbed Hayley.

He said something, but Ari couldn't hear what it was from

here, then he shoved both her sister and Sophie into the back of his van, climbing in after them.

"Ari, no."

Hands clamped on her arm, holding her back. She hadn't even realized that she was trying to move toward the van.

Someone was kidnapping her sister.

She couldn't do nothing.

"You can't," Rosie said, keeping hold of her. "He'll see us."

"He has my sister."

"He'll kill us, or take us too," Rosie said.

"I have to stop him." She fought to get free. She couldn't just let this man take her sister.

"How?" Rosie was struggling to keep hold of her. "We're ten. He's a grown-up. And he has a gun. How are you going to stop him?"

She didn't know.

But she had to try.

Managing to get out of Rosie's grip, she ran toward the van. Just as she did, it took off, tires squealing.

It was gone.

With her sister.

She ran down to the street just in time to see the van turning a corner.

Should she try to go after it?

How could she catch it when she'd have to run?

She couldn't.

Ari couldn't believe this was really happening.

Had it?

Had she just imagined it?

Maybe she was so busy pretending to be a private detective that she had just conjured up the whole thing.

"What should we do?" Rosie asked, joining her in the road, tears streaming down her face.

Arianna could tell she was crying, too, because the wind was icy cold on her wet cheeks. "We have to get help." Her parents said she was too young to have her own cell phone so she couldn't call 911. And she didn't want 911 anyway. She wanted her mom. "We have to get to the station. My mom and your dad, they'll know what to do."

Her mom was a cop. She was the strongest, smartest woman on the planet. Ari didn't know the details, but she knew that her mom had been through some horrible stuff, and yet, she still dedicated her life to helping people.

"I'm sorry, Ari." Rosie threw her arms around her.

Arianna hugged her best friend back as tightly as she could. If they'd been a little closer to Hayley and Sophie, the man with the gun would have taken them, too, and her mom would have lost both of her daughters in one moment.

But her mom would find Hayley.

She would.

She had to.

* * * * *

4:18 P.M.

"Finally," Paige sighed as a car pulled up in the driveway. They had been waiting outside Davis Hilliard's house for almost ninety minutes waiting for him to get home so they could interview him.

"Think he was delaying on purpose?" Ryan asked as they climbed out of the car.

The chilly weather was a nice change from the stuffy car, and she stretched her stiff muscles. She glanced at her watch. It was approaching four-thirty, and she'd told the girls she would be home around six, but it was looking like it would be closer to seven. She was looking forward to hanging out with her girls tonight, and Rosie Xander was always a delight to have stay over.

"He knew we were waiting here for him," she answered her

partner's question.

"What could he have been doing for the last hour and a half?"

"I guess we're about to find out," she said as they approached the teacher. "Mr. Hilliard?"

Davis Hilliard turned toward them. From the look on his face, he had no idea why they were here. "Oh, detectives."

"We called earlier," Ryan reminded him. "Said we'd be here about three. It's now nearly four-thirty."

"Oh. Right. Sorry." The teacher didn't really look sorry as he led them up the path to the front door.

The house was beautiful—a large, three-story colonial, painted bright white, with red shutters, and a large porch. The yard was also perfectly manicured with hedges, flower beds, and neatly trimmed trees.

"Come in." Davis led them through a large entrance foyer and into a huge lounge. The décor was distinctly feminine. The wallpaper was floral and there were several landscape watercolor paintings hanging on the walls. There were vases of flowers, knickknacks, throw pillows and frilly curtains.

"Where were you, Mr. Hilliard?" Paige asked once she and Ryan were seated. They had learned some things about the math teacher who had found Brianna Lester's body. Some things that pointed to the man standing before them being their killer.

"Just about," the man shrugged.

About abducting his next victim?

If this man was the killer they were hunting for, they needed to get something to prove it before anyone else died.

"Sit down, Mr. Hilliard," she said.

The man looked like he was going to disagree, but then shook his head and sank down into an overstuffed armchair. "I'm sorry. I should have been here at three like we discussed. It's just that everything that happened today, finding that poor girl's body … I just needed to clear my mind and I lost track of time."

Entirely plausible, or he was off luring another teenage girl into a trap.

"Did you go anywhere special?" she asked. If they could catch him in a lie, they could use that against him to get a confession.

"Just drove around."

"Anywhere in particular?" Ryan asked.

"No, I just drove around." Davis gave them an odd look like he knew they were up to something. He just hadn't figured out what.

"Did you remember anything that might be helpful?" Paige asked.

"No, I'm sorry. I really didn't see anything other than the girl's body."

"And you didn't touch her?"

"I didn't touch her."

"Not even to check that she was deceased?"

"When I got closer, it was pretty clear by her pallor and the lifeless look in her eyes that she was already dead. I had my phone by then, so I just called the office and asked them to call the cops."

"Was Brianna Lester one of your students?" Ryan asked.

"No. I don't teach freshman or sophomores, just juniors and seniors."

"So, you knew Ally Brown and Talia Canuck?"

"I taught both of them," Davis nodded.

"How did they do in your classes?" she asked. "Did you have any problems with them?"

"No, both girls were like all the rest of my students. They talked too much and weren't particularly into math, just like every other teenager I've ever taught, bar a handful who really enjoyed mathematics."

It didn't sound like Davis Hilliard had much to do with the victims, but since they were assuming he picked the victims at random based on who responded to his message on the bathroom mirror, that didn't mean much.

"We heard you lost your wife and daughters," she brought up the reason for their visit.

"I did." Davis's gaze moved to the framed family portrait hanging above the fireplace. In the picture, Davis was beaming, his arm around the shoulders of a pretty brunette with big brown eyes and a beautiful smile. Two brown-haired girls, both clones of their mother, were also smiling at the camera, only a little less enthusiastically than their parents.

"Your daughters were beautiful," Paige said. Although she was sorry for the man's loss, it wasn't an excuse for abducting and murdering teenage girls.

"Thank you." Davis nodded solemnly. "Liza was nineteen, and Bridget was only nine."

Nines.

That fit with their killer.

When they'd spoken with the principal about Davis Hilliard, she'd said that the man had a breakdown after losing his family, but hadn't mentioned specifics other than to say it was some time over the summer, and that he had only recently returned to work.

"How long has it been since you lost them?" she asked. From the looks of things, Davis had been having a hard time letting go. The feminine touches in the house had no doubt been his wife's, and he clearly wasn't ready to change anything yet. Paige imagined that the girls' rooms had remained untouched and would probably remain virtual shrines for a long time to come. If anything ever happened to one of her daughters, she didn't think she would ever be able to face getting rid of—or even moving—their things.

"Nine months," Davis replied. "Nine months and thirteen days."

It had been thirteen days since Talia Canuck went missing.

Add nine months to that and Davis Hilliard had lost his entire family in one fell swoop.

That was three number nines. *Nine* months since he had lost his *nineteen*-year-old and *nine*-year-old daughters.

"It was a boating accident?" Ryan asked.

"We were at my parents' lake house for the weekend. My parents bought it when they retired. My dad loves to fish, and my mom loved to sit out by the water and read. We would go down there on the weekends in the summer. My wife was an executive at a finance company, and she liked to get away for the weekends. And even though school was out, I tutored and taught summer school during the week. We all looked forward to those weekends."

"You weren't on the boat?" Paige asked.

"No. I was supposed to be, but the porch steps were wobbly, and the rest of the family were coming for a barbeque. My dad and I were fixing them when we heard the explosion. A fault with the engine. That's what took my family from me."

Losing his wife and children could definitely have been the trigger. But why kidnap and abduct girls from the school where he worked? Was it just because he needed to lash out at the world to cope with what had happened and the school was just a convenient way to get access to victims or did they hold some special significance?

"We understand you had some problems at the start of the school year," Ryan said.

Davis' brows knit together, and he glared at them. "They weren't problems, I just came back too soon. I wasn't ready."

From what they'd heard, that was downplaying it.

"We heard that you lost it in a class on the first day because one of the kids dropped their book on the floor."

"The noise startled me," Davis said defensively.

"So much so that you started screaming hysterically at them. The kids said they were all afraid that you were going to hit the boy who dropped his books. The principal said they were all sympathetic to your situation, but that they thought you were a risk to the safety of the students. She said it was either lose your job or get some psychiatric help."

"I got the help," he growled at them.

Was that it? He was angry at the school for threatening him into getting counseling? That didn't really seem like something that would trigger him to start killing students.

Or maybe he blamed the kids?

Thought they were somehow responsible for what happened?

Or maybe she was just reading too much into motive. Maybe he was just angry and grieving, and he just snapped.

They would check with the school and see if he was in class at the time of Brianna Lester's abduction.

"Did you kill those girls?" she confronted him. "Did you drown them because your family drowned in the lake?"

Davis bounded to his feet, his cheeks turning bright red, and she saw in his eyes what those kids had seen. He wanted to hit them, only he knew better. "I think you should leave. Now."

"We'll be back, Mr. Hilliard," she warned him as she and Ryan stood. "Don't leave town."

They finally had a direction to move in.

She and Ryan would go back to the station and find out everything they could about Davis Hilliard.

Then she'd go home and unwind with her kids.

* * * * *

5:01 P.M.

She had no idea where they were.

None.

They had been walking around for an hour, and she didn't think they were anywhere near the police station.

Rosie just wanted to go home.

She was scared.

Terrified.

And she didn't know what to do.

114

Arianna's plan that they walk to the police station so they could tell their parents what they'd seen was never going to work. They were never going to find it.

They were lost.

They were probably going to be grabbed off the street and shoved into some car by some bad person, just like what had happened to her cousin Sophie and Ari's sister Hayley.

With every step they took, Rosie kept expecting the bogeyman to come jumping out from behind a car or a bush or a mailbox and grab them. She wanted to be someplace safe. What if the man in the van had seen them? What if he was worried that they could identify him? What if he thought he better come back and kill them?

They should have gone back to Ari's house and called for help from there.

That would have been the smart thing to do, but her best friend always liked to walk on the wild side. Arianna wanted to be a cop like her mom when she was grown up. That was fine. But right now, they weren't grown up. They were ten-year-old kids, and they shouldn't be wandering the streets by themselves.

When her parents found out, they were going to be so mad.

She never should have let Ari talk her into leaving the house and following Hayley. She knew better, but the idea of finding out what the big girls were up to was too exciting to resist. She and Arianna were tired of always being treated like little kids. They were ten now, old enough to be included, but the older kids never wanted to. Just for once, they wanted to know what was going on, even if they had to sneak and snoop to find out.

Neither of them had spoken since they'd started walking. They were both lost in thought. If she knew Arianna, her friend was running through what had happened over and over again, trying to figure out a scenario where they'd been able to do something to stop the kidnapping from happening. She was refusing to think about it.

Rosie was cold and tired. They hadn't grabbed jackets when they left the house because they wanted to catch up to Hayley before she disappeared. If she could figure out where they were, she'd turn around and just go home, or at least back to Arianna's house or one of her aunts' or uncles'.

They turned the corner, and she looked up and down the street. There were lots of cars, large houses, and a few people walking dogs.

Nothing looked familiar.

And it was starting to get dark.

She wasn't allowed to be out alone after dark. The streetlights were blinking on, and lots of the houses had lights shining from their windows. She wished so badly that she was at home.

It was cold, it was getting dark, and she was scared.

She'd had enough.

"Ari, we're lost, we should just—"

"There," Ari said triumphantly, pointing at a street to their right.

"What?" All she saw was another street. One that looked just the same as all the others they'd trekked down tonight.

"It's Hood Street," Arianna said, like that explained everything.

"And?"

"Hood Street is only two streets over from the police station where your dad and my mom work."

"Are you sure?" It sounded too good to be true. After walking around for so long, she'd been convinced that they were lost and never going to get to the precinct or anywhere else.

"Of course, I'm sure." Arianna rolled her eyes. "I always thought it was cool that there was a street with my last name so close to the police station. Come on, let's go."

Rejuvenated by the relief of finally almost being someplace safe, they both began to run.

They darted across the street, then ran up the sidewalk. Now that they were close, Arianna seemed to know where they were going—or maybe she had all along—and Rosie just followed her.

"There it is," Ari said as they turned another corner.

Although she was exhausted, her feet seemed to move faster. She just wanted to get inside.

By the time they burst through the door, she was breathless. Her chest was heaving, her legs quivering, but she had never been so relieved in all her life.

They were here.

They were safe.

Rosie just wanted to curl up and cry.

No.

She was too big to cry.

"Rosie Xander? Arianna Hood?"

She looked up—way, way up—at a man who was standing over them.

A man.

A big man.

For a moment she panicked.

Had the man in the van come here?

Did he know who they were?

Was he here for them?

Then she noticed he was in uniform. He wasn't just a man; he was a cop.

"Yes, is my mom here?" Arianna was asking.

"I don't think so, honey. Is there something I can help you with?"

"No," Ari said emphatically. "I need my mom. Now."

"Is my dad here?" Rosie asked. She might be a big girl, but right now she didn't feel like one. Right now, she needed her parents.

"He might be. How about I call up and see." The cop led them both over to the desk where he picked up a phone and dialed.

The world started to blur around her.

She was warm and safe, and now that she was, she was starting to struggle to block out the kidnapping.

She kept seeing the gun, the man shoving her cousin and best friend's sister into the van, the tires squealing as it took off.

Sophie and Hayley were gone.

Really gone.

What if they never found them?

What if they never came back?

"Rosie?"

She spun around.

Her father was standing behind her.

"Daddy."

Rosie burst into tears and flung herself into her father's arms. She didn't care if crying made her a baby like her big brother was always telling her. She was scared, and she needed her daddy.

"Baby, what's wrong?" Jack asked as he crouched down and held her.

She wanted to answer. She wanted to tell him about how someone had taken Sophie and Hayley and how she and Ari had walked for an hour to get here to get help.

"Where's my mom?" Arianna demanded.

Rosie felt her father tense. His cop instincts must be kicking in, and he realized something was wrong. "What are you girls doing here? You're supposed to be at Ari's house, and Hayley is supposed to be babysitting you. How did you get here?"

"We walked," Ari replied.

"You walked? You girls know better than to walk here on your own. Where's Hayley?"

"We don't know," Ari said.

"You don't know?" her dad echoed. "Ari, tell me right now, what's going on?"

"We were following Hayley. She went to see Sophie and some guys. Then there was a van. The man had a gun. He put them in the van and drove off. We didn't know what else to do. So, we came here. Where's my mom?" Ari finished on a sob.

"Come here." Her dad rearranged her in his arms so he could hold Ari as well. Then he was standing up with both of them in his arms. "Call Paige and Ryan; get them here immediately," he called out over his shoulders as he carried them both upstairs.

"What's going on?" someone asked. It sounded like her dad's partner Xavier Montague.

"The girls walked here on their own; they said someone kidnapped Hayley and Sophie." Her dad set both her and Arianna down in a chair.

Rosie couldn't stop crying.

What was happening to Sophie and Hayley right now?

Were they still alive?

Were they being hurt?

"Girls, I need you to tell me everything you saw." Dad was crouched in front of them, wearing his cop face.

"I don't know," she said through her tears. She hadn't been paying attention too much other than making sure Ari didn't get them both killed. And everything had happened so quickly, there hadn't been time to memorize everything.

"Ari?"

It didn't look like Arianna was paying much attention. She was wriggling in the chair and trying to look down the hall.

"Ari?"

"Where's my mom?" Ari asked.

"She's coming, honey. Right now, I need you to tell me what you remember so we can find your sister and Sophie."

"The man had a gun. He's probably hurting them," Ari said, her voice a little too high, and even Rosie could tell that her friend was starting to lose control.

"Arianna?"

All three of them turned as Ari's mom, Paige, came running toward them, Uncle Ryan right behind her.

"Mommy." Ari flew off the seat and into her mother's arms. "I'm sorry. I should have stopped him. I'm sorry, Mommy. You have to find her. Please, Mommy, find her."

Even at ten, Rosie knew that the chances of finding Hayley and Sophie weren't good.

They were virtually zero.

* * * * *

5:32 P.M.

Her worst nightmare had just come true.

She could barely breathe.

Barely think.

Barely function.

There were a million things she wanted to do at once, and yet, she was paralyzed. There were too many things running through her mind, too many emotions buzzing through her body.

"She's not picking up." Paige threw her phone across the car. She couldn't hold on to it, dialing her daughter's number over and over again—never getting any response, it was killing her.

"I'm not getting any response either," Ryan said, tossing his phone down along with hers.

"It's not surprising that Sophie hasn't answered, maybe she told Hayley not to answer either," Jack suggested.

That was not the case, and they all knew it.

Paige knew what Jack was trying to do; he was trying to keep her and Ryan at least marginally calm.

But that was impossible.

Her daughter had been kidnapped.

Kidnapped.

That was a word she never wanted in a sentence with one of her children.

She wanted to take it back, to erase it, to rewind the clock and never go to work today so she would have been home, and Hayley would never have snuck out. It wasn't like her daughter to do that. Hayley was such a good kid, she never talked back, she always did as she was asked, she didn't argue or manipulate to get her way. Sneaking out of the house when she was meant to be babysitting was so unlike Hayley.

There must have been a good reason for her to do it.

Hayley would never have left Ari and Rosie home alone otherwise.

"If Sophie and Hayley were just hanging out and not wanting to be disturbed, then why would Rosie and Ari say they saw them being shoved at gunpoint into a van?" Ryan demanded.

"Is there any way they could have gotten it wrong?" Xavier asked. "Maybe they weren't close enough to see what was really going on. Or maybe they just saw the girls getting into a van with people they knew, and they mistook something else for the gun?"

Xavier was clutching at straws.

As much as she wished that what he was saying was true and Hayley was just hanging out with Sophie doing something she knew she wasn't supposed to be doing, they all knew it wasn't true.

Hayley was gone.

Possibly forever.

"You saw Ari and Rosie; did they look like they were confused about what they saw?" Ryan growled. "They were terrified. They walked the streets for an hour to get to the station to get help. Those girls were petrified. They looked like they'd just witnessed an abduction."

Abduction.

The word almost made her spin into hysteria.

She curled her hands into fists and dug her fingernails into her palms deep enough to draw blood. She needed the pain to keep her sane, to keep her focused. Her daughter's life depended on her holding it together.

"That's not going to help." Jack's hands closed over hers and gently, but firmly, pried them open, then put a tissue into her hands so she could clean away the blood.

"I think you two should have stayed at the precinct," Xavier said.

"This is my daughter. I am not sitting on the sidelines," she said immediately.

"Neither am I," Ryan added.

"That is exactly why you two shouldn't be here," Xavier persisted.

Paige would have continued to argue, but she was already jumping out of the car as Xavier had pulled it to a stop, and she didn't want to waste another second. Convincing her colleagues that she was capable of working this case wasn't worth her time.

In kidnappings, every second counted.

Every single second.

Around fifteen hundred children under the age of eighteen were abducted every year. Approximately two hundred of those were taken by someone who wasn't a relative. Ninety percent of those children were usually reunited with their families.

But ten percent weren't.

She was not going to allow her daughter to be one of those ten percent.

There were already a dozen cops swarming all over the place where Arianna and Rosie had said the girls were taken from. The crime scene unit was there too.

This didn't feel real.

She had been to hundreds of crime scenes before, including crime scenes where people she loved and cared about had been involved.

But nothing like this.

Memories of the first time she'd met Hayley and Arianna flooded her mind. She remembered finding the girls in a hospital room, Hayley's scared little face looking up at her. She remembered holding the child on her lap and assuring her that they would find her a family who would care for her, who would show her what life was supposed to be like and who would love her unconditionally.

Even then, she'd already loved Hayley.

"We'll find them," Xavier's voice rumbled behind her, and he wrapped an arm around her shoulders. "Don't give up. Hayley is counting on you to never give up."

"Yeah, okay," she said shakily. She didn't want to give up on her daughter, but what if Hayley was already dead?

Or what if she wasn't?

What was happening to her little girl right this second?

"Stop." Xavier gave her a small shake. "Stop running *what if* scenarios in your head or you're going to drive yourself crazy. Hayley is counting on you, and so are Elias and Arianna."

She felt a stab of guilt about leaving Ari.

Elias had arrived at the station and was with their daughter, and Ari had told her to go and do whatever she had to, to find Hayley, but Ari was just a terrified ten-year-old girl. She needed her mother.

"Have you found anything?" Ryan was growling at everyone and no one in particular.

"We'll find something." Stephanie Cantini came over to them. "No one is leaving until we have something," she assured them. "I'm so sorry." Stephanie hugged Ryan and then her. Paige tried to return the hug, but she didn't want comfort or sympathy. All she wanted was information that would lead her to her daughter.

"Do any of the buildings have security cameras?" she asked, scanning the neighboring shops. The area was quiet. There were mostly restaurants that didn't open until dinnertime, and according to the girls, the kidnapping had occurred too early for many of the workers to have arrived, so there weren't likely to be any witnesses. The security footage could be their only hope at finding the van and who took her daughter.

"Yes, a few do. I have people speaking with all of the businesses," Stephanie told them. "There are also some tire tracks." The crime scene tech pointed to the road just a few yards away from where they were standing. "We'll see if we can get anything from those. I understand that the, uh, there might be, um, another case where …"

"Just spit it out, Stephanie," Ryan snapped. If he hadn't, she would have. Their daughters were missing and beating around the bush and wasting time was only going to get them killed.

Stephanie nodded and continued. "I understand that the man who found Brianna Lester's body said that he saw a white van driving out of the parking lot. The Number Nine Killer should be abducting another victim today, assuming he sticks with his pattern," she finished and appeared to hold her breath as she awaited their response.

It wasn't like she hadn't already thought that.

Ryan probably had too.

But hearing someone else say it made it seem real.

If the Number Nine Killer had her daughter, then they had just under ninety-nine hours to find Hayley and Sophie alive.

Davis Hilliard had deliberately kept them waiting at his house for almost ninety minutes, even though they'd made plans to see him at three.

He'd had ample time to abduct the girls and then stash them someplace before coming to speak with them.

If that man had her child, she would kill him.

"We have no proof," Jack said as though he had read her mind. "We will look into Davis Hilliard, and if he did this, he will be arrested and sent to prison, but right now we don't have enough to go after him."

Paige hated that he was right.

"We're also trying to track the girls' phones," Stephanie continued.

"We haven't been able to get through to either of them. Keeps going straight to voice mail," Ryan said.

"The phones are probably turned off," Stephanie said. "But

we'll keep trying. As soon as they turn back on, we'll be able to get a location."

If *they get turned back on*, Paige thought.

She didn't believe it was going to happen, but at least, it gave her some hope.

"Excuse me." A cop came running over. "I found these just up the street."

He held out two cell phones.

Broken cell phones.

One of which she recognized.

It had little gold diamantes in the shape of a treble clef on the back.

It was Hayley's cell phone, and it looked like someone had stomped on it.

There went that one little piece of hope she'd had.

And with it, the last thread holding her together.

* * * * *

6:44 P.M.

"Should I come down to the station?"

"No, there's not really anything you can do here," Xavier Montague assured his wife. With everything that was going on, he'd needed to hear her voice. Needed the reassurance of knowing that his wife and children were okay. That they were safe.

He couldn't imagine what Ryan and Sofia and Paige and Elias were going through.

He didn't want to imagine.

"I could just come down and be there, offer whatever comfort I can," Annabelle protested. He understood her desire to be here. They were a close group of friends, and she wanted to do anything she could, no matter how small, that might make this easier.

"I know you want to help, but right now, I just don't think there's anything that's going to help them. They know you care. They just need answers, and we're doing whatever we can to get them."

"What about the kids? They can come and stay here," she pressed. He could hear the pain in her voice, and he wished that he was there to take it away. He wanted to hold her, kiss her until her fears melted away, make love to her until both their worries disappeared.

But he wasn't leaving this building until they knew where Sophie Xander and Hayley Hood were.

"I don't think Arianna is going to leave here until we find her sister. Same goes for Ned. Rosie and Zach are here, too, because Laura wants to stay and help however she can. You just stay at home with JP and Katie. I don't want them finding out what happened." His five-year-old twins were too young to know that the older kids they idolized and thought of as cousins had been abducted.

"Okay," Annabelle finally conceded. "Just keep me updated. I'm praying for the girls, for everyone."

"I'll let you know the second we know anything. Belle, the kids, you're sure they're okay?"

"They're fine." He could hear the smile in his wife's voice. "They're eating chocolate sundaes and making such a mess they're going to need an hour in the bath to get clean."

He loved bath time. He loved watching his kids so excited to play with the bubbles making funny moustaches and beards, and squirting water at each other with their array of animals. "And Katie's cold hasn't gotten worse?"

"She hasn't coughed or sneezed since lunchtime."

"JP isn't coming down with one yet?" That was life with two small children—when one got sick, the other inevitably followed suit.

"So far, so good, but I wouldn't be surprised if he wakes up with the sniffles tomorrow morning."

"Give them a big cuddle from me and tell them that I love them."

"I will," Annabelle promised. "I love you, too."

Xavier never got tired of hearing Annabelle say that. There had been a time when he hadn't been sure that things would work out between them, but now he had everything he'd ever wanted. A wife, two beautiful children, a family that he felt like he belonged in.

"I love you, too. I'll talk to you later."

As he hung up, he felt himself slipping out of dad mode and into cop mode. Crime scene was still combing the abduction site, searching for anything that would help them, but Xavier already knew they weren't going to find anything.

If this was the Number Nine Killer, he never left anything behind.

In his mind, he had already decided that it was the same killer. Everything fit. Hayley and Sophie attended the same school as the other victims and the timeline fit. Who else could it be? He wasn't going to close down any other avenue of the investigation, but until he knew otherwise, he was working this case as though the Number Nine Killer was the perpetrator.

And the next thing he needed to do was interview Arianna and Rosie.

The entire Xander and Hood families had descended on the station. Ryan and Sofia, Jack and Laura, Mark Xander and his wife Daisy, Ryan's parents, all the kids, Paige and Elias, Paige's parents, Elias's parents. Ryan was harassing every detective who came within range, while Paige was sitting on a chair, Arianna on her lap, staring into space. He knew she was running the case in her mind; he could practically see the cogs spinning at record speed.

Rosie was also sitting on her mother's lap, both little girls had tear-streaked faces, but both were managing to remain calm. Or, at least, reasonably calm.

"Hey, girls." He crouched in front of them. "We need to talk about what happened today."

Arianna immediately looked to her mother. "I'll come with you," Paige said.

"And I'm coming with Rosie," Laura piped up.

He had been expecting that response. He understood. If it were one of his kids who'd just witnessed an abduction and was going to be interviewed by a cop, he wouldn't want to leave their side either. But he was going to get more out of the girls if they weren't worried about upsetting their mothers.

"I think it's better if I speak to the girls alone," he said gently.

"I'm not leaving my daughter," Paige said adamantly. Laura looked just as determined.

"You're not leaving her," he reminded them. "They'll be with me, and we're only going to be over there." He pointed to an interview room a mere four or five yards from where they were sitting. "Girls, you ready?"

Ari and Rosie exchanged glances, but both slid off their mothers' laps.

"Don't worry, I'll be in there with her," Jack told his wife.

Xavier had been anticipating this response from his partner as well. "Jack, you can't come either."

"I'm a cop."

"Not with this. With this, you're a father of a witness. The girls and I will be fine. We won't be long," he said firmly before they could waste any more time arguing.

He took Rosie and Arianna by the hand and led them to the interview room. He had known these two girls since they were babies. He hated that they had been dragged into the dark side of life and wished he could erase what had happened from their minds. But they were the only ones to have seen this killer and walk away alive. They were the best chance they had of finding Sophie and Hayley.

"We told you what we saw already," Ari said the moment the door closed behind them.

"I know you did, but I want to ask you a few more questions. Sometimes, after a little bit of time goes by and we think about what we saw again, we remember things we'd forgotten the first time."

Neither girl looked convinced, but they both sat down

"You said that Hayley and Sophie were with two teenage boys. Did you recognize them?"

"I think it was Sophie's boyfriend," Rosie replied.

"Think? You're not sure?"

"They were in a car," Ari said.

"Did they drive away together?"

"I think so. Sophie and Hayley got out of the car, and we ran and hid, but I think I remember the sound of a car driving off." Ari looked at Rosie who nodded.

"When Sophie and Hayley walked past you, did you hear anything they said?" Xavier didn't think the teenagers would have said anything relevant to the case. They'd most likely been with Sophie's boyfriend Dominick Tremaine, but that didn't mean they hadn't said anything useful.

"No," Rosie replied.

"No," Ari echoed.

"The man with the gun, were you able to see anything about him? Was he tall or short? Old or young? Did you see his skin color?" If they could get a description of the man, then they could either disprove that Davis Hilliard was the killer or help prove it.

"He was wearing all black——"

"But no gloves," Rosie interrupted. "He was white."

"And he was tall." Ari's blue eyes gleamed as the girls got on a roll once they started remembering things. "He was at least a head taller than my sister."

"That's great, girls." He smiled at them. They were doing just as well as he'd known they would. "Did you see his face?"

"He had on one of those things, you know that cover someone's face, but you can still see their eyes and their mouth," Rosie said, gesturing at her face as she explained.

"A balaclava?"

"Yeah, one of those," Rosie said, a little of the wind coming out of her sails.

Wanting to keep the girls moving without time to dwell, Xavier moved on to the next question. "Did he say anything?"

"No," Arianna said immediately, but then her face clouded over as she thought. "Wait, I think he did," she said excitedly.

"He did." Rosie nodded so quickly her long, dark hair bounced about.

"What did he say?"

"He knew their names," Arianna replied. "He said 'Get in the car, Sophie; you too, Hayley.' He knew them. He knew my sister."

That definitely fit with the Number Nine Killer.

The only thing that was bothering him about it was that he didn't think either Sophie or Hayley would have called a phone number about a date. Sophie was too into Dominick Tremaine, and he just couldn't see Hayley doing something like that. She was too quiet, too sensible.

But who else could it be?

They didn't know if Davis Hilliard's white with a blue logo van existed, but this van definitely did.

"Girls, one last question, do you remember any logos on the van?"

"I think it had something blue on it," Rosie said.

Just like the one Davis had seen.

Maybe he wasn't the killer after all.

They needed to find that van.

* * * * *

8:16 P.M.

"You should go home." Ryan stood behind his wife and rested his hands on her shoulders, kneading gently.

"No."

"There's nothing you can do here." There was nothing *he* could do here. That was the worst feeling in the world. Knowing that his baby girl was in trouble and there was nothing he could do to make it better.

That was his job.

He was the dad. He fixed things.

He was a cop. He saved people.

But he couldn't bring back his daughter. He didn't know where she was; he didn't know who had her, and he didn't know how to find her.

"There's nothing you can do here." Sofia turned to face him.

Ryan flinched at her words.

It was like she had reached inside his mind, read his greatest failure, then threw it back at him.

"Oh, Ryan, I'm sorry," she said as she obviously noticed the flinch and realized its cause. "I didn't mean it that way. I just don't want to leave here. I know it doesn't make sense, but it's like I feel connected to her here. I feel like we're doing something to find her. If I go home, I'm not going to sleep anyway."

He understood; he felt the same way.

Being here was doing something. He could help work the case, he could track down who took his daughter. If he went home, he definitely couldn't see himself lying in bed and going to sleep. If they didn't find Sophie, he doubted he'd ever sleep again.

"It's okay," he assured his wife. He didn't want to fight with her. They needed each other right now; they couldn't turn on each other. In his job he had seen it happen countless times before. Parents who were torn apart by losing a child, and unable to take the grief and the guilt, they channeled those emotions into anger and hurled them at the most convenient target, each other. He didn't want that to happen to them.

"Did we do this, Ryan?" Sofia's silvery eyes shimmered with unshed tears. "Is this our fault?"

"No," he said firmly.

Or *lied* firmly.

"I don't know," he said softly. They had messed up with Sophie. They shouldn't have let her get away with her bad behavior as long as they had. If they'd put a stop to it right away, then instead of being out with the boy they'd forbidden her to see, she would have been at home doing her homework.

Now it was too late to do things right.

If they didn't get Sophie back, the rest of their lives would be an unending cycle of what ifs, should haves, and self-recrimination.

"She knows we love her, right?" Sofia's bottom lip wobbled, and he wished he could do something to take away her fears and her pain.

He wished more that he could tell her that their daughter knew they loved her, but he honestly wasn't sure.

Sophie was so angry, and she had let that anger cloud everything. The girl he had known since she was a tiny baby was someone who cared more about others than she did herself. Who was never happier than when she was doing something for someone else. But since she learned the truth about her parentage, it was like she'd lost herself.

Ryan had to believe, though, that deep down she knew they loved her. Deep down—maybe deep, *deep* down—under all the anger and hurt, Sophie knew that their love for her was unconditional and unending.

Leaning down, he touched his forehead to his wife's. "Our daughter knows we love her."

"Thank you," Sofia said in a way that let him know she had the same mix of doubts and conviction swirling around inside her.

"I love you." Ryan hooked a finger under her chin and tilted her face up, brushing his lips across hers. Then he drew her against his chest and just held her.

"Dad? Mom?"

They turned to find Ned standing beside them. His blond hair was mussed, and his blue eyes were wet. He looked so much younger than his twelve years.

"How are you doing?" he asked his son.

"Is Sophie dead?" Ned asked.

"Why do you think that?" Sofia asked.

"I thought most people who were kidnapped were killed within the first few hours," Ned said anxiously.

Unfortunately, his son wasn't wrong.

Three quarters of the abducted children who were murdered were killed in the first three hours.

Sophie had been gone for over four hours now.

That meant she could already be dead.

He was almost hoping that it was the Number Nine Killer who had taken Sophie and Hayley. At least, that way, they still had four days left to find them before they were killed.

His gut didn't know for sure that it was the killer he and Paige had been looking for, but he didn't think his daughter was dead. He didn't *feel* it.

"Your sister isn't dead," he said adamantly.

"Are you sure?" Ned's pleading eyes looked up at him.

"I'm sure," he said, drawing his son close.

"Are you sure?" Sofia whispered in his ear.

"I'm sure," he whispered back.

Both his wife and his son leaned against him, and he held them up. He hadn't been there for his daughter when she needed him. He hadn't sat her down and made her tell him what was going on inside her head. He hadn't been the parent she needed during the worst time of her life. He hadn't gotten her the help she needed. He was going to be here for the family he had left.

And he did have a lot of family.

His parents were standing hand in hand over by the other window. His sister-in-law Laura was sitting on a row of chairs. Rosie was asleep—her head in her mother's lap. His brother Jack and Xavier were over in the corner, sitting at a table full of files, poring over them. His other brother Mark and sister-in-law Daisy were playing cards with their twenty-one-year-old son, eighteen-year-old twins, fifteen-year-old son, and Jack's eleven-year-old son trying to keep the kids busy and occupied. Elias Hood was sitting in a chair, his leg bouncing continuously, Arianna curled up on his lap asleep. And his partner Paige was moving restlessly about the room.

He wasn't alone.

He had a lot of people who were here for him and his daughter.

A lot of people who were here to support him and his wife and son if the worst happened.

No.

He couldn't allow himself to think that way.

He couldn't allow the possibility that Sophie wasn't coming home to enter his mind. If it did, Ryan was afraid he was going to fall apart, and then, what good would he be to Sophie? Or to his family?

"I'll be right back." He kissed the top of Sofia's head, then left her with Ned and headed over to Jack and Xavier. "Do you have anything?"

"I'm sorry, Ryan. Nothing yet," Jack answered. He had to give his older brother credit. He'd been asking the same question every fifteen minutes or so since this nightmare began, and every single time Jack had replied calmly.

"There has to be something. We have to grill Davis Hilliard, push him hard to tell us what he was really doing when he stood Paige and I up," he said. He didn't know if the man was the killer, but they had to do something.

"And the Tremaine boys," Paige joined them. "Ari and Rosie

said they thought that Hayley was sneaking out to meet up with Sophie and Dominick. He might have seen something and just be afraid to come forward because he knows that Ryan doesn't like him."

Guilt sliced through him.

It wasn't just his fault that Sophie had been abducted, but that Hayley had been dragged into this as well. Hayley would never have been there if it wasn't for Sophie. And Sophie would never have been there if he and Sofia had been able to get her behavior under control.

How was he ever going to face his partner again if her daughter died because of him?

Avoiding making eye contact with Paige, he said, "You're going to speak with them, aren't you? Why don't we go over there now? It's not that late, and we don't have time to waste."

"We'll interview them tomorrow," Xavier assured him. "We'll do all of our interviews tomorrow."

By *all* of the interviews, Ryan knew that they meant speaking with him and Sofia, and Paige and Elias as well. "You can interview us now. We're all here. No one's going anywhere."

"No," Jack said firmly. "No interviews tonight. Everyone is too tired. No one's going to be thinking clearly. Since we're all staying here, we might as well at least try to get some rest. I know no one wants to sleep, but the facts are that we aren't going to help Sophie and Hayley by pushing ourselves into exhaustion. If we're going to find them, we need to be clearheaded. Everything we do is about them, not about us. We do whatever it takes to bring them home alive."

Ryan couldn't argue with that.

I'm coming for you, Sophie. I won't rest until you're home safe and sound, he said to himself.

* * * * *

9:51 P.M.

"I'm sorry."

"Sophie," Hayley groaned. "You said that already—several times—and I already said it wasn't your fault."

"Of course, it's my fault," her friend contradicted. "If I hadn't ignored my mom and gotten into a car with Dom this morning, if I hadn't skipped school and made wedding plans with Dom, if I hadn't called you and dragged you over there, then you wouldn't be here."

"We don't know that," she said, just like she had every other time Sophie had said that. And since they'd been shoved at gunpoint into a van, tied up and driven here, Sophie had said it a lot.

"I'm sorry. I'm sorry that I got you into this," Sophie said again. This time, tears began to slide slowly down her cheeks. "If I hadn't called, you'd be at home right now, and I'd be with Dom or at home too. We'd both be safe. But now ..."

Now they were in some basement, their hands bound to pipes in the wall with plastic zip ties.

They had gone through all the stages of emotion you'd expect when you'd been abducted. Over the last few hours, they had gone through denial. They'd gone through anger; they had gone through depression and bargaining and they were hovering on the edges of acceptance.

Not that they would give up without a fight.

Hayley would never do that to her family. She would never allow anyone to kill her without doing everything in her power to stop it from happening.

"This isn't your fault, Soph," she said firmly. "You couldn't have known this would happen. Of course, you would call me when you were planning on getting married. And, of course, I would come. Neither of us could have known that we would get shoved into a van and brought here. None of this is your fault.

We're best friends, we're a team, we are in this together."

Together was the only way they were going to make it out of this alive.

If Sophie continued to blame herself and let guilt weigh her down, they didn't stand a chance.

"No more talk like that. We need each other right now. We have to stay strong and be smart. We have to keep our eyes and ears open so we can take advantage of any opportunities that present themselves. So, promise me—promise me—you're not going to waste any more time feeling guilty for something that wasn't your fault and apologizing to me for something you don't have to be sorry about."

Sophie drew in a long, ragged breath, then lifted her free hand and wiped at her cheeks. "Okay. You're right. We're in this together, and we can find a way to get home. My dad and your mom are cops. They'll be looking for us, and we're smart, we can figure this out." Sophie offered her a watery smile.

Hayley returned it with a weak smile of her own. She needed Sophie right now. She was terrified, beyond terrified, barely able to hold it together terrified. Memories of the first five years of her life were filling up her mind, flooding it with images of blood and smoke and darkness. Screams and moans of pain echoed inside her head.

Was the life she'd been rescued from going to claim her anyway?

Was this where she would live out the rest of her days?

Would she be hurt and raped in this dark, dingy basement?

Would she die down here?

What would happen to her body?

Would it be hidden where it would never be found?

Would her family ever get it back so they could have a funeral and get some closure?

What would happen to them?

Would her mom ever get over the loss?

Would her dad?

What about Arianna?

Would her sister be able to cope with the loss and learn how to live in a house with two grieving parents?

Would her abduction and murder forever shape Arianna's life and the person she would become?

A sob broke free despite her best efforts to hold it back and remain calm.

Just because she'd been through hell like this before didn't make going through this again any easier.

"It's okay, Hayley, you can let it out," Sophie said quietly.

She hadn't cried yet. Not when the cold metal of the gun had touched her skin. Not when she'd been shoved into the van. Not when she'd been tied up. Not when she'd been threatened that if she ran her friend would be shot. Not when she was brought down here and tied up. Not when she'd ripped all the skin off her wrist wrestling against the plastic tie.

Not at all.

Until now.

Now all her fears came out in a flood of tears. She sobbed until she was out of breath and her throat was raw, and her chest ached. She cried until she was so exhausted all she could do was sink down against the cold concrete floor and shake.

"We have to stop tag teaming like this." Sophie gave a small laugh. "We both have to hold it together at the same time if this is going to work."

She tried to laugh back.

Sophie was right.

They had both taken a turn to fall apart. Now they both needed to focus. They both needed to be strong even if they had to fake that strength until they felt it. *Fake it till you make it*, her dad always said.

"Okay, I'm all right now. Well, as all right as I can be, given—"

"Given someone kidnapped us," Sophie finished.

"Right." She still couldn't quite believe it was true. How unlucky could she be? Kidnapped twice in her life, and she wasn't even sixteen yet. That had to be some sort of record.

"He knows our names," Sophie said. "He knows us."

"Do you know who he is?" The man had been dressed in black and wearing a balaclava, so they hadn't been able to get a good look at him. Plus, the gun had been kind of a distraction. She'd seen guns before, but she'd never had one pointed at her.

"I don't know." Sophie looked thoughtful. "There was something familiar about him, but I couldn't put my finger on it. It was like I'd seen him before, but I can't remember where."

Hayley had gotten the same feeling.

They definitely knew him, and he knew them.

"Do you think it's that guy? The one who killed those other girls from our school?" she asked. She hadn't known Brianna Lester or Talia Canuck, but she had been tutoring Ally Brown. She liked her. They'd had fun together, and Hayley had felt at ease with her, something she didn't often experience with kids her own age. But things with Ally had been good. They'd both been a little socially awkward, not like all the other kids, and they'd bonded over that.

Now Ally was dead.

And she and Sophie could be next.

"It was all over school today, Brianna Lester's body was found in the teachers' parking lot," she told Sophie. Since Sophie had skipped school, she had missed out on the stories that had been passed about all day.

"You think the killer is someone from our school?"

"That could be why we think the man who took us is somehow familiar."

Why would someone from the school be abducting and killing girls?

Who from the school would be abducting and killing girls?

She wished she had something to go on. One concrete little

thing so she didn't feel like her world was spinning entirely out of control.

"Do you think they're looking for us?" Sophie asked quietly, her gaze fixed firmly on the ground.

"Yes." Hayley knew without a doubt that when her mom returned home and found Ari and Rosie alone, she would have known something was wrong.

"My parents think I ran away." Sophie still wouldn't look up. "They think I ignored them and ran off with Dom. They think that I hate them."

"They don't think that." She knew that Ryan and Sofia didn't really believe that Sophie hated them, but it didn't matter what she thought, Sophie had to believe it.

"They do." Sophie finally looked up. "They really do. I've told them that almost every day since they told me the truth. I ignored them, I lashed out at them, I was so angry that I couldn't see straight. But I don't hate them. I love them so much. I love them for giving me a home and for loving me even when I don't deserve it. I just want a chance to tell them I'm sorry. Even if I'm going to die, I just want one second—one second to tell them how much I love them and apologize."

They might never get one more second with their families.

Sophie might never get to apologize to her parents and tell them she loves them one more time.

She might never get a chance to tell her parents one last time that she loves them. Seconds had always seemed so normal, just a part of everyday life. Now, the one second she wanted, she might never get.

MARCH 8TH

7:00 A.M.

"It's seven." Paige and Ryan appeared before him.

"And?" Jack Xander asked. He was tired, stressed, and trying his best to hold it together because he loved his brother and his friend, and he knew that they needed him calm right now.

Both Ryan and Paige were holding on by a thread.

And he suspected it wouldn't take much to snap that thread.

Although he was only eighteen months older than Ryan, and three years older than Mark, he'd always thought of himself as the much older big brother, rather than just the oldest. He knew people thought he was bossy, and he supposed he could be, but it was only because he cared and wanted the best for the people he loved.

He and Paige had dated for a while many years ago. They had quickly realized they were better friends than lovers. She had then been partnered with his brother, and they'd become close friends. She was like a sister to him, and they'd spent a lot of time together in the aftermath of the death of his old partner and Paige's best friend, Rose Lace. They'd been the closest to Rose, and her death had hit them both hard. Grieving together and talking about Rose had helped them both to heal.

As a tribute to the partner he would never forget, he had named his daughter after Rose. That his child, his ten-year-old daughter, had witnessed the darkness in the world firsthand filled him with a mixture of rage and fear that left him feeling impotent.

He couldn't take away what she'd seen.

He couldn't make it better.

He couldn't erase it from her mind.

He couldn't give her back her innocence.

He couldn't make her feel safe.

Rosie had lost something yesterday, and she could never get it back.

All he could do was whatever it took to find Sophie and Hayley and bring them safely home.

His daughter was every bit as tough as her namesake. She'd been born premature and had been strong from the very second she entered the world. She was bright and bubbly and full of life and energy. She worked hard at everything she did, and she was a smart, creative, warm, and caring child. She was everything he wanted his children to be, and he prayed that this wasn't going to change her.

"Jack?"

"Yeah?" He blinked and focused. It had been a long night. He and Xavier had worked until after midnight, then he'd held Rosie in his arms and gotten a couple of hours of restless sleep before getting back to work. He had accepted that none of the family were leaving until the girls were found. Neither were any of them going to get a full night's sleep until the girls were home.

"Interviews," Ryan snapped. "You said you weren't going to do interviews until this morning. Well, it's morning now. Let's get this over with."

"I'll take Ryan and Sofia since Ryan is your brother, and you can do Paige and Elias," Xavier said.

It was as good a way as any to decide who interviewed whom, and it meant they'd be done twice as quickly. Whether Hayley and Sophie were the Number Nine Killer's next victims or victims of someone else, time was of the essence.

"Okay," he agreed. "Let's go," he said to Paige.

Paige nodded to Elias who left Arianna with Paige's parents and followed them out of the conference room their families had taken over and into a small interview room.

"There have been no unusual phone calls, emails, messages, or anything on Hayley's social media," Paige said the second the door closed behind them. "And no one unusual hanging around. This wasn't a case of someone stalking her."

Paige attempting to preempt his questions by giving answers to what she already knew he was going to ask wasn't going to help. This case wasn't Ryan and Paige's, nor had they conclusively proved it was related to the Number Nine Killer, so Paige was going to have to take a back seat whether she liked it or not. This was his case, and she was the parent of a victim—not a cop—on this one.

"Paige, I know this is hard. I know that you want us to move quickly, and we will, but if we move too quickly, we could miss something important," he reminded her. "Now how do you know that Hayley hasn't received any unusual phone calls, emails, or messages? Have you been checking her phone?" His kids were eleven-and-a-half and ten. Although lots of kids their age had their own phones, his kids didn't. He wasn't ready for them to have that kind of unfiltered access to the world.

"We don't check her phone," Paige replied. "But we do make sure that it and her computer only have access to certain apps. Whatever good that does," she sighed. "She's fifteen; she can access anything she wants if she really wants to. But you know Hayley, Jack. You know she's a good kid. I didn't worry about her meeting some guy who wasn't who she thought he was over the internet and sneaking off to meet him."

He had to agree it didn't seem like something Hayley Hood would do. She was a mature and sensible kid, but even the smartest of kids—or adults—sometimes did stupid things. "Can we take a look at her computer?"

"Of course," Elias agreed immediately. "You know we have nothing to hide. Anything you need to look at to bring our daughter home, you can."

That was the answer he expected. He knew that neither Paige

nor Elias had done anything to their daughter, and they weren't suspects, which meant they could focus on people who might be. "What about boys? Is there anyone she's interested in?"

"She hasn't mentioned one, but ..." Elias trailed off.

"But?" he prompted.

"But I think there's a boy she was interested in," Paige finished for her husband. "I think his name is Zane Bishop. Hayley never talked about him, but I saw his name all over a couple of her notebooks, and when I asked her about it, she went bright red and denied everything."

Teenage girls.

Jack had to admit he was making the most of his time with his daughter before she became more interested in boys and her friends than she was in him and Laura. It was already starting to happen. Rosie and Ari had been whispering about some boys in their class they thought were cute just a week ago.

"We'll interview Zane Bishop," he said, jotting down the name.

"He's a piano prodigy," Paige said. "I can't see him abducting Hayley and Sophie."

"Do you think it could be the same man who kidnapped and killed Talia Canuck, Ally Brown, and Brianna Lester?" Jack asked. He hadn't been involved in the case, although he and Paige and Ryan had discussed it a couple of times. He and Xavier had read through all the case files, but he'd rather get Paige's feelings on the case.

"I don't know." Her brown eyes were thoughtful, and she twirled a curl around her finger that had fallen loose from her hair tie. "That the girls attend the same school as the other victims fits, and the timing fits, but I don't think that either of them would have called a number they saw on the bathroom mirror to get a date. Which doesn't necessarily mean that it isn't him. He changed up the drop site of the bodies because he knew we were on to him. Maybe he changed up the way he got his victims as well."

That was true. The killer had already changed one aspect of his MO—there was nothing to say he couldn't change another. "Do you like Davis Hilliard for it or not?"

"He's the only suspect we have," Paige began, which wasn't the most convincing of affirmations. "I don't know. He has an anger problem, and he suffered a loss nine months ago that could have been a trigger. But I don't know, I think if he were going to kill anyone because of his family's deaths it would be … I couldn't even say. They died in a freak boating accident, it didn't have anything to do with the school. He has a number nine connection, and he works at the school, so he has access to the bathrooms. When Ryan and I looked into him, we did find one thing that, I guess, could have given him a reason to go after teenage girls."

Both he and Elias looked at her expectantly, waiting for her to continue.

"Davis Hilliard's older daughter Liza was nineteen when she died, but she had only just graduated that spring before the accident. She missed a year of school between her sophomore and junior years, she spent that year in a psychiatric facility. Apparently, she was bullied so badly by the other girls in her classes that she attempted suicide. I guess if he blamed high school girls for what happened to his daughter, maybe he thought if she hadn't missed a year of school and graduated when she was supposed to, she might not have been in that boat. It's stretching a little, but I guess it's a motive, and he is the only suspect we have. Plus, he kept Ryan and I waiting ninety minutes, which means he could have grabbed the girls, stashed them, then come home. We checked with the school. He wasn't there the morning Brianna Lester was abducted, and he didn't have any classes before her body was found. He has motive, means, and opportunity."

* * * * *

NINE

"It's Dominick Tremaine," Ryan said adamantly, for at least the twentieth time in the last five minutes.

Xavier resisted the urge to roll his eyes only because he knew that Ryan and Sofia were out of their minds with worry over their daughter. He wondered if Jack was having better luck getting information out of Paige.

As far as he knew, Dominick Tremaine had no motive to kidnap Sophie and Hayley. He already had Sophie. She was head over heels in love with him, as only a teenager could be, and was ready to give up anything and everything to be with him.

"We'll come to Dominick in a moment," he assured Ryan. "But first, I want to go through a few other things."

Ryan looked like he wanted to argue and try to prove his case, but Sofia put a hand on his arm to quiet him. "Whatever you need to ask, Xavier," she told him. Fear covered every inch of her features, but she was doing her best to hold it together. Probably mostly for Ryan and their son Ned. Sometimes it was easier to be strong for the people you loved than it was to be strong for yourself.

That was something he'd learned in his journey with Annabelle.

They'd met fifteen years ago when Annabelle was at the lowest point of her life. She had lost her entire family in one night and been used as a pawn by the killer so he could escape. It had taken Annabelle a long time to recover, and he thought part of that was because she had wanted to live only for him. She hadn't wanted to get better for herself, and that had almost cost them their relationship and her life.

Now he looked back on those dark days with that sense of peace which came from knowing as awful as it'd been at the time, everything had worked out okay.

He prayed that one day Ryan and Sofia and Paige and Elias,

could look back on these days like that. That although they were horrible, terrifying, scar-inducing days, in the end, they'd gotten their girls back, and their lives could go on, even if they would never be the same.

"I know that Sophie was involved." He deliberately avoided using Dominick's name in case it set off another rant about the boy. "But has there been anyone else she was interested in or anyone else who was interested in her, but it wasn't mutual?"

Ryan glared back at him.

Sofia's pale cheeks tinted pink, and she fixed her gaze on the floor. "This time last year I would have been able to answer that. This time last year, I would have been able to tell you everything that had been going on in her life. This time last year, I'd have been able to tell you the name of every boy who'd asked her out or showed interest in her. But now, I'm sorry, Xavier, I have no idea if there was anyone who liked her."

He should have known that.

Xavier felt terrible that he'd made Sofia and Ryan feel worse when they were already feeling as low as it was possible to be. Unfortunately, the questions he had to ask next were only going to make them feel worse yet.

"I know Sophie had her phone on her when she disappeared because it was found broken on the next street over—"

"She must have taken it out of my office before she came downstairs yesterday morning," Ryan inserted.

"Before that, after you confiscated it, did you look through it? Was there anything to be concerned about in her messages or on any of her social media profiles?"

"I looked through it," Ryan said. "But I didn't see anything that alarmed me. Pretty much everything revolved around Dominick."

And just like that, they were right back to Dominick.

Was it a possibility that Dominick had taken the girls?

Xavier couldn't see why.

It didn't make sense.

Dominick was already dating Sophie, and even if he *had* grabbed her for some reason, why would he take Hayley? Xavier could see it might have been possible that if Sophie had broken up with Dom like her parents had ordered, he might have been pushed into abducting Sophie, but that was it.

And even *that* was stretching things.

They had looked into Dominick Tremaine when the little girls said he'd been there right before the abduction, and he didn't have a criminal record. He had never been in trouble at school, all his teachers liked him, all the students liked him, all the girls liked him.

Maybe that was an avenue to pursue.

Someone who wanted Dominick and thought that getting his girlfriend out of the way would help them get him.

But again, why take Hayley?

Collateral damage?

Wrong place, wrong time?

"What are you thinking?" Ryan asked, looking more cop and less frantic father.

"You keep saying you think Dominick Tremaine kidnapped Sophie and Hayley at gunpoint, but why do you think that? Is it just because you don't like the boy and don't want him dating your daughter? Or is there something specific that makes you think he's capable of committing a crime like this?"

"Dominick was the last person seen with Sophie. She got in the car with him yesterday morning, even though I warned him to stay away from her, and Sophie was forbidden to see him. Neither of them ever turned up at school. We don't know what they did all day. Sophie could have ended things, and he got angry. Maybe Sophie called Hayley to come and get her, and that's why Dominick took her too."

Although he had wondered something similar, Xavier wasn't sure that breaking up with Dominick was on Sophie Xander's to-do list.

"Rosie and Ari said that they saw Sophie and Hayley get out of Dominick's car," Xavier reminded him. "Then the girls walked down the alley, turned down the street heading back toward the Hood house and were grabbed by someone in a van at the intersection. How could Dominick have gotten out of his car, into a van, out of the alley, and around to the intersection in time to grab them? It probably only took the girls two, three minutes tops, to walk that far. It wasn't feasible that Dominick Tremaine is the man in black with the gun that Rosie and Arianna saw grab the girls."

"He had a partner," Ryan said quietly.

"Who?" He wasn't discounting Ryan's theory, but they needed something more than a father who disapproved of his daughter's boyfriend to look into Dominick as a viable suspect.

"What about this other boy?" Sofia asked. "The one that Arianna and Rosie saw standing outside the car with Hayley."

"Didn't they say he got into the car at the same time Hayley did? And, according to them, he never got back out. The same reason that means Dominick couldn't have been driving the van goes for him as well. The timing just doesn't fit. Neither Dominick nor the other boy was the one with the gun."

"Then who is it?" Ryan ran his fingers through his hair in frustration. "Who has Sophie? If it's not Dominick and this other boy, then who? The Number Nine Killer? Some random guy? A rapist? A murderer? A sex trafficker? An old guy? A young guy? Does he live here? Out of state? Out of the country? Does he have brown hair? Blond hair? Red hair? Gray hair? Blue eyes? Brown eyes? What's his job? What are his hobbies? Does he have a family? Siblings? A wife? Kids? We know absolutely nothing about this man other than he owns a gun and a white van and he abducted two teenage girls."

Xavier felt his friend's frustration, his sense of helplessness. He knew how he felt when Annabelle had been in the hands of a lunatic, and he had no idea as to the man's identity or why and where he'd taken her. That kind of helplessness made you feel like you were lost in the middle of the ocean, tossed about by the waves, dragged along by the currents. Every direction you looked, you saw the same thing—endless miles of water. There was nothing to hold on to, nothing to give you direction, nothing to keep you up as exhaustion wanted to pull you down.

"We're going to find them, Ryan. Jack and I will interview Davis Hilliard. If he did this, then we'll find proof. We'll interview Dominick Tremaine and see whether he saw anything when he was leaving the alley or whether it's a possibility that he's responsible for Sophie and Hayley's abduction. No one is going to rest until the girls are home safely."

"What can I do?" Ryan asked.

As much as he hated it, there was only one answer Xavier could give his friend right now. "Nothing. You just have to trust us to do our jobs."

To lay the life of their child in someone else's hands—*that* was perhaps the hardest you could ever ask of a person.

* * * * *

9:23 A.M.

"I'm not staying out of this, so don't bother asking again," Ryan warned as he, Paige, Jack, and Xavier all took seats at the conference table. Every file and piece of evidence they had about the girls' disappearance, and the Number Nine Killer, and every other sexual predator who kidnapped teenage girls and lived in the vicinity, was all laid out.

"Ryan," Jack started.

"I can't do it," he said firmly. "I can't leave Sophie's fate—her life—in anyone else's hands. I'm sorry. It's not that I don't trust you, I do. But this is my daughter, my baby, I can't sit on the sidelines and do nothing. So, don't ask me to."

"I'm with Ryan," Paige added. "We are in on this case; besides, the more people working on this, the greater the chances that we find the girls quickly."

That his partner had phrased her comment that finding the girls was a foregone conclusion, didn't elude him.

He understood.

That was precisely how he was thinking about it.

Sophie *would* come home.

They *would* find her alive.

Anything else was unacceptable.

Sofia would never survive losing their daughter—neither would he, and Ned's life would be forever shaped by the loss.

"Since we don't know that Hayley and Sophie's abductions are related to the Number Nine Killer why don't you two keep working that case," Xavier suggested. "You can go through missing persons reports, see if any other teenage girls who attended the high school went missing yesterday. If there was one, and she fits the requirements of the killer, then we might be able to discount the killer as the one who took the girls."

"And Xavier and I will interview Dominick Tremaine," Jack said. "And then, we'll start going through all the sexual offenders in the area, see if the girls fit any of their MOs and then start interviewing them."

Ryan couldn't help but tense at the mention of Dominick Tremaine.

He couldn't shake the feeling that the kid was bad news.

Yes, he knew that plenty of fathers didn't like the boys their daughters dated. And he couldn't deny that there was a chance that he would never see any man as good enough for his little girl. But he was sure that wasn't all this was. He was sure—positive— that there was more to it than that.

He just wasn't sure exactly what it was.

There was just a niggling doubt inside him that he was right, and that Dominick was somehow involved.

As hard as it was, for now, he was just going to have to trust that if Dominick was involved, they would find out. And then, he would make sure the man was punished to the full extent of the law. He would make sure that he never saw the light of day again.

"Paige and I will go and interview Davis Hilliard now," he said, pushing his chair back and standing. "You good with that?" he asked when Paige hesitated.

"Yes," she said, but her gaze travelled the room and settled on Arianna who was playing snap with Rosie and Laura.

He couldn't imagine what Paige and Elias were going through. Not only was their older daughter missing, but their younger one had witnessed the abduction. Both of her children had been affected by this, and it was all because of him. As soon as they were in the car on the way to Davis Hilliard's house, he would apologize to her and hope that she could forgive him, although he didn't know how they were going to be able to remain partners if they didn't find the girls in time.

Stop, he ordered himself.

He couldn't start thinking like that.

They would find the girls.

They. Would. Find. The. Girls.

"I'll just say goodbye to Ari, tell her where I'm going and when I'll be back, then I'll meet you in the car," Paige said.

Shrugging into his coat, Ryan was just pushing his chair in when the door swung open. "Mail for you, Ryan. You too, Paige," a colleague announced.

Ryan took his letter and held out the other envelope to Paige as she walked over.

A sick feeling settled on him.

A premonition of sorts.

Whatever was inside this simple white envelope was terrible news.

He probably should have listened to his gut, but he was so

anxious to get it open, he ripped through the seal and pulled out a single piece of paper.

On the paper, there was one typed line.

Payback. Payment will be your daughter.

Ryan was pretty sure his heart actually stopped beating for a moment. That air stopped filling his lungs, and his blood stopped flowing around his body.

Sophie hadn't been taken by chance.

She was targeted.

Because of him.

Someone had taken his daughter to punish him for something they believed he'd done to them.

What was worse was that the letter was signed.

With one single word, the world seemed to stop spinning.

Time stood still.

The note was signed, *Nine.*

The Number Nine Killer had killed Talia, Ally, and Brianna to get to them. And then to punish them further, he had taken their daughters.

Ryan knew the exact second that Paige opened her envelope and read the same thing he had because she gasped.

The sharp intake of air caught everyone's attention, and when Paige's knees buckled, Xavier snapped an arm around her waist before she hit the ground.

"What's going on?" Elias demanded as everyone rushed over. Elias wrapped an arm around his wife's shoulders, and Xavier released his hold on Paige.

"Mom, Dad, take the kids outside," Ryan ordered. He didn't want them overhearing this.

Thankfully, the look on his face must have been enough to convince his parents to round up the kids without protest. All, except Arianna.

"Mom?" The little girl looked worried.

"Go with the others, Ari," Elias said.

Ari looked conflicted but obeyed her father and the second the door closed behind his parents and the kids, leaving only him, Paige, Jack, Xavier, Elias, and Sofia, he said, "He took them on purpose. To punish us."

"Punish us?" Jack looked confused.

"Me and Paige," Ryan elaborated tightly.

"What?" Elias looked a combination of shocked and perplexed.

"That's what it says," Ryan said. He could feel himself starting to spin out of control.

He was losing it.

Quickly.

He was unraveling.

When Sophie was eight, she asked for a kitten for her birthday. After much discussion, he and Sofia had decided she was mature enough to have a pet of her own, so they'd bought her a gorgeous little smoky gray kitten that she had named Silverbelle. The cat's favorite game had been chasing a ball of wool around the house. It didn't matter how many times one of them rewound the yarn into a ball, it took the cat less than a minute to unravel the entire thing.

That was what he felt like right now.

Like some giant cat—life, he guessed—had taken hold of him and was batting him around and around until he had unraveled into a useless, long string of wool.

He was responsible for what had happened to his daughter.

Whatever Sophie was going through right now, whatever she was going to go through before this ended, either in her homecoming or her death, was because of something he had done.

"Someone sent you a letter saying that they took the girls because of you?" Elias asked.

"As payment," Paige said quietly. She was visibly shaking and was so pale that Ryan wondered if she could remain standing if

Elias let her go.

"Does it say who the killer is?" Jack asked.

"It's signed *Nine*," Ryan replied. All this time he and Paige had been searching for a motive. Looking at Talia's family, looking for links between Talia and Ally, looking at someone at the school who would have reason to kill Talia, Ally, and Brianna, and all this time, they should have been looking at themselves.

"So, it was the Number Nine Killer who took the girls," Xavier said.

"Only he doesn't really care about them; he's really going after Ryan and Paige," Jack added, shaking his head as though he was struggling to comprehend it all.

"This guy has to be someone from a case you worked." Xavier was looking excited now; this was the break they needed, only Ryan couldn't summon any enthusiasm.

How could he?

How could he feel anything other than crushing guilt?

"We have to go through all our old cases." Paige roused herself, straightening and tugging herself out of Elias's arms. Then she spun around and threw her arms around her husband's neck, burying her face against his chest. "I'm so sorry."

"Shh, it's not your fault," Elias said, dragging her closer.

Ryan turned to face his wife.

He wanted to apologize.

He wanted to hold her.

He wanted them to help carry each other's pain and fear.

But Sofia just looked up at him, burst into tears, and went running from the room.

He had to fix this.

For his wife.

For his daughter.

For his family.

Only he had no idea how.

* * * * *

10:34 A.M.

"I didn't think this day could get any worse," Jack said to his partner as they drove to the Tremaine house.

"Neither did I," Xavier agreed.

His partner sounded just as shell-shocked as he felt.

While the letters Ryan and Paige had received were, in a sense, good news, giving them a direction to move in as well as several clues to the killer's identity. On the flip side, it also presented a whole new set of challenges.

First and foremost, that someone had made their intentions clear.

Ryan and Paige were the endgame.

This was about payback. For what, they didn't know yet but abducting the girls was only a precursor. It was an added layer of punishment, but it wasn't the primary goal.

However, since it was an added layer of punishment, they couldn't predict what the killer would do to Hayley and Sophie. Jack would bet almost anything he wasn't going to just hold them for ninety-nine hours and then kill them. He had already worked his way through that stage of the plan and moved closer to his ultimate goal.

The killer had been violent with Brianna Lester, even though he hadn't with Talia and Ally. He wasn't just progressing through the stages of his plan but progressing in his confidence as well. He was enjoying what he was doing, and now that he had a taste for blood, he could do anything to Sophie and Hayley.

Perhaps he already had.

The girls had been gone for around eighteen hours now. That was plenty of time for the killer to have done anything to them.

Plenty of time to kill them.

They had no proof that the girls were still alive, and just

because he had kept his other victims for ninety-nine hours before he killed them didn't mean he would do the same with Hayley and Sophie. They weren't like his other victims. He had already changed the script. Now they were walking blind.

All they knew was that this man wanted Ryan and Paige to suffer, and he was going to do whatever it took to make it happen, regardless of how many innocent people he dragged into it.

"We're here," Xavier said as he parked the car in front of a small Cape Cod style house. It was pretty with cute dormer windows, a bright yellow front door, and several garden beds that he suspected would be full of an array of colorful flowers once spring came.

"Ryan was convinced Dominick had something to do with this?" he asked Xavier as they got out of the car.

"Adamant."

"What do you think?"

"I think that logistically it doesn't seem feasible, but he could be working with a partner, I guess."

"But you don't think so?"

"I'd be more likely to believe it was a possibility if the theory wasn't presented by an emotional father who didn't like the boy his daughter was dating and already forbidden her to see him."

Jack felt the same way.

It was hard to take Ryan's theory seriously when he just plain didn't like Dominick Tremaine for no other reason than that Sophie did.

"For now, let's just interview him as a potential witness in the abduction," Xavier said.

"Agreed," Jack said and rapped on the door whose cheerful yellow color was incongruous with the reason for their visit here.

"Hello?" A pretty middle-aged woman, dressed in a bright floral dress and a full head of gray hair pulled back into a neat bun at the nape of her neck, greeted them.

"Mrs. Tremaine?" Jack asked.

"Yes, and you are?" Her smile didn't waver, but she scanned the street behind them as though that held the answers to their identities.

"I'm Detective Xander, and this is my partner Detective Montague," Jack introduced them.

Panic flashed briefly through her brown eyes. In his job, he'd seen that look many times before. A cop turning up on your doorstep was never good news. But then, Jodie Tremaine's expression turned suspicious. "My boys are home. I don't have any other family, why are you here?"

"We actually need to talk to your sons," Xavier said. "Dominick, specifically. We believe that he witnessed an abduction."

"Oh." Mrs. Tremaine's hands flew to her mouth. "Oh my. I had no idea. He never mentioned anything, but then again eighteen-year-old boys don't talk much to their mothers. Come in." She ushered them into the house.

The inside of the house was much like the outside and like Jodie Tremaine herself. It was bright and colorful, the wallpaper was floral, and there were several vases of flowers dotted about. The woman obviously loved flowers.

She led them into a living room and indicated they should sit on a sofa—a floral sofa—then said, "I'll get the boys."

"This house is too flowery." Xavier squirmed, the second Mrs. Tremaine left the room.

Jack laughed. Laura loved flowers, and although their house wasn't as overrun by them as the Tremaine house, he was used to having lots of bouquets about everywhere. "Hard to see a woman like that raising a son who would kill three teenage girls and then kidnap the daughters of two cops just to punish them for something."

"And punish them for what?"

"I don't know. Neither of the Tremaine boys or their mother

has been in trouble with the law. And the boys are only eighteen. This seems too sophisticated a plan to be committed by an eighteen-year-old."

"Oh."

They looked over at the door where Dominick Tremaine was standing.

"My mother said Detective Xander was here; I was expecting Sophie's father, but you're not him."

"I'm Ryan's brother, Jack," he told the teenager.

"Is this about Sophie?" Dominick asked as he took a seat on the other couch.

"When was the last time you saw Sophie?" Xavier asked.

"Yesterday." The boy's cheeks heated. "I picked her up for school. She said that she'd spoken with her parents and that they'd agreed to let us keep seeing each other. Only when I turned up, that ... uh ... wasn't the case. We drove off together, but Sophie didn't want to go to school, so we just hung out."

"What were you doing together all day?" Jack asked.

"Just talking."

The way Dominick refused to make eye contact made it clear there was more to it than that. "Talking about what?"

"Sophie wanted to get married."

Married?

Ryan was going to go ballistic when he heard that.

"She's only fifteen; she can't get married," Xavier reminded Dominick.

"We knew that. We were going to have a ceremony and then move in together, then when she turned eighteen, we could make it official. We were going to do it last night, but then Hayley convinced Sophie to wait until today. So they could get a dress and do her hair and make it special. But they never came. I tried calling Sophie, but she didn't answer. I assumed her parents found out and they took her phone and wouldn't let her leave the house. Did something happen to her?"

From the look on his face, Dominick Tremaine genuinely cared about Sophie. Jack knew better than most that sometimes young love really was the real thing. He had loved Laura since they were kids. They had dated all through high school, but he'd messed things up and lost her. He'd thought that she was gone from his life for good, but then, almost fifteen years ago fate had thrown them back together. He'd had to work hard to regain Laura's trust, but their love had never died. Now they were happily married with two kids and planning to grow old side by side.

Who knows, maybe Sophie and Dominick Tremaine really were in love and really would somehow find a way to be together forever.

If they ever got Sophie back alive.

"Hayley was there as well?" Xavier asked.

"Sophie called her, and she came. Victor too. They weren't there long. Hayley convinced Sophie to hold off on the ceremony, then the girls left, and Victor and I went to Mom's shop to help her close up, then came back here for dinner. Now would you please tell me what is going on?"

"Sophie and Hayley were abducted just minutes after they left you." Jack broke the news as gently as he could.

"Sophie's gone?" Dominick lunged to his feet.

"She is. Did you see anything?" Jack added.

"No. I thought she and Hayley just went home."

"Do you remember seeing any vans?" Xavier asked.

"I don't remember seeing anything. Victor and I were talking about the wedding. I kind of remember hearing tires screeching," Dominick said thoughtfully. "But I don't remember seeing anything."

The story was believable.

It was entirely plausible that excited to get his girl, Dominick Tremaine wasn't paying attention to anything else other than talking to his brother about his planned illicit wedding ceremony.

"Mrs. Tremaine." He turned to Dominick's mother who was listening quietly to their conversation. "What time did the boys get to the store?"

"A little before closing. Maybe quarter to five," Mrs. Tremaine replied. "I know they were there before the last customer of the day left, so it was definitely before five o'clock."

If the boys had driven from the alley near where the girls were taken to their mother's store, then it didn't seem likely they would have been able to commit a double abduction, then take the girls somewhere and stash them.

Ryan might not like Dominick Tremaine, but Jack thought the teenager was a good kid who genuinely loved Sophie.

* * * * *

11:08 A.M.

She hadn't shaken this much since she'd almost been killed and suffered severe hypothermia.

She was shaking so much; her muscles were beginning to ache.

She had tried to control it, but it was useless, so she was trying to ignore it.

Paige flicked through another file, trying to make herself concentrate enough to read it. Which was as pointless as trying to stop herself from shaking.

But she had to find a way to stay focused.

They had to figure out who was angry enough with her and Ryan to want to kidnap their daughters to punish them.

No one sprang to mind.

That seemed ridiculous.

This man had gone to so much trouble to trick Talia, Ally, and Brianna into walking into his trap. He'd been restrained in keeping them prisoner for exactly ninety-nine hours, touching them only to put a number nine tattoo on them, then killing them and posing their bodies. There was no way he could have known that they were going to wind up with this case, but it had certainly worked out well for him.

Now he had her sweet, beautiful, precious little girl.

And if she couldn't figure out who he was, she was never going to get Hayley back.

She and Ryan were going through all of their cases, starting with the most recent ones, looking for anyone that stood out at them as a suspect. Or any cases that had a number nine connection. They were looking at all suspects, witnesses, victims, and family members in their cases because they couldn't know who the killer was. Davis Hilliard was also not out as a suspect. No one was.

Until this was over, Arianna and Elias were not leaving this building.

She couldn't risk the killer going after them.

Since they now knew that she and Ryan were the real targets and that Hayley and Sophie hadn't been taken by chance, there was a chance that the killer could take her other daughter or her husband too. It was lucky that he hadn't seen Ari yesterday when he was grabbing the older girls, or he probably would have taken her too.

That would have killed her.

This was hell enough, but to lose both her children in one moment would crush her.

"Paige."

She looked up at her partner. She and Ryan had been going through files for the last hour, but they'd been working in silence, each lost in their own thoughts. Each battling their own guilt. Each fighting their own struggles.

"I'm sorry."

"For what?" she asked, confused.

"For this." He waved his hands at stacks of files on the table.

"That we haven't found anything yet? We never expected to

find anything this quickly. We have worked thousands of cases over the years. It could take us days to find the one we're looking for." She hated admitting that, but it was a reality. They might not find this man before he came for them.

"No, not for that. For this. For what happened to the girls," Ryan said quietly.

"Why are you sorry for that?" She understood guilt and blame. She was blaming herself, and she had already apologized to her husband a dozen times for their daughter's abduction. She had apologized to Arianna and to her parents and her in-laws and the rest of her family.

Seeing their terrified faces was like sticking a thousand tiny pins into her flesh.

She almost couldn't bear to be around them.

If Hayley never came home, she didn't know how she was going to live out the rest of her life knowing that her child had been kidnapped and killed because of her.

But with Ryan, she didn't feel that way.

With Ryan, she could let a little of the guilt slide, because she knew he felt the same way and was going through the same thing.

"Sophie got Hayley into this mess," Ryan said.

"How do you figure that?"

"We let Sophie get out of control. She ran off with Dominick, then called Hayley, dragged her away from the house, and they were abducted. If it weren't for Sophie calling Hayley, she would have been safe. And if it weren't for me, then Sophie would never have gotten to this place. I'm so sorry."

She and Ryan had been friends for a long time.

A *really* long time.

They had been through a lot together. They had watched each other's backs; they had kept each other safe; they had relied on each other, and every time they needed each other, they'd been there. They had talked about everything from marriage problems and kid problems, to sports and the weather, and everything in between.

Ryan had saved her life, most literally, on more than one occasion. Besides her husband, he was her best friend. She couldn't imagine life without him. Paige didn't think a day had gone by in the nearly twenty years that they'd known each other where they hadn't spoken or texted.

And she had to say she was a little offended by that statement.

"Don't you ever say that again," she snapped at him. "How dare you say that. Or even think it."

"What?" Ryan looked surprised by her reaction. What had he expected, that she would thank him for the apology? That she would agree with him that this was his fault?

"How dare you think that you can spin this so it's your fault. This man is after both of us, and he took our kids to get to us. You are the one person I can be around without feeling like I'm going to explode with guilt, and now you want to ruin that by making this about you."

"I-I'm sorry," Ryan stammered.

"Don't be sorry … just don't say that again. It's not true, okay? This isn't Sophie's fault or yours."

"But the girls wouldn't have been alone and vulnerable if it wasn't for Sophie," Ryan protested.

"You know it doesn't work that way," she rebuked. "This guy hates us. Enough to kill innocent girls just to get to us. He wanted Hayley and Sophie; that was probably his plan all along. If he hadn't gotten them then, then he would have just waited and taken them some other time."

"I guess you're right," Ryan agreed.

"He hates us, Ryan. Hates us. Enough to take our daughters because he thinks it will crush us, render us useless. But it won't. We're too strong for that, and our girls are strong too. They'll hold on until we find them."

She had to believe that.

Paige knew her daughter was strong and that she'd been

through more in the first five years of her life than most people did in an entire lifetime, but this was asking so much from her.

"Do you really believe that?" Ryan asked. He looked and sounded like he needed reassurance, but she was hardly in a place to be offering much of that. She needed someone to tell her that everything was going to be okay, even if they were lying. She just needed to hear the words. She needed someone to lie to her, to give her something to hold on to, to give her faith when her own was faltering badly.

But right now, Ryan needed her.

He needed to hear the same things she did.

"I believe that," she told him. "I believe that our girls are strong enough to get through this. They have each other, and they know that we're going to be doing whatever it takes to find them. They're smart girls, and we've always told them what they should do if something ever happened to them. They know what to do. We just have to keep the faith."

Ryan reached over and covered one of her hands with one of his, squeezing tightly. "Thanks for lying."

She huffed a small laugh and mustered a half smile for him. "You're welcome."

"I don't know who it is and that drives me crazy. He has my baby."

He didn't have to say more. "I know, Ryan. I know."

"Is there *any* of our cases that you can think of that have anything to do with the number nine?" Ryan asked.

"Nothing that jumps out at me." How could that be? How could there be someone in her life who hated her so much that they wanted to destroy her, and she didn't even know who they were?

"We should keep looking." Ryan picked up another file and began to flick through it.

"We should," she agreed, also picking up a file. Paige opened it and tried to read it, but the words all blurred together into one large indecipherable black smudge.

She couldn't do this.

She couldn't just sit here and read files and hope that something jumped out at her.

She couldn't just go on as though this was any other case.

She was about to fall apart.

She could feel it coming.

Ryan's hand covered hers again. "It's going to be okay, Paige. Sophie and Hayley are strong. They can do this. They can hold on until we find them. And we *will* find them."

"Thanks for lying." She managed to regain a hold on her emotions.

"You're welcome."

Paige started to read the file in her hands. What choice did she have? If she didn't, she didn't stand a chance at getting her daughter back.

* * * * *

11:53 A.M.

He wondered if they had figured it out yet.

Did they know who he was?

He didn't think so, or they would have shown up at his door already and hauled him off to jail.

He loved this stage of the plan; it was even more fun than the first stage had been. If this phase was this much fun, how much fun was it going to be when he got the people he really wanted here?

They knew now that this wasn't about girls at the high school. He couldn't have cared less about Talia Canuck, Ally Brown, or Brianna Lester. He'd had fun with them; he'd enjoyed their time together. He'd learned from them some of what a person went through when you tied them up and trapped them someplace.

He'd learned a lot about himself too. Before this, he'd never known that he enjoyed hitting another person. He hadn't known that he enjoyed stealing their freedom and then their life. He hadn't known that he was evil inside.

But apparently, he was.

He had to be, to do the kind of things he'd done, and the sort of things he was going to do.

It wasn't like he'd been born this way; at least, he didn't think that he had. He'd been made this way by circumstance. Circumstances that were well and truly outside his control.

It was the cops.

They were to blame.

They had done this to him.

They had taken a once nice, sweet, innocent person and turned him into a killing machine. A machine that had only one purpose in life and didn't care who it had to destroy to get there.

All he cared about was punishing those responsible.

He wanted to make them suffer like he had suffered.

He wanted them to feel pain.

Unimaginable pain.

And he was going to make it happen.

Detective Ryan Xander and Detective Paige Hood had ruined his life, and now he was going to return the favor.

Taking their daughters was just the beginning. He was going to do so, so much more.

Speaking of Sophie Xander and Hayley Hood, he thought it might be time to go down to the basement, hang out a little with his newest guests. He wasn't quite ready for the girls to learn his identity. He wanted to save that reveal for something he had planned for later, but he could still have a little fun with them.

Grabbing the keys from the hidden drawer in the back of the desk, he headed for the basement. He took a moment to peer through the little glass window and see what his little houseguests were up to.

Hayley and Sophie were sitting side by side, their bound hands hanging from the pipe by their wrists, their free arms locked around each other's shoulders. They appeared to be whispering to each other, but unless he turned on the TV connected to the hidden cameras in the basement, he couldn't hear what they were saying.

Not that it really mattered, but he was kind of interested to know what two people being held captive together talked about. He'd never had two girls here at the same time before. Maybe once he had a little fun with them, he might watch the recordings.

For now, though, he slid the key into the lock, then threw open the basement door.

Immediately, both girls' heads whipped in his direction.

Neither Hayley nor Sophie said anything, but they watched his every step as he descended the staircase.

"Hungry?" he asked as he held up a plate of sandwiches. He knew they had to be because they'd been here for around twenty hours now, and in all that time, he hadn't given them anything to eat. He had been gracious enough to leave them some bottles of water. He didn't want dehydration getting in the way of the fun he had planned.

"Let us go, please." Sophie ignored his question to ask.

"That was rude." He shook his head at her. "I went to all the trouble of making these for you, and then bringing them all the way down here, and you can't even answer a simple question or show a mite of gratefulness. Would you prefer I just threw these on the floor?"

Both girls tentatively shook their heads, and he set the two plates down and slid them over to the girls. He didn't want to get too close. These two weren't like his other guests; they had cops for parents who had no doubt taught them well in self-defense.

Although Sophie and Hayley eyed the sandwiches, they didn't pick them up. Instead, Hayley said, "My mom and Sophie's dad and uncle are cops. They'll be looking for us. They'll find us.

Please just let us go. We don't even know who you are, so we can't tell them anything. Please."

Please.

Always so polite.

Whenever you abducted someone and kept them prisoner, they always so politely asked you to let them go.

It was very amusing.

"I really don't think so," he said and smiled at them, although they couldn't see it from behind his simple black balaclava. He had toyed with the idea of using a different mask, something a little more elaborate and frightening, but then he'd decided what was scarier than a simple black balaclava.

Black was the color of death and destruction, after all.

"Please, we won't—"

"I've had enough of this game," he said, cutting Sophie off. "I didn't come down here to debate this with you. I'm not letting you go. End of story. It's as simple as that, and I don't care to hear another word on the topic. Now eat your sandwiches, or I won't be nice and bring you anything else to eat."

The girls exchanged glances and then both picked up their lunch and nibbled on their food.

For the next few minutes, no one spoke. They just ate in a kind of companionable silence. Like they were old friends getting together for a meal. Only they weren't old friends; he was their captor, and they were his prisoners, which made things so much more fun.

"So ..." he drawled, when they finished their lunch. He couldn't decide what he wanted to do next. Well, he *did* know what he wanted to do next; he just wasn't sure that it was a good idea.

Still, after all, wasn't that what this was all about?

He wanted his revenge.

He wanted some fun.

He wanted to punish the cops who ruined his life and what

better way than this?

It was risky to get too close to the girls in case they'd cooked up a plan of sorts. He didn't think anything they could do would work. They were bound to the pipes with plastic zip ties, and he'd made sure there wasn't anything in this entire room that was sharp enough to cut through them.

"Why did you kidnap us?" Sophie asked.

He sighed. Hadn't they put a stop to this line of questioning?

"Do you want money?" Hayley asked. "Did you kidnap us for ransom?"

"No," he replied—at least, not the kind of ransom she meant. He wasn't interested in money. Although, that did give him an interesting idea. Something to file away for later. "I didn't kidnap you for ransom."

"Then why?" Sophie asked. Tears brimmed in her eyes—in both girls' eyes—but they held them back. They were doing an excellent job of keeping it together, better than that stupid Brianna Lester with her ridiculous incessant crying.

"Because I want to punish someone," he answered. It really couldn't hurt to let them in on what he wanted. After all, that was the whole point. He wanted Detective Xander and Detective Hood to know that they were responsible for what was going to happen to their daughters, and he wanted the girls to know who to blame for where they were and what they were going through.

"Punish who?" Hayley asked.

"Your mother. And your father," he turned to Sophie.

Sophie's gray eyes and Hayley's blue eyes grew wide as saucers, and they simultaneously sucked in a breath.

"That's right. Your precious parents are the reason you're sitting here right now."

"What?" Sophie asked.

"Why?" Hayley asked.

He'd had enough of this. He was getting bored. He hadn't taken time out of his day to spend in the basement talking.

"You're very pretty." He sidled up to Hayley Hood and brushed the back of his hand across her milky white cheek. Her skin was so soft, the kind of skin that begged to be kissed.

Hayley shrank away from his touch, and Sophie glared at him. "Get your hands off my friend!" she shrieked.

He ignored her.

He had stripped the girls' clothes off them when he'd brought them here, leaving them in just their underwear. It was so much easier to clean up after if he didn't have to worry about clothes grabbing hold of fibers and hairs and handing the cops his DNA on a silver platter.

His hand dropped to her shoulder, then let his fingers trail down her bare arm.

This was going to be fun.

* * * * *

12:40 P.M.

The sun was shining.

Sofia hated that.

The sun shouldn't be shining when her daughter was being held captive by some deranged serial killer.

It should be dark out. The sky should be a mix of black and gray clouds that would block out any light and brightness.

People were buzzing about, making the most of the sunshine, anxious for the long winter to be behind them and spring to arrive. There were small buds on the trees which would soon be a mess of pretty delicate blossoms. Fresh, little green leaves were beginning to uncurl, making the drab landscape look new and clean and ready to shrug off the dreary winter.

It was wrong.

The world shouldn't be full of color when her life was full of black.

What was happening to Sophie right this second?

Was she hurt?

If she wasn't, she would be soon. Sofia had no doubt about that. After all, it was the whole point, wasn't it? To make the child pay for the sins of the father.

She wanted to go running out there and turn over every rock and look in every shadow and in every single house in the city, if that was what it took. And, at the same time, she was petrified of leaving this room in case they got news.

It was comforting to have the whole family here. At least she wasn't alone.

And, although Sofia thought it probably made her a bad person, she was glad that Sophie wasn't alone either. She hated that Paige and Elias were suffering as well and that Hayley's life also hung in the balance, but at least, the girls had each other. She didn't think she would be able to cope with this if she knew her daughter was alone and scared in some dark, dank basement or some old warehouse or an attic or wherever else this lunatic might have stashed them.

"I brought you a sandwich."

Sofia jumped at the voice. She had been standing at the window, staring out for so long that she'd almost forgotten that there was anyone else around.

"You haven't eaten anything since Sophie went missing, and you have to keep your strength up."

She turned slowly.

She seemed to do everything slowly since her world had been destroyed.

Everything took such effort. Turning around was now the equivalent of running a couple of miles.

When she managed to turn all the way around so that horrible sunshine poured through the window, streaming onto her back and warming it a little, she found her husband standing before her.

He held a plate in his hands; a sandwich sat on the plate. The sight of it made her stomach churn, and she had to press a hand to her mouth, so she didn't throw up.

She shook her head at the sandwich and turned back to the window. She wasn't interested in eating. She knew she should. She knew it was the right thing to do, and she knew she needed to keep up her strength because when Sophie came home, her daughter was going to need her, but ... blah, blah, blah.

She couldn't care less about the right thing to do right now. Who cared about strength and eating when her heart—her very heart—had been ripped out of her body?

The sun continued to stream through the window.

Its warm rays seemed to caress her face and Sofia decided that maybe it wasn't so bad after all. Perhaps the sunshine was a good thing. Maybe it was an omen. Perhaps it meant that, although she was trapped in a thick, suffocating fog right now, eventually the sun would come out and clear it all away, and her baby would come back to her.

"I'm sorry."

The words were blurted out in a rush as though he expected her to grab hold of them and throw them back in his face.

Sofia sighed inwardly.

She and Ryan hadn't spoken since he and Paige had gotten letters saying they were to blame for the girls' abductions, and she had burst into tears and rushed out of the room. Her sisters-in-law, Laura and Daisy, had come running after her and spent a good thirty minutes or so talking her into unlocking the bathroom door. Eventually, she had because she realized that they were all hurting, and it was better to hurt together than to hurt alone.

By the time she'd come back into the conference room where they were all camping out, Ryan was already off with Paige going through their cases to see if they could figure out who was behind this. She knew she should have gone to him, spoken with him, but instead, all she'd done was stand and stare out the window.

"I'm sorry," Ryan said again, and she realized she hadn't spoken yet.

"Don't say that again," she said a little more forcefully than she had intended, but she didn't want apologies. She wanted her daughter.

"You're right, I'm—" He stopped abruptly, but she knew what he had been going to say.

He had been going to apologize.

Again.

"You don't have to apologize to me, Ryan."

"I don't know what else to do. This is all my fault. I'm the reason that Sophie is gone. I'm the reason that you and Ned and the rest of the family is suffering. If it weren't for me, then Sophie would be at home right now. I'm so sorry." Ryan reached out a hand to cup her cheek, but his hand stopped millimeters away as though he were afraid that touching her would make things worse.

"Oh, Ryan." Tears pricked the back of her eyes again. She thought she'd have run out of tears by now. "Why would I blame you for this? It's not your fault."

"It is. He took her because he wants to punish me." Ryan's blue eyes held more pain and anguish and guilt than she'd ever seen.

She hated it.

She hated this man for doing this to her husband and her daughter and to her.

Revenge.

She was so sick of hearing it as an excuse for people to hurt other people.

You weren't the center of the universe. The world didn't revolve around you; you weren't up on a pedestal, and you didn't get to hurt people just because you had been hurt or imagined that you'd been hurt.

"Ryan." She put her hand over his and moved it the last few millimeters until it caressed her cheek. "What did you say to me when my stalker started stalking Paige?"

A half smile tilted one side of his mouth. "That it wasn't your fault, that you weren't responsible for his actions. But this is different."

"How?"

"Because that really wasn't your fault. You didn't do anything to him to make him obsessed with you, or with Paige. But this is my fault. He's doing this because I arrested him or arrested a family member or couldn't find the person who hurt him."

She stood on tiptoes so she could press a kiss to her husband's lips. "It's not different, Ryan. It's the same." Those years that her stalker had fixated on Paige, repeatedly trying to kill her and nearly succeeding on several occasions, had been hell. She hadn't known who her stalker was, and each time she'd seen Paige suffering, and knew it was because of her, she had beaten herself up because she hadn't been able to stop it from happening. Ryan had told her over and over again that it wasn't her fault, but she still wasn't sure she believed it.

As if reading her mind, Ryan said, "You never stopped blaming yourself."

"And you might never get over blaming yourself, but it doesn't change the facts. What happened to Sophie isn't your fault. And it's not why I'm upset. I mean, I *am* upset about Sophie, but I was never upset about those letters. I just keep thinking about the last time I saw Sophie." A couple of tears escaped and rolled slowly down her cheeks, splashing onto Ryan's hand.

"Don't do that, sweetheart." Ryan wrapped an arm around her waist and drew her against his chest. "You're going to drive yourself crazy if you do."

"I can't help it. I keep wondering if there was something I could have said or done to stop her from leaving."

"There wasn't."

"But if I'd just told her again that we love her and that we were sorry—"

"We've told her hundreds of time in the last few months that we're sorry we didn't tell her earlier," Ryan reminded her.

"I know, but maybe she just needed to hear it one more time. Just one more time to know that we love her, that we will always love her, that nothing could ever change that. Maybe she just needed us to be more understanding or to be tougher or—"

"Do you hear yourself? You're clutching at straws. There was nothing you could have done differently that would have gotten a different outcome. Sophie was struggling. It would have happened no matter when we told her; it was a lot for anyone to handle."

Ryan was right about that.

If anyone knew about learning that your parents weren't who you thought they were and were the kind of people nightmares were made of, it was her.

"Sophie is a Xander," Ryan said firmly. "Xanders are strong, they never give up. Sophie will come home, and when she does, she'll find a way to deal with who her parents were."

Ryan was right again.

Sophie was a strong, smart girl who could do anything.

And if she couldn't, then Sofia would send her all the telepathic help she could.

A mother could do that for her child, right?

* * * * *

1:01 P.M.

For some reason, a sudden burst of renewed energy surged through her veins, and Sophie Xander pulled the wadded-up piece of material away from the cut on her face.

"It's still bleeding a little," Hayley said, leaning in closer to get a better look at the welt.

"No worse than yours," she said and gestured at the gash on her friend's shoulder.

Their abductor had *not* been pleased when they had tried to fight off his attempted sexual assault of Hayley. When he had come at her friend, they hadn't been sure what to do. They had discussed fighting back and any possible ways they could do it. Their options were limited since they both had one hand bound to the pipes on the wall rendering it virtually useless.

But they were strong girls, and they weren't going to do nothing.

So when the masked man had started talking about how pretty he thought Hayley was and then come toward her, running his hands over Hayley's face and then down her arm, they prepared themselves. The second his hand moved toward Hayley's breasts, they had both lashed out with their feet and their remaining free hands.

Hayley had grabbed hold of the man's arm and sunk her teeth into his flesh. Sophie, although she was a little farther away and not at a great angle to do much, slammed her foot into his knee— immensely satisfied when she managed to pop the joint out of place.

The man had screeched in agony, staggering backward out of reach and popping his dislocated joint back into place with a grunt of pain.

Then he had turned on them.

He had lunged at her, backhanding her across the face, causing the skin over her left cheekbone to split. The blow hadn't knocked her out, but it had been hard enough to stun her. And while her free hand had flown automatically to the bleeding cut on her cheek, the masked man had turned his attentions to Hayley. He had wrapped a hand around her neck, then sunk his teeth into the tender skin just above Hayley's breasts.

Then he had stood back, breathing hard, his chest heaving, his hands clenched into tight fists at his side, his brown eyes glittering with a madness she had never seen before.

Once, when she was ten, there had been a hostage situation at the center for abused women and children that her mother ran with her friends. Her mom, as well as a couple of other women, had been held at gunpoint by a man determined to reclaim the wife and daughter who had fled from his violent temper.

She had almost walked in on the hostage situation.

She had opened the door, seen what was going on, and frozen. If it hadn't been for her mother, the man might have seen her, dragged her inside, shot her, and the others.

Her mom had saved her that day.

Given her the strength to run and tell someone what was going on.

Thankfully, the only one who'd died in that room was the hostage taker himself, but Sophie had nightmares for months after. In her dreams, her fears of what might have happened had played themselves out, torturing her night after night until she dreaded the going down of the sun.

She had never seen that man's eyes, his back had been to her, but she suspected they had looked a little like this man's eyes. Filled with a terrifying mixture of evil and coldness and a weird sense of enjoyment. Like hurting other people gave him some sort of pleasure.

Sophie had a feeling the masked man had intended to do a whole lot more to her and Hayley, only someone had interrupted him. A voice from upstairs had called out to him.

For a second, that sound had been like a beacon of hope.

Someone was coming.

Someone would find them.

Someone would save them.

This whole ordeal had seemed so close to being over, she could taste it. She could go home. She could tell her parents how much she loved them and how sorry she was for how she'd treated them. She'd tell them all about her fears that her biological parents' DNA would be too strong to overcome. Her parents had given her a wonderful home, and she didn't want to be like the people who'd created her.

But it hadn't happened that way.

The voice had asked if *he* was down there but hadn't used a name, so they still didn't know who their abductor was. The basement door had been flung open, and a pair of boots had been visible at the top of the stairs.

She and Hayley had started begging for help. Explaining that this man had kidnapped them and hurt them and that whoever the person up there was they needed to run for their life and get help.

The boots hadn't moved.

And the relaxed stance of their abductor made it clear that whoever was at the top of the stairs didn't want to go and get help.

Because he already knew what was going on down there.

He knew because he was in on it.

There were two of them.

The masked man had a partner.

The only thing she and Hayley had going in their favor was the fact that there were two of them against their one kidnapper.

Now they didn't even have that.

Maybe there was one thing they still had that leveled the playing field a little.

Anger.

She was *so* angry at this man.

How dare he kidnap her and Hayley. How dare he tie them up and think it was okay to try to rape them. How dare he hurt them and make them bleed. How dare he think that their parents had done anything that made them deserving of being punished.

Her dad and Hayley's mom were kind, compassionate people who had dedicated their lives to helping the community and keeping people safe.

"I hate him," she said aloud.

"Me too," Hayley said, her blue eyes filled with a darkness that

Sophie had never seen before.

"Do you think my dad and your mom know who he is?"

"Not yet. If they did, they'd have found us already. But they will. If he hates them as much as he says and blames them for something, then he didn't just take us to keep us here. He has something else planned."

"I wish I knew what. Maybe we could get him to tell us what he thinks they did." Knowledge was power, and if they could find out why the masked man and his partner hated their parents, maybe they could find a way to use it against him.

"Maybe," Hayley agreed. "It has to be a case that they worked."

"What do you know about the other girls from our school who were killed?" She had been so wrapped up in herself and her pain that she hadn't been able to pay attention to anything else. She didn't want to be that selfish person ever again.

"You think it's the same guy?"

"Yes."

"I thought so, too, at first, until he said that he took us for a reason, but I guess they could still be related. All I know is that the rumors going around the school were that it was someone from the school. A teacher. The one that went crazy after he lost his family in the boating accident."

"Mr. Hilliard." Sophie had never had him as a teacher, but there were always rumors of one sort or another floating around the school about him. "I don't know why he'd hate your mom and my dad. Do you think maybe his family's deaths weren't really an accident?"

Before Hayley could answer, they heard the sound of a key sliding into a lock.

He was back.

Or maybe it would be both of them this time.

Sophie felt her stomach drop.

She wanted to believe that she and Hayley were strong enough

180

to survive whatever happened to them down here. But what if this man succeeded in raping them this time? How would she deal with that? Or what if he was going to hit them again, only worse this time? How would she deal with that?

"Hello, girls," the man called out cheerfully.

She hated that.

Why did hurting another living being make him so happy?

He had to be some sort of sociopath.

Two sets of boots clomped down the stairs and she instinctively shrank as far away from them as she could get. Hayley edged closer and held out her hand. Sophie grabbed it and held on tight. At least, whatever happened, they had each other.

"It's time to send a little message to your parents. A little something to let them know just how serious we are. And we need your help."

The man held up a pair of pruning shears.

Sophie couldn't help it, as strong as she wanted to be, her fear got the best of her, and she screamed.

* * * * *

3:29 P.M.

"I need a break," Paige announced, setting down the file she'd been flipping through and pushing back from the table. She knew she should keep going. The answers they were seeking had to be in there somewhere. It was so frustrating to know that those answers were lying on the table before her, but she just hadn't found them yet.

As much as she wanted to keep going, her eyes were burning, and her head was swimming. Her hands had cramped from clutching files for so many hours, and she just couldn't go on for another minute until she took a short break.

"Why don't you go and see if Jack and Xavier have anything,"

Ryan suggested. He also pushed away from the table and scrubbed a hand over his tired face.

"Yeah, okay," she agreed, even though they both knew that if Jack or Xavier had found anything, the first thing they would have done, would have been to come in here and tell them.

She was so tired.

She could feel her pulse thumping in her temples, pounding a steady beat.

It was beating so loudly it almost drowned out the rest of the world.

Paige knew she was going to have to get some sleep soon, no matter how much she didn't want to. It wasn't just that she was afraid of nightmares haunting her sleep, but she was also afraid they would get a break in the case the second she closed her eyes and drifted off.

It wasn't that she didn't trust Jack and Xavier and the entire rest of the police force and crime scene unit to find her daughter, it was just that she had to be here.

She *had* to be.

This was the only link she had to Hayley right now, and she couldn't bear to let it go.

"I have a headache," she murmured more to herself than to Ryan as she pressed her thumbs to her temples and massaged her aching head.

"Of course, you do; you haven't eaten anything in over a day," Ryan said, picking up a bottle of water from the table and tossing it to her.

She caught it with one hand and unscrewed the cap, downing half the bottle in one go. She hadn't realized how thirsty she was until she started drinking. The water helped to refresh her and dulled the headache a smidgen. "Did you find anything?" she asked her partner.

"No." He stifled a yawn. "Nothing has stood out, and I haven't found anything that relates to the number nine."

"You know we're going to have to sleep soon."

"I know. I convinced Sofia to take a nap by promising I'd take one later." The look on Ryan's face said he had no plans on taking a nap until he crashed, and his body and brain wouldn't take no for an answer.

"Elias tried that same deal with me. He and Ari were asleep last time I checked. I'm glad he's getting some rest. Ryan?"

"Yeah?"

"I don't want to, but I also don't want to get too tired that I miss something important. I'll take a nap if you do," she bargained. Admitting that she couldn't go on much longer and getting some sleep while her little girl was out there somewhere, suffering, was the hardest thing in the world to do, but maybe it wouldn't be so bad if they both got some sleep at the same time.

"Okay," Ryan agreed, somewhat reluctantly. "You go check on Jack and Xavier, see if they have any leads. I'll organize the files in here, so we know where we're up to after we sleep. Then we can go lie down for a bit."

"All right, I'll meet you in the conference room in a few minutes." Their family had virtually taken over the police station. Everyone was set up in one of the conference rooms, Jack and Xavier were working out of another, and she and Ryan were reading files in a third.

Her whole body was stiff and sore from too much tension, too little rest, and too many hours sitting hunched over a table poring over files. She stretched her arms above her head as she crossed the busy bull pen where other detectives were working on their cases, and probably Hayley and Sophie's on the side.

"Hey, guys," she said as she pushed open the door to the other conference room.

Jack and Xavier, and Stephanie from the crime scene unit were all standing around a brown box that sat on the table.

"Oh, Paige," Stephanie said.

All three of them turned to face her, Xavier trying to

surreptitiously move to block her view of the table.

Immediately, she was suspicious.

They were trying to hide something from her.

"What's in the box?" she asked, walking over.

"We don't know yet," Jack replied.

"Well, it's something. Stephanie is here. Did the kidnapper send something else? Is that addressed to Ryan and me?"

"You should go, Paige," Jack said firmly.

Her heart began to beat in time with the headache pounding at her temples. "It is, isn't it? The kidnapper sent something."

Something.

She was a cop.

She knew the kinds of things kidnappers sent.

Things.

They didn't send *things;* they sent body parts.

"Xavier, take her out of here."

Paige heard Jack say the words, but they seemed to float across the room from him to her.

Xavier's arm wrapped around her waist and he guided her back toward the door. She felt limp, hollow inside, like the last bit of her had disappeared with the realization that her baby had been hurt.

If it weren't for Xavier's arms holding her up, she would probably be a little puddle on the floor right now.

What had the kidnapper done to Hayley?

That there wasn't a piece of her daughter lying in that box never even occurred to her.

She could feel it.

She could feel that her baby was here in the room.

At least one part of her.

This wasn't just her worst nightmare come true, it was like she had descended into hell and was forced to watch her daughter dragged down to hell with her.

What had they done to her?

Paige had to know.

She had to know what those monsters had done to her child so when she found them, she would do that and so much more to them.

Stephanie was very slowly and carefully cutting through the tape and easing the box open. Jack was watching, a grim look on his face. He knew what was inside that box just as she did. It was why he didn't want her to see. But it didn't make any difference. Xavier could drag her out of this room, but he couldn't drag those thoughts out of her head.

Xavier almost had her to the door, but she couldn't leave now.

Not until she knew.

Paige wrenched herself free from Xavier's grip just as Stephanie opened the box.

"Paige, don't," Jack said as she came up beside him. He tried to grab hold of her and pull her away before she saw what was lying inside the box.

But he was too late.

She saw.

She saw what was in there.

She collapsed.

She would have hit the floor hard, but Jack caught her and scooped her up, cradling her in his arms.

"I told you to get her out of here," he said, presumably to Xavier, but Paige wasn't altogether sure.

The world was alarmingly shimmering around her, and she hung in Jack's arms like a rag doll.

"She wrenched herself free," Xavier said.

"Here, take her, get her out of here." Jack passed her to Xavier, and she hung just as limply in his arms as she had in Jack's.

She seemed to have lost the ability to move.

Hayley really had been hurt.

Her precious little girl, who would never hurt a fly, who was smart and serious and kind and caring, and who always looked for the good in someone, had been hurt.

Although she'd known it all along, it suddenly became very real.

Horrifyingly real.

This man who thought she and Ryan had done something to wrong him hadn't just stolen her daughter, but he'd also stolen a piece of Hayley that she could never get back.

One of Hayley's pinkie fingers lay in that box.

Lying on a piece of white paper that was stained with blood.

Hayley's blood.

Hayley's finger.

How was she going to tell Elias what the kidnapper had done?

How was she going to face him if Hayley's body was delivered piece by piece to the police station?

How was she going to face her daughter if they found her and Hayley learned that it was her fault that she'd been abducted and tortured?

Her tears came in a mad rush. Xavier carried her from the room she didn't think she'd ever be able to step into again. She was passed from his arms to her husband's, and from the whispered voices and then Elias's sharp intake of air, she knew that Xavier had broken the news.

She expected Elias to pass her straight back to Xavier or to drop her on the floor. She certainly deserved it. Instead, his arms curled tightly around her, and he clutched her close. Paige could feel his tears mix with her own as they sobbed for their daughter who would forever bear the deformity of one man's campaign for revenge.

Paige lost track of time, unsure how long she held her husband and cried.

Eventually, she cried herself to sleep.

* * * * *

4:13 P.M.

"How's Paige?"

"She's still asleep. Which is probably for the best," Jack answered his partner. He couldn't imagine what it would be like to see his daughter's severed finger lying in a box.

Well, actually, he *could* imagine what it would be like.

Which was worse.

He had worked a couple of kidnapping-for-ransom before, but none where the relatives of the victim were working the case—or at least trying to. That the relatives were his own family and friends made things that much harder. He had to keep resisting the urge to sugarcoat things to try to make them easier to deal with.

But none of this was easy to deal with for any of them.

Jack wished that he and Stephanie had waited another minute before opening that box. He'd thought that Xavier already had Paige out of the room. If he'd known she was still there, he would never have risked her seeing what was in the box.

It was inevitable that sooner or later—probably sooner—Paige and Ryan would have found out what the kidnapper had sent, but hearing about it and seeing it with your own eyes were two completely different things.

For as long as he lived, he would never forget the look on Paige's face or her agonized moan as she collapsed.

"Is Elias with her?" Xavier asked.

"Yes. He's just sitting in the conference room holding Paige and Arianna." The three of them were clinging to each other; they were all each other might have by the time this was over. He was praying it wouldn't end that way and doing everything within his power to bring the girls home, but there were no guarantees.

"Are Ryan and Sofia in there too?"

"Holding each other and crying."

Tears.

So many tears.

He hated tears.

He hated seeing the people he loved in so much pain.

It made him angry; it made him feel powerless, and it made him feel grateful.

Jack was so grateful that his family was safe.

If the kidnapper had seen Rosie and Arianna, he could have taken them as well. It could be him and Laura clinging to each other and trying to comprehend that someone had stolen their child and cut off a piece of them.

It made him feel guilty that he was so thankful that his wife and his son and daughter were safe while his brother and someone he considered a sister's children were in so much danger.

"There's nothing wrong with being grateful your family is safe," Xavier said quietly.

He glanced up, surprised, but he shouldn't be. He and Xavier had been partners for over a decade now; they often knew what the other was thinking. And right now, he was guessing that Xavier was thinking the same thing he was. "You're feeling guilty too."

"I know there's no reason to, but every time I look at Paige or Ryan, or Elias or Sofia, I can't help it. All I can think of is how thankful I am that my wife and my kids are safe. And then I feel so guilty. But enough of that. We have to stop worrying about that. There's nothing wrong with being grateful that we aren't suffering too. We just have to focus on finding them."

Xavier was right.

Feeling guilty about feeling grateful wasn't productive.

"Hey guys." Stephanie Cantini opened the door and came into the room, plopping down into a chair at the table and resting her head in her hands.

"You okay, Steph?" Jack asked.

"No. I hate this. I hate that the people I love are hurting. I hate that two innocent girls are being punished for something they didn't do. I hate that someone is targeting Paige and Ryan for just doing their job. I just ... hate this," she finished glumly.

"We all hate this," Xavier said. "But we're doing everything we can to end it."

"You're right, I guess." Stephanie lifted her head and straightened in her chair. "It just doesn't seem like enough."

"Did you get anything from the box?" Jack asked, unable to make himself more specific about the contents.

"Everything to do with this case is getting top priority," Stephanie said. "First thing I did was run DNA from the ...uh ...the fingers, and compare it to the DNA samples from the toothbrushes Ryan and Sofia and Paige and Elias supplied us with."

"And?" Jack asked. He could already read the answer in the crime scene tech's face, but he wasn't quite ready to accept confirmation yet.

Confirmation was so final.

"And it's them. The fingers are Sophie and Hayley's," Stephanie replied.

Although he'd known that was what she was going to say, he couldn't help the crushing disappointment. He'd been hoping against hope that this was all just some big crazy misunderstanding. That Sophie and Hayley had just run off because Sophie was angry with her parents, and that Rosie and Ari had been mistaken when they'd thought they'd seen the older girls being kidnapped. That the letters Paige and Ryan had received earlier were just some horrible hoax; it wasn't completely unheard of for people to fake their own abductions, even going so far as to collect ransoms.

But there was no denying it now.

They had irrevocable proof that Sophie and Hayley had been kidnapped.

"Did you get anything else from the fingers?" Xavier asked tightly.

"There was no DNA, no fibers, or anything else. Whoever cut the fingers off washed them before he put them in the box," Stephanie answered.

"Just like the Number Nine Killer," he said thoughtfully.

"We're sure that's who we're looking for?" Xavier asked.

"I don't know. I know the letters were signed with the number nine, but I think we should still keep every single avenue open. Ryan and Paige hadn't been able to find anyone whom they thought might have a grudge against them. Maybe the Number Nine Killer just targeted them because they were the cops working the case. The girls went to the school, and the theory was that the killer worked at the school so he would have already known who Hayley and Sophie were. Maybe that's all this is. Maybe it wasn't any more personal than that. Or maybe the person who took the girls just thought he could hide and pin the blame on the Number Nine Killer so we wouldn't find him," he suggested.

"No, it wasn't." Stephanie shook her head.

"Why not?" Jack asked.

"I found something on the note."

In the box with the fingers was a handwritten note that was addressed to Ryan and Paige telling them that he was going to send their daughters back to them in pieces so they could feel the pain of loss that he'd felt. Thankfully, Paige hadn't seen the note earlier, and he and Xavier had decided that there was no point in telling either her or Ryan or their partners about the note right now. It didn't seem to serve any purpose.

"Hairs? Fibers? Fingerprints?" Xavier asked.

"No, none of those."

"Then what?" Jack asked.

"Well, I was looking over the note, which I've already sent off to a handwriting expert, just in case they can give us anything helpful," she added. "Anyway, when I was analyzing the note there were marks on it—impressions. The paper was from a notepad, and there had been another page on top; I could make out what had been written on it. It was a list of numbers. Phone numbers. I cross referenced them with the numbers that Talia Canuck, Ally Brown, Brianna Lester, and the other girls from the school found on the bathroom mirror and called. They're the same. The same man who killed those girls is holding Hayley and Sophie prisoner."

Jack took a moment to let that sink in.

What was the connection between luring teenage girls from the high school with promises of a date and love, then holding them for ninety-nine hours, tattooing them with a number nine, then drowning them and posing their bodies, and kidnapping two girls because you wanted to punish their cop parents?

Right now, he couldn't see one.

But it had to exist.

Maybe knowing that the Number Nine Killer was indeed the person who had taken the girls would help Ryan and Paige to see a link to a case that they hadn't seen before.

"Was there anything else on there?" Xavier asked.

"Nothing that I could see."

"What about the box?" Jack asked. "Was there anything on there that was helpful?"

"I didn't find any forensics."

"We're trying to track the sender through the courier company, but so far, all they've told us is that the person paid cash and gave the name John Smith." While they would look into any John Smiths in the area, and anyone related to any of Paige and Ryan's cases with the name John or Smith, Jack already knew the name was a fake.

"I hope you find something. Anything. If this is the same killer and he plans on sticking with the ninety-nine hours thing, then he's already had the girls for around forty-eight hours," Stephanie said, her hazel eyes full of concern.

Which meant they might have as little as fifty hours left to find them alive.

And after he killed Hayley and Sophie, who was next?

Elias? Sofia? Arianna? Ned?

Ryan and Paige?

That had to be the endgame, but there was no way to know who else this man would go after before he came for Ryan and Paige.

If they couldn't find out who he was and stop him, he could lose half his family.

* * * * *

5:50 P.M.

Ryan woke with a start.

In his dreams, he'd been chasing the man who had his daughter.

He'd found him standing over Sophie's naked dead body, holding a rope in his hands which had been wrapped around his daughter's neck, choking the life out of her. He had told the man to give himself up, but instead, the man had turned, a horrible smug, mocking smile on his face, then started running.

Ryan had run after him, but no matter how fast he went, the man just seemed to get farther and farther away from him. It was like he was running in slow motion. The faster he tried to go, the slower he actually went until his feet didn't seem to move at all. As though they had been cemented in place.

The man had just laughed.

Laughed and then told him that he was going to lose every single person he loved.

First his daughter, then his son, then his wife, then the rest of his family until he was left all alone in the world.

For someone who'd grown up in a family where they loved and valued each other, where his parents had provided him a happy and stable home that had inspired him to one day make a home like that for his own family, to lose them and be left alone was a terrifying thought.

He couldn't let that happen.

He wouldn't.

In the dream, he'd seen the face of the man who had stolen his child.

It was Dominick Tremaine.

His subconscious merely acting out his fears or a premonition?

Usually, he didn't believe in premonitions or that dreams were some sort of prophecy, but right about now, he was ready to clutch at any and all straws that presented themselves.

"Ryan?" Sofia's anxious face came into view.

His wife had gotten a little sleep earlier, she'd crashed in his arms and clearly been plagued with bad dreams of her own that had her whimpering and moaning. He'd wanted to wake her, pull her out of the nightmares she was trapped in, but what would be the point? Awake she would only have to deal with real life nightmares. At least the ones that haunted her sleep would end, but this one might never be over. Despite the rest Sofia had gotten, dark circles were marring the skin under her eyes, and she was too pale. She seemed to have aged over the last day, making her look so much older than her forty-three years.

"Are you all right?" Sofia asked, and he realized he hadn't answered her yet.

"I'm fine," he answered distractedly, his eyes scanning the room. After learning that the man who had Sophie had cut off her finger and had it delivered to the police station, he realized just how serious this killer was. The man wanted to destroy him, and someone that dangerous was a risk to the rest of his family as well as Sophie. "Where's Ned?" he asked, bolting upright when he couldn't see his son anywhere.

"Relax." Sofia's small hands rested on his shoulders. "He's in the bathroom. Your dad is with him," she added as though she knew his next concern was that his son would be anywhere alone when there was a madman on the loose. Even though they were in a police station, it reassured him more to know that his retired cop father was with his son. His dad wouldn't let anyone get Ned.

"You should get some more sleep," he told his wife. He was worried about her. Sofia was going to let guilt about arguing with Sophie the last time she saw her, and not being able to stop her getting into that car, consume her if they didn't get their daughter back.

Sofia had been through so much thanks to her family from hell and her relentless stalker. She didn't deserve to be suffering again. She didn't deserve to be faced with losing her daughter.

While he'd grown up with the picture-perfect family, Sofia had grown up in a wealthy family raised by nannies. Her father was a judge who ruled his family with an iron fist, a stepmother—who turned out to be her biological mother—who didn't want her but the son she'd lost. Her three brothers were much older and her sister much younger, and although she had friends Ryan knew, she'd been lonely. Her one wish was for a family that would love her.

And she had it.

Only now, it was being torn to shreds, and he was powerless to stop it from happening.

"I don't want to sleep." Sofia shuddered as she said the words. "But you should try to get a couple more hours, you were barely asleep for an hour."

He felt about sleep the exact way as his wife did right now. "I'm fine. A power nap was all I needed." Ryan was about to say more when he saw the conference room door open, and Paige step through.

She was looking even worse than she had last time he'd seen her, and he knew immediately that something was wrong.

Like the rest of them, he had heard Paige's weeping two hours ago and had dropped the stack of files he'd been organizing, ready for them to get to work on after a nap, to rush out and see what had happened. While Xavier had passed Paige to Elias, Jack had come and collected him and Sofia, leading them into an empty interview room, where his brother had sat them down and explained as gently as he could that Sophie and Hayley's fingers had been found in a box addressed to him and Paige that had been delivered to the precinct

The words had fractured him into two halves.

The father half wanted to rage and scream and weep about someone harming his precious child. The cop half wanted to see the evidence and then use it to nail this psycho to the wall.

But Jack had nixed the cop part when he refused to let him see the finger, so the father part had won out. He'd held his wife; they'd wept together, clinging to one another and holding each other up when the world was trying to throw them down then stomp them into nothingness.

Now, something else had happened, but since he didn't want to worry Sofia until he knew what, he said, "Paige and I are going to go sort through some more files." He dropped a quick kiss to her lips before all but running over to his partner to find out what was going on. "What?" he asked Paige when he got to her.

"Not in here," she said, her brown eyes were red rimmed, her curly hair a frizzy halo around her paper pale face. She was a mess, and he assumed he looked no better.

He followed her out to their desks, then asked again, "What?"

"I got this." She shoved a piece of paper at him.

Detective Hood

You have a choice. I can continue to deliver your daughter to you piece by piece or you can trade yourself. Your life for hers. You have until midnight tonight to make your decision. If you do not surrender yourself to me, I will send you another piece of your daughter.

If you want to make the trade, then call this number for directions on where to meet. 032 473 4738

For a moment, he just stared at the piece of paper in his hands, speechless.

This got more surreal by the second.

"I assume you got one too," Paige said quietly.

Ryan didn't need to look through the pile of mail sitting on his desk to know his partner was right.

"What do we do?" Paige asked.

"Make the trade," he said immediately. It wasn't something he even needed to consider. His life for his daughter's was a trade he would gladly make.

"No, I mean about the letters," Paige said. "Of course we're going to give ourselves to him so the girls can go home; but do we leave these letters here so Jack and Xavier and the others know where we are in the hopes they can get some forensics from them? Or should we throw them out in case they find them before we make the trade and do something to make him kill the girls?"

"Let's leave them," he replied. "We don't know what he's going to do with the girls when we make the trade. If they know what's going on, they'll be able to find the girls, make sure they're safe."

"Okay, let's go before anyone notices," Paige said, already heading for the elevator.

Ryan followed, saying a silent goodbye to his wife and son. This might be the last time he ever saw them alive, and he knew that part of Sofia would be furious with him for handing himself over to a killer with a grudge. But at least Sophie would be alive, and that was really all that mattered.

* * * * *

6:12 P.M.

Her hand hurt so badly it was hard to concentrate on anything else.

Hayley still couldn't believe it had really happened.

That any of this had really happened.

It had to be some horrible nightmare, and any minute now, she would wake up in her bed, in her room, in her house, with her little sister and parents asleep down the hall.

Only with every painful thump in her hand, she was reminded that this was real.

All too real.

Every time she looked at the bloody stump where the pinkie finger on her right hand used to be, she flashed back to it happening.

To the second man coming down the stairs and holding a gun on Sophie, threatening to shoot her friend if she tried to fight back. Of the man who had tried to sexually assault her using his entire bodyweight to press her against the wall so she couldn't do anything to fight back even if she was willing to risk her best friend getting shot, which she wasn't. Of his hand curling around her wrist that was bound to the pipes and holding her hand still. Of the cold metal circling her small finger. Of the snapping sound it made as the pruning shears easily crunched through the bones. Of her finger falling in what seemed to be slow motion down to the ground where it landed with a small plop. Of nausea swelling up through her stomach as she threw up. Of the sounds of her screams. Of the blood that poured out and the pain that tidal waved through her entire body.

Then of having to watch the same thing happen to her best

friend.

The men hadn't given them any first aid. They'd merely tossed some towels at them, collected the fingers and left.

Hayley wondered if the finger had made it to its destination already. Had her mom seen it? It made her feel sick all over again thinking of what her family would go through when they saw her severed finger. Maybe at first they could live in denial and pretend it wasn't really her finger, but they would run DNA tests, and it would show that the fingers were hers and Sophie's. And then that attempt at denial would be over.

"Are you okay?" she asked Sophie. Watching out for her friend was the only thing keeping her going. If she were alone here, she'd probably have given up already. Just curled into a ball and waited for death to come.

Slowly.

She was sure that these men were going to keep cutting pieces off her and sending them to her mother until she was dead.

Sophie lifted her head slowly. She had pulled her knees up to her chest and had been resting her head on them, her free arm curled tightly around her legs as though she were physically holding herself together. "I'm all right. You?"

"I'm all right, too," she said. Hayley knew Sophie was lying when she said that she was okay, and she knew Sophie knew she was lying when she said the same thing. But by unspoken mutual agreement, they both pretended to believe each other's lies.

What else could they do?

They had been abducted, nearly raped, and had their fingers amputated. There was no way they could be okay. But they had each other, and that was enough to keep their strength up so they hadn't given up yet.

Any time Hayley felt like letting go, that it was getting increasingly difficult to keep enough inner light shining to keep her hopes up, she thought of Sophie. What would happen to her friend if she gave up and left Sophie to deal with those men on her own?

She couldn't do that.

Not to the friend who'd done so much for her. When she had first come to live with Paige and Elias, she hadn't known anything about how to be a normal little girl. How could she? She had grown up in a house where they were never allowed to leave, barely able to go outside, where they were threatened daily, and where even at five, she had understood what their captor was doing to her older sisters.

As much as Paige and Elias's love had helped her adjust, it had been Sophie who'd helped to ease her into living in the real world. Sophie had taught her how to play with dolls and climb trees; she'd taught her not to be afraid of other children and how to laugh and have fun. Hayley would be forever grateful, and while there was no way she could ever repay Sophie for all she'd done, she could spend the rest of her life being the best, best friend in the world.

"I'm scared, Hayley." Sophie's soft voice floated into her thoughts. "Really, *really* scared."

"Me too," she admitted, reaching out a hand to her friend.

Sophie grasped her hand tightly. "I don't want to give up, but I don't know that I can go through this again. What is he going to take next? Another finger? A toe? An ear? What if he decides to go for something bigger? Like an arm or a leg?"

Her friend's voice was getting increasingly hysterical, and Hayley shuffled over as close as she could get and wrapped an arm around Sophie's shoulders. "Shh, Soph. It'll be okay. I don't know how, but we just have to keep believing that. You know our parents, and probably the entire police department are looking for us. Every time he contacts them, it gives them more to work with. They'll figure out who the men are, and they'll come for us."

"How?" Sophie asked. "How will they figure out who they are when we've been in the same room as them, and we don't even know?"

"I don't know," she said honestly. But she also knew that just because you couldn't see a way out from a dark place you were trapped in didn't mean one didn't exist. She'd been rescued before, and she and her sisters had thought they were never getting out of that house. She knew that Eliza had tried over and over again to find a way to escape to the point that the man who had abducted them had to resort to brainwashing to keep her in line.

The unexpected had happened then, and it could happen now too.

The door to the basement was flung open, and light flooded the dingy space.

"How're my girls?" a cheerful voice called out.

The man who'd cut off their fingers clomped happily down the stairs; the other man trailed after him. While the second man was clearly in on the plan and was prepared to help when he had to, it didn't seem like he got any pleasure from this.

Surely, there had to be a way to use that to their benefit.

That was what you were supposed to do, right? Try to get the submissive partner to realize that he really didn't want to be doing this and get him to turn on the dominant one. It had to be easier than getting the dominant partner to let them go. He was enjoying this. He wanted to hurt them; it gave him a rush. She remembered the look on his face when he had hit Sophie and bitten her earlier, and when he had cut off their fingers.

It excited him, but not the other man. He'd barely been able to look at them. In fact, she didn't think he had. She thought he might have just trained the gun on them and then kept his head turned in the other direction, so he didn't have to witness them being hurt.

"Please," she said to him now. "Please don't let him hurt us again. You know it's wrong; I know you do. Please let us go. You have the gun. You don't have to shoot him; just tie him up or something and let us go. Please."

"Please," Sophie echoed.

"Nice try." The man who liked to hurt them laughed. "Gotta give you props for trying, but he's in on this just as much as I am. We both want this. While it's regrettable you had to be hurt to teach your parents a lesson, it's the way the world works. The innocent often pay for the crimes of the guilty. And now that you've served your purpose, it's time to move on to those who are the guilty party."

They'd been wrong.

These men weren't going to keep them here cutting them into pieces and sending them one by one to their parents.

They were going to kill them.

Now.

She was going to die at fifteen, after only ten years of really living life.

When the man came toward her with a syringe in his hand, she lost it. Hayley kicked and screamed and scratched and snapped her teeth at him.

But none of it did any good.

The syringe pricked her skin, and within seconds the blackness claimed her as its own.

* * * * *

6:37 P.M.

"Davis Hilliard is here," a young officer announced as she pushed open the door to the conference room where he and Jack were going through every teacher and student from the high school looking for anyone who might be the killer.

"Davis Hilliard is here?" Xavier repeated. They had been going to meet with the teacher who had found Brianna Lester's body earlier today, but it had been postponed because they'd been focusing on other things. They were supposed to meet with him at his house tomorrow morning, so why had he shown up here?

"Sitting in an interview room waiting to talk to you," the officer confirmed.

"Did he say why he's here?" Jack asked.

"He said he wanted to turn himself in," the cop replied.

Turn himself in?

Did that mean he was admitting to being the Number Nine Killer and the man who had abducted Sophie and Hayley?

Was that a good thing or a bad thing?

It could mean that the girls were already dead and that he had achieved his goal, so there was no longer a reason to hide. He could be ready for them all to know who he was so he could relish in the pain he'd caused.

Or it could mean that he had realized that hurting Hayley and Sophie was never going to get him what he wanted and make him feel better, so he had decided to just end the whole thing and turn himself in, letting the girls go alive.

Xavier hoped it was the latter.

He didn't want to have to tell Paige and Elias and Ryan and Sofia that their daughters were dead.

From the look on his partner's face, Jack was thinking the same thing.

"Let's go," Jack said, eagerly heading for the door.

He followed just as eagerly. He was ready for this to be over. He wasn't sure how much more of the Xander and Hood families' suffering he could take. This had to end one way or the other.

"Oh," Davis Hilliard looked up, disappointed when they joined him in the interview room.

"Expecting someone else?" Xavier asked.

"Well, yes, actually. Last time I spoke with Detective Hood and Detective Xander. You look like Detective Xander," Davis said to Jack, "but you're not."

"I'm his brother."

"Okay. Are they coming?" The man looked toward the door

behind them.

"No. We're working this case now." Xavier watched Davis Hilliard for his reaction; the teacher looked disappointed. Like part of the reason for his coming here tonight was to see Ryan and Paige.

"Why?"

The man sure seemed upset that he wasn't going to get to talk to the cops he'd come here to see. "As you know, that's Detective Xander, and I'm Detective Montague," Xavier introduced himself.

"Okay. Why aren't the other detectives here? Why aren't they working this case? Why is it your case now?"

Davis Hilliard asked a lot of questions. "Why do you care?" Xavier asked instead of offering any answers.

Shrugging nonchalantly, Davis folded his hands and rested them on the table. "No reason. I was just surprised, that's all."

Xavier didn't believe that.

The teacher had come here with the express purpose of seeing Ryan and Paige. If it was because he wanted to see how what he was doing was affecting them was still to be seen.

"We were told you came to surrender yourself," Jack said.

"Not surrender myself," Davis contradicted. "I came to prove that I'm not the killer you're looking for."

He might have believed that if it wasn't for the disappointment written all over the man's face, now that he knew that he wasn't going to see Paige and Ryan. "Why should we believe that? You come down here, you're disappointed you're not going to see the cops you wanted to see, and you have a motive."

"What motive? That my family was killed in a boating accident? Why would that make me want to kill girls from the school I work at?"

"You tell us," Jack said.

"Because of Liza?"

"She attempted suicide, didn't she? Because she was so severely bullied by the girls in her class."

"So?" Davis said defensively. "That's not a reason to kill innocent kids."

"I agree," Xavier said. "But you were pretty angry when you went back to work. Maybe you just got angrier the longer you spent around those kids. I mean, they tormented your daughter to the point where she wanted to end her life. Then she fights back, gets help, returns to school and graduates only to be killed in a boating accident. Then after suffering such a devastating loss, you return to work only to be forced to get help yourself because of those same kids. Maybe you thought it was time you taught them a lesson, and what better way than to have them all living in fear as you start killing them off one by one."

"I didn't kill anyone," Davis bit out. "I was angry. Yes. I don't deny that. Those kids tortured my daughter for no reason. Liza was a sweet, smart, funny young woman. She didn't deserve what those girls put her through. They were relentless. It was every day, laughing at her, excluding her, making fun of her clothes and her hair. I was the one who found her ..." He trailed off, his eyes going distant.

Xavier could sympathize.

There had been a time, not long after he and Annabelle had started dating when he'd come home to find her holding a bottle of sleeping pills in her hand. He had known how much she'd been struggling and had believed for one horrifying moment that she had already swallowed the pills. Thankfully she hadn't, but just knowing that she was contemplating suicide had been enough to terrify him. She had come a long way since then. She was no longer in that place, but that was a memory he would never forget.

He couldn't imagine coming home to find that she had succeeded.

"She ran herself a hot bath, then climbed in and slit her wrists. I don't even know what made me go in there. She was sixteen; it wasn't like I usually went into the bathroom when she was in

204

there. It was just fate, I supposed. Leading me to her when she needed me. We rushed her to the hospital. She was very lucky we got to her in time. I blamed them. I can't say I didn't. But I did not kill anyone. If I were going to do it, it would have been the girls who ruined my daughter's life, not some random kids who just happened to go to the school I worked at."

Davis Hilliard sounded sincere, and Xavier had to admit that he believed him. His admission that if he were to get revenge, it would have been on the girls who had bullied Liza had been the thing to convince him. Because it was honest. If he were Davis Hilliard, the idea would have gone through his mind too. He would never have acted on it, but he would have thought it.

"How do I convince you I didn't do this?" Davis asked. "That's what I came here to do. I want to convince you that I'm not a killer."

"You can give us a DNA sample and a sample of your fingerprints and your handwriting," Xavier said. Medical examiner Jenny Buckley had been able to get a sample of DNA from Brianna Lester's tooth which had been found in her stomach. Whoever hit her had left a little piece of himself behind, and while the sample was being run through CODIS, they could get Jenny to compare it to Davis Hilliard's DNA and see if they got a match.

"Anything. Anything at all," Davis readily agreed.

Which pretty much cemented in his mind that the teacher was innocent.

"Someone from the crime scene unit will be here shortly to—" he broke off when someone hammered frantically on the door.

His stomach dropped.

Was this the news they had all been dreading?

Were they about to learn the girls' bodies had been found?

"Excuse us," Jack said, as the two of them headed out into the hall where Jack's wife Laura met them.

Xavier had never seen her like this before.

Her violet eyes were wild, and she all but threw herself at her husband. "Oh, Jack," she sobbed.

"What is it?" Jack sounded panicked now, too, as though he were feeding off his wife's anxiety.

"Laura, what is it?" Xavier asked. If there was bad news, he would rather just hear it and be done with it.

"It's Paige and Ryan," Laura said.

"Paige and Ryan? What happened? Did they get another package?" In his mind, Xavier was running through what body part the kidnapper had cut off this time.

"No. Well, yes. I found letters on their desks, but they're gone."

"Gone?" Jack echoed.

"I couldn't find them. I looked everywhere. Then I found letters on their desks. The killer told them that they could trade themselves for Hayley and Sophie. They're gone. Ryan and Paige are gone. They must have gone to make the trade," Laura cried.

The killer would never let Sophie and Hayley go alive.

Ryan and Paige had to know that.

They had just willingly walked into a trap.

* * * * *

8:04 P.M.

"Are we sure we're making the right decision?"

Paige looked over at her partner. Even his profile, which was all she could see in the half light from the passing streetlights, was grim.

"Yes," she said immediately.

She didn't even have to think about that.

She would do anything—literally—to get her daughter back alive, even if it meant walking straight into a trap that would cost her her life.

But if Ryan was having doubts, he didn't have to do this. She would trade her life for both girls.

"Are you having doubts?" she asked.

"No. Not about trading ourselves for our girls," he said quickly. "I was just wondering if we should have told the others. Tried to set a trap of our own. Caught this guy."

"We talked about that," she reminded him. "He knows we're cops. He could be expecting us to have set a trap for him. We can't do anything to risk Hayley and Sophie. If he suspects that we're trying to trap him, then he could just kill the girls and run, go after someone else that we love."

Paige wouldn't risk her daughter's life, either daughter, or her husband, or anyone else she loved. She didn't see any other way to do this to ensure that Hayley made it out of this alive than to give the kidnapper what he wanted.

"What if they kill the girls anyway?" Ryan asked

That had been worrying her too.

She could trade herself for her daughter only to have the kidnapper kill both of them. Then she'd be leaving her husband as a widower and Arianna to grow up without a mother.

But it was a risk she was willing to take.

It was a risk she *had* to take.

"We still have our guns; we don't make the trade until we know that Hayley and Sophie are alive and safe," she said.

"They'll probably be armed as well because they know that we're not just going to hand ourselves over to them before that."

"One of us can keep a gun on them while the other checks the girls, then once we know for sure they're alive, then we can put down the gun and go with them."

"Seems like a plan." Ryan nodded once. Then he turned the car into the next street. "This is where they said to meet them."

She looked around.

The kidnapper had wanted to meet them in a residential area. It hadn't been what she and Ryan had been expecting, but she supposed he thought it would make them more likely to be compliant because they wouldn't want to risk any innocent people getting caught up in the crossfire.

It was probably a good idea.

While getting her daughter and Sophie to safety was her number one priority, she wouldn't do anything to needlessly endanger someone else's daughter, son, mother, father, husband, or wife. She wanted everyone to walk out of this alive.

Including Ryan and herself, if they could make it happen.

They didn't really have a plan after they handed themselves over.

Neither of them really wanted to talk about it. They were too focused on making sure they didn't screw up the handover so their girls didn't die.

"There's the van," she said, spotting it just up ahead.

Ryan pulled in behind it, and they both climbed out of the car. Her stomach was churning, and she was so nervous she was shaking. There was so much at stake. One wrong move and Hayley could be killed.

As soon as they were out of the car, the back of the van slid open, and a man in a black ski mask pointed a gun at them. A second man climbed out of the driver's seat.

There were two of them.

The kidnapper had a partner.

That information probably would have helped them figure out who they were looking for when they'd been going through their case files, but right now she didn't care.

All she cared about was Hayley.

She tried to look into the back of the van. Two lumps were lying under gray blankets.

Hayley.

Automatically, she took a step forward, Ryan snapped a hand around her wrist and held her in place before she could go any closer.

The man who'd gotten out of the front of the vehicle also had a gun, and he waved it at them. "Anyone tries anything stupid, he shoots your kids," he announced, indicating his partner.

"Neither of us wants to do anything stupid, but we're not just handing ourselves over to you until we know that they're alive," Ryan said.

"One of you can check, then we'll dump the girls and get out of here before anyone sees us," the driver of the van said. He was clearly the dominant one in the partnership.

"You go," Ryan told her.

She shot him a grateful smile. She knew how hard it would be for him to be this close to his daughter and not get to touch her, knowing that he might never get another chance. Especially given how rocky his relationship had been with Sophie these last few months.

Crossing the short distance to the back of the van, Paige barely cast a glance at the man with the gun. She just jumped up and in and hurried to the lumps under the blanket, throwing it aside.

Tears filled her eyes, trickling down her cheeks as she stared at her daughter.

Hayley was dressed only in her underwear. She was lying on her back, a bite wound visible on her shoulder, her right hand, with its bloody stump where her pinkie finger used to be, rested on her stomach. Her chest rose and fell with each breath.

She was alive.

Sophie too.

She dropped to her knees and pressed a kiss to her daughter's forehead. This could be the last time she ever saw her, ever got to touch her or hold her. It wasn't enough. She wanted to pull Hayley into her arms and hold her, rock her, and apologize to her for everything that had happened.

"Are they alive?" Ryan called out.

"Yes," she called back. "Ryan should get a chance to say goodbye," she said to the man behind her.

"Okay," he replied.

Surprised, she turned to look at him. Since he was the submissive in the partnership, she hadn't expected him to reply, and if he did, she hadn't expected it to be in the positive.

"He can get them out of the van," he said to his partner.

"Whatever," the other man said. "But you have sixty seconds, then we're out of here. And you leave your gun on the ground over there."

Ryan didn't hesitate. She heard the clunk as the gun hit the pavement, then he was jumping up beside her, dragging his daughter into his arms. Paige held Hayley while Ryan picked up Sophie and carried her out of the van, setting her gently down on the sidewalk before returning to get Hayley.

She didn't want to let her baby go, but at least if she died, it would be knowing that she'd saved her daughter in the process.

The second Hayley was out of her arms, the man behind her wrapped his arm around her neck and shoved the gun against her temple.

"Try anything stupid, we kill your partner, then the girls," the dominant man warned.

Paige watched Ryan leave Hayley beside Sophie then rejoin her in the back of the van. As soon as Hayley was safely out of harm's way, she relaxed a bit.

"Put these on your partner." The dominant man shoved plastic zip ties into Ryan's hands.

"Sorry," he murmured as he took her hands and bound them together.

"Not your fault," she reminded him.

"Now do her ankles."

The submissive shoved her down, and without the use of her hands, she landed awkwardly, pain shooting up through her hips and back. Ryan put the zip ties around her ankles then the gun was shoved back against her temple.

"Do anything stupid and we shoot your partner," the

dominant warned again, tentatively coming toward Ryan who sat beside her and let the man cuff him as well.

When they were both restrained, the two men jumped out of the van.

"Now this is fun," the dominant beamed. Then the door was slammed shut.

The claustrophobia hit her immediately.

Paige had suffered from it ever since her stalker had run her car off the road and into a river leaving her trapped inside as the car slowly filled with water.

Ryan knew her well enough to know that her sudden intense shaking and hyperventilating meant only one thing.

"It's okay, Paige." He tried to move closer as the van took off down the street, making them both nearly topple over. "Try to breathe through it."

Breathe through it.

It sounded so simple.

Like she actually had some control over the phobia.

"Come on, Paige." Ryan managed to maneuver himself close enough that their shoulders touched.

The physical contact was enough to jar her marginally away from completely losing it.

Hayley was safe now, but she was going to need her whole family to rally around her if she was going to make it through this. Including her mother.

She had to get it together.

She and Ryan needed to work together if there was any chance of them getting out of this alive.

Her ragged breathing calmed a little.

"You're doing great," Ryan encouraged. "Just breathe in slowly ... count to ten ... let it out. There you go, keep going. In and out, nice and slow."

It took several minutes, but she managed to regain control of her breathing.

"You okay?" Ryan asked.

"Yeah." She was still breathing too fast, and she was still shaking uncontrollably, but she was all right. "They're safe."

"They are," her partner agreed. She could hear the relief in his voice, both that their daughters were alive and that she was back in control.

"Now *we* just have to figure a way out of this."

* * * * *

9:21 P.M.

She could never get enough of watching her children sleep.

Annabelle could stare at them for hours.

When they were small babies, she would sneak into their room after Xavier had fallen asleep and scoop one of them up out of their cribs and sit in the rocking chair and just hold them. She hadn't cared about the lack of sleep back then. In fact, she'd kind of enjoyed it. She enjoyed most housekeeping tasks and would get them done in between changing diapers and breastfeeding. The rest of the time, she just held her babies and soaked in the fact that she was a mother.

She missed those days when they were that little.

They were growing up way too fast.

They'd even discussed them having their own room.

JP and Katie had always shared a room. When they were infants, it was just easier to do all the middle of the night breastfeeds in the one place. And then, when they'd gotten a little older, they had loved playing together, and both had been a bit nervous about sleeping alone.

But they were five now.

They'd be starting kindergarten in the fall, and she and Xavier had decided that it was time.

So, this summer, they would be doing some shuffling around

and redecorating.

Her babies were getting too big.

Annabelle wasn't sure if more children were in the cards for her and Xavier. She was thirty-eight now, and he was forty-seven. They were probably too old, but she didn't want to discount it. She would love to have a little baby around the house again. But even if they didn't, she would always be unbelievably grateful for JP and Katie.

She'd never had a family like this before.

As a kid, she'd been kidnapped, and when she was returned home, her parents had been different, colder toward her. At the time, she had believed it was because the physical scars she had received had made her unworthy of love. A few years ago, she'd learned the truth.

Her mother was really her aunt who had adopted her to keep her away from her biological father—her mother's brother.

He was an evil man, and she was forever grateful to the woman who would always be her mom for rescuing her. Although she knew the truth now, it didn't change the facts that her childhood had been lonely and miserable. She had wanted love and friends but been afraid to seek out either

Now she had it.

She loved Xavier with all her heart, and although their relationship had been rocky at times, now they were in a good place, and she was happy.

Happy.

For so long she hadn't believed she would ever get to that place.

Now she was there.

She really was.

And it was all thanks to these two amazing little people and their daddy.

Tiptoeing quietly across the room, she ran a hand over Katie's soft little head. Her braids were a tangled mess, and she knew it would be a struggle in the morning to get her little girl to sit still long enough to redo them. Katie never liked to be still. She loved to run and play and sing and dance; she was just like Annabelle wished she'd been when she was Katie's age.

JP had tossed his covers half onto the floor. He was such a restless sleeper and every bit as energetic as his twin sister. He loved to ride his bike and climb trees, and she was always terrified he was going to fall out and break his neck, but he never did. She gently straightened the covers and tucked him back in, then kissed his forehead.

She was so lucky.

Annabelle was just straightening, when she saw something out the window.

Two lumps were lying in her front yard illuminated by a streetlight.

No, not lumps.

People.

Two people were lying unmoving in her front yard.

She moved closer to the window, which didn't have any drapes because both her kids liked to sleep with the light of the moon streaming through, so she could get a better look. The light wasn't good, but the people looked like girls. She could see long, dark hair and long, red ...

Annabelle gasped.

Was it Sophie Xander and Hayley Hood?

Rushing from the room, she eased the bedroom door closed and then hurried downstairs. Her cell phone was on the kitchen table, and she snatched it up and rushed outside as she dialed Xavier's number.

"What's wrong?" her husband asked as soon as he answered. It was just like him to worry, but it wasn't entirely out of the ordinary for her to call him when he was working late.

"I think Hayley and Sophie are in our front yard," she blurted out as she grabbed the keys and locked the front door behind her.

If this was some sort of trap and the killer was lurking around out here someplace, she didn't want him getting inside to her children.

"Stay inside, make sure all the doors are locked, and I'll be there as soon as I can."

"I'm already outside," she informed him. Her children were tucked up safely in their beds. She wasn't standing by while the children of four people she loved were lying hurt outside.

"Annabelle," Xavier hissed, clearly exasperated.

She scanned the yard as she ran to the girls; when she reached them, she dropped to her knees and pulled back the gray blanket so she could see them better. "It *is* them," she told Xavier.

"Get back inside," he said tightly.

"I can't, they're not moving." She pressed her fingertips to Hayley's neck, a pulse thumped weakly. She checked Sophie, who also had a pulse, but both girls were cold. Too cold.

"Are they alive?"

"Yes, but hypothermic. Send an ambulance as well."

"I will. Jack and I are on our way." She could hear thumping in the background, and then the ding of the lift opening.

The precinct was only about a ten-minute drive from their house so her husband and Jack would be here soon, but she had to get the girls inside. She wasn't very tall, and the girls were fifteen, already about the same height as she was. It wasn't going to be easy to get them inside, but she couldn't leave them out here.

"I'm going to hang up now," she told Xavier. "I'll get the girls inside and try to warm them up a little. See you soon."

"Be safe," he said before he disconnected the call.

Annabelle gave the yard another once-over. Nothing looked out of the ordinary, and nothing moved. But it was dark, and there were plenty of places for someone to hide if they wanted to.

She couldn't worry about that right now though.

The girls were her number one priority.

What were they doing here?

Why had the kidnapper let them go?

And why leave them here?

She spread the blanket over Sophie and hooked her hands under Hayley's armpits and began to drag her toward the house. Hayley wasn't wearing any shoes, and she was worried that she was hurting her, but whatever injuries that might cause wouldn't be life threatening. Hypothermia was.

Balancing Hayley, she just managed to unlock the door without dropping her, then dragged her inside and draped her on the sofa. Grabbing the blanket she and the kids loved to snuggle under when they watched a little TV after dinner, she tucked it around Hayley.

Just as she was stepping back outside to retrieve Sophie, she heard sirens, and seconds later, flashing lights filled the night, and Xavier's car pulled to a stop in the driveway.

"You okay?" Xavier ran to her and gave her a hard hug, while Jack scooped up his niece.

"Fine, Hayley is already inside," she said.

The four of them headed inside. Xavier locked the door behind them. "Just in case he's out there."

"I don't think he is. If he was, he had plenty of time to get me," Annabelle said, catching the shudder that rocketed through her husband.

"The kids okay?"

"Asleep. They're fine, Xavier. Why did the kidnapper leave Sophie and Hayley on our front lawn?"

"Because Ryan and Paige are idiots," Jack said, spreading more blankets over the still unconscious teenagers.

"What?" She looked to Xavier for more information.

"Ryan and Paige received a letter from the kidnapper telling them they could trade themselves for their daughters."

Her eyes grew wide. "The kidnapper has Paige and Ryan?"

"They snuck out of the station to make the swap. We didn't think that he would really let the girls go alive. We thought that he'd kill all four of them or keep all four of them until he finished playing with them," Xavier explained.

"But he *did* let the girls go," she said, stating the obvious.

"But why?" Xavier asked.

That was a question they would only find the answer to once they knew who the kidnapper was.

MARCH 9TH

12:22 A.M.

"We should have killed them," he told his partner. He was sure it was a mistake not to have, but it was too late now.

That hadn't been part of the plan.

Hayley Hood and Sophie Xander were alive and had probably been found by now. They'd left the girls in front of Detective Xavier Montague's house. He was supposedly one of the detectives working the case now, along with Detective Jack Xander, Ryan Xander's brother.

They were supposed to deliver the teenagers piece by piece to their cop parents, and when they grew bored of that, use the girls as bait to lure their parents into a trap. Then they were going to kill the kids, dump their bodies in front of the police station, using a stolen van so the cops wouldn't be able to track them.

Making the swap this soon seemed like a waste.

There was so much more suffering they could have inflicted on the detectives who'd ruined his life.

If they were going to mess with the plan, then he had at least managed to add a little fun to things. It was a risk to make the swap in such a residential area. Particularly, at the time they had. Eight in the evening was still pretty early. People were still up, cooking dinner or eating dessert or relaxing watching some TV at the end of a long day. Many were still only just arriving home or out walking the dog; anyone could have noticed them at any time.

But what was the fun in taking the easy road?

There wasn't any.

He liked to live life on the edge, take risks, and everything had

219

worked out okay.

They'd gotten what they wanted.

He just couldn't shake the feeling that leaving those girls alive was a mistake that was going to come back to bite them.

But he'd let his partner talk him into letting the girls live.

"We should have killed them," he said again.

"We didn't have to. They were innocent. They shouldn't have had to pay for someone else's mistakes."

"And what about the others? Talia Canuck, Ally Brown, Brianna Lester, you didn't seem to mind when they were paying for someone else's mistakes," he snarled.

His partner shuddered.

He had minded.

He had cared.

He had begged and bargained for those girls' lives.

He had pleaded so much it had actually become disgusting to watch.

That wasn't how a man behaved.

A man did what had to be done.

His partner didn't get that.

They might have shared a goal, but that was it. His partner wasn't enjoying any of this, and he probably would have backed out by now if it weren't for him. While he was enjoying this more and more with each passing hour.

He had enjoyed biting Hayley Hood as payback for her biting him first. The taste of blood and sweat, seasoned with fear. It was delicious. Intoxicating. He just wished that his stupid partner hadn't interrupted him before he'd had a chance to taste more than just her blood.

"No one else now, though, right?" his partner asked. "I mean, we have who we wanted. We don't need to go after anyone else."

Pathetic.

That attitude was absolutely pathetic.

His partner had actually thrown up when they'd been cutting

off the girls' fingers.

Thrown up.

There wasn't anything he found more disgusting than vomit.

There was just something about the smell, the look of it, those chunks in that liquid.

It was vile.

Disgusting.

He expected better from his partner.

If that idiot threw up again, he might just find himself on the other end of the pruning shears next time around.

"I decide who dies and when. You used up your one chance to get your way when you asked to let Sophie and Hayley live. You don't get another. Now go and check on our guests, make sure they're settled in." He gestured at the door to the basement.

His partner started toward it then stopped, standing there, hovering nervously from foot to foot.

He rolled his eyes.

Why did he get stuck having to work with such an idiot?

He guessed it was a case of beggars couldn't be choosers. It wasn't like you could just go up to some smart, sensible person and ask them if they wanted to help you get revenge by kidnapping, killing, and torturing people.

If you did, you'd either get committed as a lunatic or thrown into prison as a criminal.

Neither option was particularly appealing.

So he was stuck with this idiot for the foreseeable future.

But … maybe when this was all over, he'd have a little fun with his partner.

"What?" he snapped when the other man didn't make any move to do as he'd been instructed.

"Couldn't you go and check on them?" he asked anxiously.

"Why?" he asked irritably. It was midnight, and it had been a long day. Between organizing deliveries to the police station, then doing the trade, then driving back here, and getting his guests settled in their new accommodations, he was tired. He just wanted to make sure everything was as it should be then go and get some sleep.

"I don't like dealing with them," the man said, his eyes dropping to the floor.

"I know," he said dryly. He didn't even think that most of his guests had known there were two of them. He'd been the one to leave the notes in the bathroom; he'd been the one to take the phone calls and set up the meetings. He'd been the one to do the abductions and to bring the girls down here to the basement. He'd been the one who brought them their meals and who killed them when the time came. He wasn't even sure why he had bothered to work with a partner if he was the one who was going to end up doing all the work anyway.

Well, actually, he *was* sure why he was working with a partner.

Because he wanted a fall guy.

Someone who, when he got what he wanted, he could leave behind and let the cops think they had their man. Detective Hood and Detective Xander knew that there were two of them, but they wouldn't be leaving this house alive, so that wasn't really a problem. And although Hayley and Sophie knew, he was sure that their claims could just be written off as the overactive imaginings of two traumatized teenagers.

Besides, when the cops found this place and came to catch their killer, they would only find one man.

And it wouldn't be him.

"Please," his partner started.

If there was one thing he couldn't stand, it was a man whining.

"Fine. *I'll* go and check on them. Then *I'll* make sure that this place is locked up securely. Just like *I* do everything else." It was tedious and tiresome, but anything was better than listening to his partner whine.

"Thank you." The other man sighed in relief.

"You better toughen up because things are going to really get started later today. I've waited a long time to do this, and it's going to go perfectly. I won't have anyone ruining this. I won't have *you* ruining this." He let the threat hang in the air for a moment. "Understand?"

"I understand."

He really hoped his partner did. Because if he didn't, he was going to find himself sitting in the basement, bound to the pipes, right alongside those cops.

"Get out of here," he snapped. If he had to go and make sure everything was safe and secure for the night, then he wanted to get on with it.

Getting the cops here had been exhausting—exhilarating, but exhausting. Two adult police detectives were much more work than one teenage girl or even two teenage girls. He couldn't just pick the cops up and cart them around like they had with the girls. He'd had to resort to threats to make sure they hadn't cooked up some plan while they were in the back of the truck on the drive here and tried to enact it. He'd had to get Detective Xander to jump the distance from the van to the basement, as he'd been too scared to cut the zip ties binding his ankles. His partner carried Detective Hood, and he kept a gun trained on Detective Xander just in case he tried anything funny.

Stifling a yawn, he pulled out the keys and unlocked the basement door.

Immediately, he felt eyes on him.

The cops were smarter than the kids had been; he was going to have to watch himself, be very careful about every move he made.

But these cops better not think that they could beat him.

He was in charge here.

This was *his* show, and he was going to get what he wanted.

They were going to scream for him; they were going to suffer for him, and then they were going to die for him.

"Just popping in to say goodnight," he said as he walked down the stairs. "If I were you, I'd make sure I got some rest. I have some fun planned for us tomorrow. You got what you wanted. Your daughters are alive. But you two are soon going to wish that you were dead."

* * * * *

2:34 A.M.

"Why haven't they woken up yet?" Sofia asked for probably the thousandth time in the last few hours.

She didn't know whether to be deliriously happy, heart-stoppingly terrified, or so furious her blood pressure rose.

Maybe a mix of all three.

Sofia couldn't be happier and more relived that her daughter was back home, safe and sound. But Ryan had traded himself for Sophie. So, while she had her daughter back, she'd lost her husband.

How dare he make that kind of decision without consulting her.

When she couldn't find Ryan around dinnertime, she and Laura had started searching the police station. While she had gone to check outside to see if Ryan and Paige had needed some fresh air, Laura had found the note on Ryan's desk.

The note that had changed everything.

She was so angry with her husband.

Angry and hurt, and mostly terrified because now she had to worry all over again.

As much as she wanted to have her daughter back alive, she didn't want to trade one loved one for another. She wanted her daughter *and* her husband, not one or the other. Only she wasn't sure that she was ever going to get Ryan back.

He could be gone forever.

And she hadn't even gotten to say goodbye.

If Ryan was intent on trading himself for Sophie, the least he could have done was kiss her one last time, tell her he loved her, and then said goodbye.

Why wouldn't he have done that?

Because he'd known that she'd never let him do it.

How could she choose between the man she loved—the father of her children, her soul mate—and the daughter she would gladly give her life for.

Ryan felt the same way.

And he knew that she wouldn't have wanted to beg him to stay, while at the same time, beg him to get their daughter back.

So, he'd taken the decision out of her hands and made it for her.

His life for Sophie's.

Now she was sitting perched on the edge of her daughter's hospital bed, clutching Sophie's hand so tightly she was afraid she was going to crush the bones, and asking every minute or so why Sophie didn't wake up.

"The drugs are still working their way out of her system," Mark replied patiently.

When they'd gotten the call from Xavier saying that the girls had been found alive in his and Annabelle's front yard, they had all piled into cars and driven straight to the hospital to meet the ambulance. Although the girls had already been checked out by the paramedics who had said that they were stable and had just been sedated, both she and Elias had insisted that Mark check them out as well. They wanted to be reassured by someone they knew and trusted who'd examined their children.

"How much longer will it be?" Elias asked. He, too, was sitting on the edge of his daughter's bed with the same mix of relief, joy, fear, and anger on his face that she knew she had on hers. Arianna had also refused to wait in the waiting room with the rest of the family. She was sitting on her father's lap, her eyes glued to her sister's face.

"I don't know. Since we don't know exactly what they were

given, what dosage, or how long ago it was administered, it's hard to say. But given that we know Paige and Ryan left around six, and Annabelle found them around nine-thirty, by their body temperature, they'd been out there for possibly around an hour. I'd say that they should be waking up soon," Mark explained.

As if in response to Mark's words, Sophie moved slightly on the bed, then moaned a little and squirmed a little more. "Hayley?" Sophie's croaky voice asked, then she winced as if talking hurt her throat.

"Baby?" Sofia leaned in closer, keeping hold of Sophie's hand and running her other hand through her daughter's long red hair.

Sophie froze. "M-mom?"

Tears welled up in her eyes. Nothing had ever sounded so beautiful to her ears. She hadn't thought that she would ever hear her daughter call her that again.

"I'm here, baby, I'm right here," she assured her daughter.

Sophie gave one nod but didn't open her eyes. "Hayley?"

"Is here too," she told her daughter. The two girls had always been close, but Sofia thought the two would likely be inseparable after what they'd been through together.

"Where is here?" Sophie asked. There was fear in her voice like she still wasn't sure she could believe what was going on. Sofia hated that fear would always be a part of her daughter's life. It would fade in time, but it would never completely go away.

"You're in the hospital. You and Hayley were found in Xavier and Annabelle's front yard. You were drugged and a little hypothermic. You were brought to the hospital in an ambulance, but you're going to be okay. You both are."

Sophie gave another nod but still wouldn't open her eyes.

"You're really safe now, sweetheart." She pressed a kiss to her daughter's forehead.

Very slowly, Sophie opened her eyes.

She scanned the room, taking in the hospital beds, a still sleeping Hayley, Elias and Arianna, Mark, and then finally

Sophie's gaze settled on her.

They stared at each other in silence for what felt like an eternity.

Then Sophie burst into tears and threw her arms around her neck.

The whole world blurred around her until all it consisted of was her and her daughter. They clung to each other and wept, both trying to believe that this was real. That Sophie was back, and although she would forever bear the physical and psychological scars of her abduction, she was going to be okay. With time and family support, she would find a way to get through this.

"Sophie?"

They both turned at the sound of Hayley's voice.

"It's okay, Hayley. We're not dead, we're in the hospital," Sophie assured her friend.

Hayley reacted quicker than Sophie had. She immediately bolted upright, and upon seeing her father and little sister, she did the same thing Sophie had done. Burst into tears and hugged them.

"Mommy, I'm sorry." Sophie's large gray eyes were brimming with more tears. They caught the light and shimmered, making her eyes look all silvery.

A week ago, hearing those words fall from her daughter's lips would have made her suspicious, wondering what Sophie was up to and what angle she was trying to play.

Today, she heard the anguish in her daughter's voice.

The pain.

The fear that the way she had behaved could never be forgiven.

The need to be held in her mother's arms like she was still a small girl, and that a mother's arms still solved all the problems in the world was evident in her tone and her expression.

"It's okay, baby," Sofia said, drawing Sophie into her arms.

"No, it's not. I was so mean to you and Daddy. I was so angry at you for lying to me, and I didn't want to see things from your point of view, but I get it now. I get why you didn't tell me. I wish you had, but I understand why it was hard for you. I didn't think I'd ever get a chance to tell you and Daddy how sorry I was, and …" Sophie trailed off, looking around the room. "Where is Daddy?"

"And Mom," Hayley added. "Daddy, where's Mom? Why isn't she here? Is she out in the hall?"

Both girls were looking at them expectantly.

Sofia didn't want to tell the girls—who had already been through so much—that while they were safe now, it was only because Ryan and Paige had traded themselves.

How was that going to make the girls feel?

If she had to guess, in a word, guilty.

Not that they had anything to feel guilty about.

That's what parents did for their children. They would do anything to make sure that they were safe. Although she was so angry with Ryan for doing what he did, she understood, and if their positions had been reversed, she would have made the same choice.

"Wait, you said we were found in Xavier and Annabelle's yard," Sophie said. "Does that mean that the kidnapper hasn't been caught yet? Is he still out there?"

"The man who took you is still out there," Elias acknowledged.

Hayley inched closer to her father, and Sophie's hand curled around hers.

"He won't get to you again," she quickly assured the girls. "You're safe here, and there's an officer right outside your door."

"Are Mom and Ryan out looking for him?" Hayley asked.

"Not exactly."

"Mom, what's going on?" Sophie asked.

"Dad?" Hayley looked at her father.

The girls were getting more anxious by the second. She could actually feel their fear filling the room. As much as she didn't want to tell them what was going on, Sofia was pretty sure that not telling them was going to be worse than just getting it over with.

She exchanged glances with Elias. When he nodded, she drew in a deep breath and began, "There's something we need to tell you."

* * * * *

6:48 A.M.

"Can you get free?" Paige asked her partner. They had been working at getting free ever since they'd been brought down to this dark, dank basement.

She didn't have to ask to know this was the same place her daughter had been held.

There was blood on the floor.

Hayley's blood.

And Sophie's.

The room had the smell of pain and fear and death. This was also where Talia, Ally, and Brianna had lost their lives.

This was where she and Ryan were going to die unless they could figure out a way to get out of here.

Right now, that wasn't looking likely.

"No," Ryan replied. "Can you?"

"No." She shook her hand in frustration. The metal clink of the handcuffs on the pipe only served to further annoy her. Hayley needed her right now, and although she knew with one hundred percent certainty that she'd made the right choice—there wasn't anything she wouldn't do for one of her children—she wanted to be there for her daughter.

"He knew that we were going to try to bring something to cut through the zip ties," Ryan said, sounding equally as irritated as she felt.

When they had decided to give the kidnappers what they wanted and make the trade, they'd hidden small blades in the bands of their watches to use to cut through the plastic zip ties they'd thought would be used to restrain them. They knew from the wounds on Talia, Ally, and Brianna that that was what he'd used, and it was what he'd used when he restrained them in the van, but as soon as he had brought them down here to the basement, he had cut off the plastic ties and replaced them with metal handcuffs.

It seemed he'd thought of everything.

"We should have brought handcuff keys." Ryan shook his hand just as she had, as though that would make the metal fall apart.

"Hindsight," she said. They should have tried to cut through the plastic ties in the van, but there hadn't been time. And they couldn't have afforded to bring much with them. They hadn't wanted to do anything that would have endangered their girls' lives. Now that the girls were safe—at least they assumed that someone would have found them by now. It had only been around eight when they'd made the switch, and early enough for someone to find them. It was time to focus on getting out of here. "Do you have any idea who they are?" she asked.

"I'm not sure. There's something familiar about them. One of them anyway. The submissive."

It was clear that one of the kidnappers was much more into this plan of theirs than the other one was.

Paige was sure that was something they could use to their advantage at some point—once they had some time to find out more about the pair. "He said he had something planned for us this morning. Maybe we can get them talking, find out what they want from us, then we can figure out who they are and use that to figure out a way out of here."

"We know what they want from us. They want us to suffer.

Hurting our girls wasn't enough."

"Think they're going to torture us?" she asked with a shudder.

"Yes," Ryan said bluntly. "Then, when they get bored, they'll kill us."

"We have to try to form a bond with the submissive, use that. I think he's the reason the girls are still alive."

"I agree," Ryan said. "It doesn't make any sense though. Why would they let them go alive?"

"Because their role was only ever to lure us here?"

"But why do it that way?" Ryan looked perplexed. "I mean, I'm unbelievably thankful they're alive, but the girls had to have seen and heard things, possibly enough to ID them. It was incredibly risky to let them go alive."

"He seems to like to take risks," she said, thinking of the way the killer had laid out the bodies on the front porches of their homes.

"You think the submissive had some sort of relationship with Sophie or Hayley before this?"

"You still think he could be Dominick Tremaine?" Paige asked.

"Maybe. It would make sense that he would want to keep Sophie alive. Or maybe that was the whole reason he was dating her in the first place. He cooked up this scheme to get back at us and thought that helping to drive a wedge between my daughter and I would be another layer of revenge. And it probably helped him to get information on me."

"If it is Dominick as the submissive, then who's the dominant?" she asked.

"Davis Hilliard?"

"It could be, but it didn't sound like him. I know he's trying to disguise his voice so we don't figure out who he is until he's ready to tell us, but I just don't know that it was the teacher's."

"Do you hear that?"

"They're coming." Paige felt herself stiffen. She could get

through anything that they threw at her knowing that Hayley was safe and alive and could live out the rest of her life and do whatever she wanted.

"You try to bond with the submissive; I'll focus on the dominant," Ryan said quickly before the basement door was thrown open.

"Good morning," the dominant singsonged as he bounced cheerfully down the stairs.

The submissive descended the stairs much slower, as though coming down to the basement to torture them was the last thing he wanted to be doing.

He could join the club.

It wasn't like she and Ryan were thrilled about this either.

"Why are you bothering with the balaclava?" Ryan asked. "Don't you want us to know who you are? Isn't that why you're doing all of this? The Number Nine murders, kidnapping our daughters, torturing them, bringing us here, it's all to punish us. But how are you punishing us if we don't even know who you are?"

"Oh, you will." The dominant stood before them.

The urge to swing out at him was strong, but she resisted, mostly because she knew it wasn't going to do any good, and a little bit because the submissive had a gun in his hand.

"I think it's self-explanatory," the dominant continued, "but my friend here has a gun, and he's not afraid to use it."

The submissive straightened at that. It was barely noticeable, but she was looking for it. The man *was* afraid to use it. He didn't want to shoot them; he didn't want to hurt them; he didn't want to be here. Maybe there was a way to talk him into letting them go.

"I brought you a little something." The dominant held up a glass tank full of water with a small, black spiky thing floating inside it.

A sea urchin.

And just like that, Paige knew who the men were.

She had no idea why they hated her and Ryan so much or what they hoped to achieve by doing this, but she knew who they were.

From the look on Ryan's face, he'd come to the same conclusion that she had.

She just wished that knowing their identities helped.

"Did you know that there are around nine hundred and fifty species of sea urchins?" The dominant was staring at the small animal as though he were enraptured by the creature.

Paige stared at it too.

Only, instead of being enraptured, she was wondering how the spiky little thing factored into what was coming next.

"They can live anywhere from tropical oceans to polar oceans. They can live as deep as sixteen thousand feet. The deepest a person has ever gone is only around a thousand feet. They're really amazing animals, and you know what I love most about them?" The dominant paused to look them straight in the eye. "Those little spikes of theirs hurt like hell when they penetrate human skin."

So that was what he had planned.

Well, that didn't seem so bad.

How much could those little spikes hurt?

They didn't look very long so they couldn't penetrate very deep.

"This little guy," the dominant said as he stepped closer, "has venomous spines. I thought that would be a little more fun."

She disagreed.

This didn't sound fun, but it did sound manageable.

"Keep the gun on Detective Xander. I don't want him trying anything stupid while his partner and I have some fun."

So, he'd decided that she was the lucky one to go first with his little game of vengeful torture. She thought about trying to take him down when he came toward her, but she was worried that his partner would shoot Ryan. The submissive didn't want to shoot anyone, but that didn't mean he wouldn't do it just to please the dominant.

"Don't do it," Ryan ordered, his voice menacing. "You want revenge, you got it. Don't make this worse for yourselves."

The man just huffed a laugh and set the tank down on the floor beside her. Then he grabbed hold of her hand and shoved it into the water, pressing it down firmly onto the poor little sea urchin.

The pain was immediate.

And intense.

But she was sure it was nothing compared to what her daughter had suffered when this man had cut off her finger.

Paige sucked in a breath and breathed through the pain.

"That is nothing compared to what you're going to feel before I kill you," the man snarled in her ear.

She didn't doubt that.

"By the time I'm done with you, you'll both be sobbing your apologies in a sniveling mess on the floor. But it won't do you any good. You'll beg for mercy, but you won't find any. You'll spend the rest of your miserable short lives trapped in this room, suffering, only unlike the innocent people you throw in prison, you'll deserve everything you get."

* * * * *

7:27 A.M.

Her dad had risked his life for her.

No, not risked his life.

He had *given* his life for her.

He was never coming home.

He was going to die.

He was going to be tortured, and then he was going to die.

Sophie couldn't think about anything else. She knew that Uncle

Jack and Xavier were coming to ask her and Hayley some questions soon, but she wasn't sure she'd be able to concentrate.

How could she, when her dad had given his life so she could live?

How could she live her life with the weight of that bearing down on her?

She didn't deserve what he'd done for her.

She had treated him so badly the last few months. She'd told him that she didn't think he loved her, that she didn't love him, that she wished he hadn't raised her, that she wasn't his daughter and never had been.

Sophie wished she could take it all back.

It wasn't true.

None of it was.

She was just scared about whether she was going to be able to be as good a person as her parents were. Her mom had used the money she inherited to start a center to help women and children who'd been abused. And her dad was a cop who risked his life every day for his family and for strangers. She had been so scared that, with the DNA of two terrible people running through her, she could never live up to their example.

And to cover her fears, she'd lashed out in anger.

Now her dad was going to die, and she would never get a chance to tell him she was sorry and to say thank you for being the best father in the world. She couldn't have asked for a better father than Ryan Xander.

"Sweetheart?" Her mother brushed a stray lock of hair off her cheek and tucked it behind her ear.

Sophie blinked and tried to focus. "Yeah?"

"Uncle Jack and Xavier are here."

"Oh," she said, mainly because she thought her mom wanted a response, but she didn't really know what to say. She didn't want to talk to her uncle and his partner about what had happened. She just wanted her dad to come walking through the door. But she knew the only way he was going to come walking through the door was if she and Hayley told them everything they remembered.

"We won't be long, girls," Uncle Jack said. "We know you must be tired."

She was tired.

A weird kind of exhaustion that seemed to run through her bloodstream. She could feel it in every part of her body from her brain to her toes and everything in between.

Her mom shifted on the bed, and for a moment Sophie panicked. "Are you leaving?"

"What? No, baby." Her mother looked as horrified by the possibility of them not being together as Sophie felt. "I was just moving over. I'm not going anywhere."

Sophie was pretty sure she heard her mom mutter *ever* under her breath.

That was okay with her.

She didn't want to be alone ever again.

"What do you remember about the abduction?" Xavier asked.

Sophie reached for her mother's hand before answering. She had to use her left hand, which felt odd because she was used to using her right, but it was swathed in bandages. The doctors must have tended to the wound while she was still unconscious. "I was with Dom; we were talking about getting married." How stupid could she be? She loved Dom but marrying him just to get away from her parents wasn't the right thing to do, for any of them.

"I was supposed to be watching Ari and Rosie, but Sophie called and asked me to come and meet her and Dom," Hayley said. She was curled up in her father's arms, her head resting on his shoulder. "I'm sorry, Daddy, I'm sorry, Jack. I shouldn't have left them alone. I knew better, but Sophie needed me."

"It's okay, baby." Elias kissed the top of Hayley's head.

"It's fine, Hayley." Jack reached over and patted her hand.

"Hayley said we should wait until the next day to get married so we could get a dress and everything," Sophie continued.

"I was hoping to talk her out of it," Hayley admitted. "Sorry, Soph."

"I kind of figured." She smiled at her friend. Hayley was the kind of best friend you dreamed about having. If it wasn't for Hayley, she doubted she would have made it through the last few days.

"We were walking back to my house and talking about Sophie marrying Dom when this van pulled up beside us. A man with a gun jumped out, he grabbed me and told us that if we didn't get in the van, he'd kill us both. We did what he said, and he shoved us inside, put plastic ties on our wrists and ankles, then drove off."

"That's what Rosie and Arianna told us," Jack said.

"What?" Hayley paled. "My sister was there?"

"She and Rosie followed you. They thought something was going on, and they didn't want to be left out," Elias gently told his daughter.

"She could have been taken, too." Hayley began to cry.

"But she wasn't, sweetheart."

"But she could have been."

Hayley sounded near hysterical, and Sophie got it. A ten-year-old girl should never have to go through what they had, and if her little brother had come as close to joining them in that basement as Hayley's sister had, she'd been feeling the same way.

"Your sister is okay, Hayley, and so are you." Xavier took Hayley's hand and tried to refocus her attention. "You and Sophie are safe now, and we want to bring your mom and Sophie's dad home safely too. Anything you girls can tell us could help us do that."

"You're right, I'm sorry." Hayley dragged in a breath and wiped away her tears.

"Don't be sorry, honey," Xavier said. "We know how hard this is. And I wish we didn't have to do this now, I wish we could give you some time to heal before we ask you all these questions, but we have to do this now."

"Did you recognize the man who took you?" Uncle Jack asked.

"Men," she corrected.

"Men?" Xavier and Uncle Jack repeated simultaneously.

"Are you saying there were two kidnappers?" Xavier asked.

"Yes." Hayley nodded.

"There was only one at first. He was the one who kidnapped us and who brought us food while we were in the basement. He liked Hayley, he tried to … you know … with her, but then he was interrupted by this other guy."

"He tried to what?" Elias asked tightly.

"It's okay, Daddy, he didn't," Hayley assured her father, snuggling against him.

"The other man," Sophie continued, "I don't think he was as into it as his friend. I think he interrupted on purpose because he didn't want his friend to hurt Hayley."

"And when the first guy was … you know … with our fingers," Hayley said, "his friend threw up. Everywhere. The other guy got angry with him about it. And when they came down the last time, he said he wasn't going to let the first guy hurt us. I think he's the reason we're still alive."

"Do you know who either of them was?" Uncle Jack asked.

"Sophie thought …" Hayley trailed off and looked over to her.

"What did you think, Sophie?" Xavier asked.

"I'm not really positive," she hedged, not wanting to commit to anything, in case she was wrong. If she was wrong, and she pointed them in the wrong direction, her dad and Hayley's mom could die.

"That's okay," Uncle Jack assured her. "Who did you think it was?"

"I thought the guy who threw up might have been Dom," she told them.

"Your boyfriend?" Xavier asked.

"Why did you think that?" Uncle Jack asked when she nodded.

She shrugged uncomfortably. She didn't like thinking that the man she loved had been involved in what had happened to her and Hayley and that he was keeping her dad from her right now. "It was just a feeling. They kept the balaclavas on the whole time, and he wasn't really around, but I don't know." She shrugged again. "I thought he was Dom."

"If it was Dom, I think he was trying to protect us, make sure we didn't get hurt," Hayley said.

"Only we did get hurt," she said, her eyes falling to her bandaged hand. How could Dom let his friend cut off her finger? Didn't he know that she could never get it back? For the rest of her life, every time she looked at her hand, she was going to remember what she'd been through.

"Do you have any idea where they might have been holding you?" Xavier asked.

"We were drugged when we left, and he put blindfolds on us when we were brought there," Sophie said. She was starting to get a headache. She didn't want to talk anymore; she just wanted to go to sleep and wake up with her dad sitting beside her bed. "I'm tired ... do we have to answer any more questions?"

Uncle Jack and Xavier looked from her to Hayley, whose eyes were already falling closed. "No," Uncle Jack said. "You two did great, telling us that there were two kidnappers and that you thought one was Dominick Tremaine was really helpful and gives us a lot to work with."

Sophie nodded tiredly and rested her head against her pillows. She was so tired. As scared as she was of nightmares, even that couldn't dampen the idea of sleep.

"Close your eyes, sweetheart." Her mom started to smooth her hair, just like she used to do when she was a little girl and was having trouble falling asleep. The motion calmed her and lulled her toward sleep.

A couple of minutes later, she was drifting away.

* * * * *

8:48 A.M.

"We thought that Davis Hilliard couldn't have been the killer because he was here at the station when Ryan and Paige traded themselves for the girls. And the sample he gave us didn't match the DNA sample we got from Brianna, but now that we know we're looking for two people, he's back in as a suspect."

Jack still couldn't believe that his brother and friend would do something that stupid.

And, at the same time, he could.

If it was his daughter who'd been abducted and tortured and the man—or men—who had her had offered him the option of trading himself for her, he would do it in a heartbeat.

He knew how lucky he was that Rosie was still alive.

If the men who'd taken Sophie and Hayley had known that Arianna and Rosie were there, they probably would have taken Ari with them, torturing Paige doubly by having both her girls gone. Rosie wouldn't have factored into the revenge, so they probably would have killed her.

But they hadn't.

The younger girls were fine, and although the older girls had a long road ahead of them, they were going to be fine too. They had been only mildly hypothermic by the time Annabelle had found them. Sophie had needed a couple of stitches to close a cut on her cheekbone, and Hayley had a bite on her shoulder that was infected. The wounds on their hands from their amputated fingers had been tended to, and although the disfigurement would be a constant reminder to the girls of their ordeal, the wounds were not life threatening.

It was the psychological wounds that would be the hardest to heal.

Laura had already made sure that the girls were set up with a counselor. The man who'd counseled Paige after her ordeal with her stalker and who'd worked with Hayley to help her adjust after she was rescued, was going to be working with both girls.

Jack was glad that Sophie and Hayley were getting help. The whole family could probably do with some counseling after this. But if Ryan and Paige didn't come home alive, he doubted any amount of counseling would make a difference.

"We have to find them, Xavier," he said to his partner.

"We will," Xavier said.

He wanted to believe that, but there was no way they could know that for sure.

"We actually have something to work with now," Xavier continued. "We have the DNA from Brianna Lester. We have DNA from the bite mark on Hayley's shoulder. And we have Hayley and Sophie's statements. The girls were pretty positive that Dominick Tremaine was one of the men who took them. We can use that to get a warrant and get a sample from him, and if it matches the samples we already have, then we know it's him. We can go and pick him up. Once we have him, we can get him to give up his partner and the location of where Ryan and Paige are being held."

Xavier made it sound so easy.

Just get a sample from their suspect and match it.

Then get the information they needed.

But nothing about this case had gone easy, so why should this?

"Actually, you don't need to get a warrant for a sample of Dominick Tremaine's DNA." Stephanie came bursting into the room.

"Why?" he asked, not ready to get his hopes up just yet. This had been a really long few days. He was exhausted—they were all exhausted—and he was worried that because of it, they were going to miss something important. And missing something important had never had such significant consequences as it did right now.

Missing something important meant two people he loved might die.

"I got a hit," Stephanie beamed, dropping down into a chair and laying some papers out in front of her.

"On the DNA samples from Brianna Lester and Hayley?" Xavier asked.

"Yep." Stephanie nodded.

"And?" he prompted, not in the mood for a guessing game. He just wanted to know whatever the crime scene tech knew so they could end this.

"And I got a hit in CODIS?"

Dominick Tremaine didn't have a criminal record so his DNA couldn't be in the combined DNA index system. "You got a hit on the partner?"

"No, I got a hit on Tremaine DNA," Stephanie explained.

"A relative is in the system?" Xavier asked.

"According to the DNA, it's Dominick Tremaine's father."

"His father?" Jack asked. They really hadn't looked particularly closely into Sophie's boyfriend because only Ryan had thought the kid could be a suspect. And that was just because he didn't like that the teenager was dating his daughter. From what they did know, the Tremaine boys' father wasn't in the picture.

"And you're going to love what I found when I looked up why the father's DNA was in the system," Stephanie said.

"Which was?" he prompted again. He knew the crime scene tech was excited, but he just wanted to know what they were up against. He had a bad feeling about this. The kidnappers had been controlled at first, but they were devolving. Other than the tattoo, they hadn't physically harmed Talia or Ally, but they'd lost their temper with Brianna, and then, even more so with Hayley and Sophie. Jack didn't think they'd keep Paige and Ryan alive for very long. They would torture them and then kill them; he'd be surprised if they kept them alive for the ninety-nine hours they had with the first three girls.

"Their father was arrested nine years ago for supposedly killing a teenage girl who attended the high school," Stephanie explained.

"Supposedly?" Xavier asked.

"He denied it, claimed he was innocent and that he was being set up. He worked as a groundskeeper, tending to the football field. The girl was a cheerleader. The murder was brutal. Apparently, she left her keys behind after a game, went back to get them, Steve was seen talking to her. The next morning, she was found lying at the fifty-yard line. She'd been cut virtually in half. That was deemed cause of death, the killer had cut through her abdomen and then watched her bleed out. She had also been sexually assaulted."

"They found his DNA inside her?" Jack asked. He hated sexual assault cases because it always reminded him of what Laura had been through when she'd been abducted while she was in college. It was a long time ago, and she'd moved past it, at least as past it as you could ever get when you'd gone through something like that, but every time he worked a rape case, he couldn't help but have a flash of his wife as the victim.

"No. The killer wore a condom. But his jacket was found close by covered in her blood. He was the last person seen with the victim. He had no alibi. And they found one of her hairs in his car. At first, he claimed he just told her that he'd found her keys and handed them over and she left. Then, when they found out about the hair in his car, he admitted he'd made out with her a little, but that was it. He was charged, pleaded not guilty, but was found guilty at the trial."

"Was this an old case of Ryan and Paige's?" he asked. If this was an old case of theirs, then he was surprised that Ryan hadn't used that as a reason to keep Sophie away from Dominick.

"It was, but Steve's last name was actually Noonan. His wife must have changed hers and her kids' names after her husband went to prison. Probably to distance herself from him. Tremaine was her maiden name. Ryan and Paige probably never made the connection, there would have been no reason to."

"And that was nine years ago?" he asked. This was what they'd been looking for. They had forensic evidence to prove that Dominick Tremaine had bitten Hayley. The girls had identified him. They had a link to the number nine. And they had a motive. If Dominick believed his father had been wrongly convicted, and Ryan and Paige were to blame for it, then this all made sense.

"Yes, and it gets better," Stephanie said.

"How so?" Xavier asked.

"Steve Noonan was killed in prison nine months ago."

Nine years ago, Steve Noonan was sent to prison.

Nine months ago, he was killed.

Nine years ago, Dominick Tremaine would have been nine years old.

Nine, nine, and nine.

Dominick Tremaine was one of their kidnappers, but according to what Sophie and Hayley had told them, he was the submissive, not the dominant.

So, who was the dominant?

Everything to do with the Number Nine murders and Sophie and Hayley's abductions and wanting to punish Ryan and Paige was all related to Dominick. But if he was the submissive in the partnership, then why was everything related to him? It seemed unlikely he would have found someone—Davis Hilliard or someone else—who would dominate him but go along with his plan of revenge.

Unless ...

"Do you think that the other man we're looking for is *Victor* Tremaine?"

* * * * *

10:33 A.M.

"How's your hand?" Ryan asked his partner.

"It's fine," Paige replied. The same response she'd given every time he had asked her that question over the last few hours.

He knew his constant questioning was annoying her, but he knew what sea urchin stings were like and how serious they could be. Two years ago, he and Sofia and the kids had gone on a family vacation to Australia. They had visited a lot of beaches, and while surfing at Point Leo beach in Victoria, he'd had the misfortune of accidentally landing on a sea urchin.

The pain had been awful, but the worst was those little spikes. A couple had broken off inside his foot, and he'd actually sustained a little nerve damage in the arch of his foot.

And that was *with* medical intervention.

Paige was sitting in a cold, dank basement, cuffed to a pipe in the wall, with no medical care, and no idea when or even if they were ever going to be found.

He was worried about infection; sea urchin stings got infected quickly. Since they couldn't make sure that all the spines were out, some had probably broken off inside which could cause damage to the tissue, bones, or nerves. Long term, there could be tissue death or joint stiffness or arthritis. And since they couldn't just head down to the hospital if it got worse, an infection could get serious quickly.

"Let me see it," he said. Their abductors had positioned them in opposite corners of the basement, probably because they were afraid that if they were too close to each other, they could work something out to get the upper hand. Being all the way over here meant he couldn't help Paige remove the spines or help monitor the wound.

Paige held up her hand, and he could see it was red and swollen, and there was black and blue bruising where the spines had punctured the skin.

"I wish we could wash that out properly," he said, more to himself than his partner.

"I rinsed it with the water," she reminded him.

"I know, but that's not enough."

"Best we have."

It was. They were going to have to do without antibiotic creams and painkillers. "How's the pain?"

"It's fine."

"Liar," he said. He remembered that his foot had hurt for days after he'd been stung.

"Okay, it hurts, but there's nothing I can do about that right now, so there's no point obsessing over it. We need to decide what we're going to do when they come back down here."

"I think we should confront them on their identities." It was Dominick and Victor Tremaine; he was sure of it. He just didn't know why they were doing this.

Was it because of Sophie?

Ryan didn't really think it could be, because why would they have abducted and killed Talia Canuck, Ally Brown, and Brianna Lester?

That made no sense.

If all Dominick wanted was revenge on him for trying to break up him and Sophie, then they would have just gone after Sophie.

And why bring Paige into this?

The fact that Dominick was the submissive also didn't make sense. If this were about Sophie, then it would be safe to assume this was his plan; therefore, he would be the dominant. But instead, his twin brother was the one in charge.

This was about something else.

They just needed to find out what, so they stood a chance of talking Dominick into doing the right thing.

Ryan was sure they could.

It didn't seem like Dominick really wanted to be doing this; he'd been dragged into it because of his twin.

Divide and conquer. That was the best chance he and Paige stood of getting out of here alive and going home to their daughters.

"They're coming," Paige said, wincing as she jostled her injured hand.

This was going to get worse before it got better, and he was starting to think that neither of them would survive. At least, whatever happened, Sophie and Hayley were alive. And that was all that really mattered. If they were going to die, then Ryan was sure both he and Paige would die content knowing they'd made the right choice and their girls would be able to live long full lives.

Dominick and Victor were still wearing their balaclavas as they carried a large tank down the steps.

At least they knew where the salt water thing had come from. It seemed the Tremaine twins were obsessed with sea life. He hadn't known that Dominick was into fish, although he hadn't really taken the time to get to know the boy his daughter claimed she loved.

Which had been a mistake.

If he had, then perhaps he would have seen that Dominick and his brother were insane.

When they set the tank down on the floor, Ryan could see some sort of blue jellyfish swimming around in there. It was a bluebottle—which wasn't actually a jellyfish. It was a siphonophore, a colonial organism. He'd read up on them when they were planning the trip to Australia since they were found in many coastal waters there.

They also had a very painful sting.

And he was guessing he was about to find out just how painful.

Paige had already been hurt with the sea urchins, so it made sense this one was for him.

"You want us to apologize to you for something, but how can we when we don't even know what we supposedly did?" Ryan asked. He and Paige had been wracking their brains trying to think of any cases they'd worked that the Tremaine boys had been linked to, but they hadn't been able to think of any.

"Not supposedly," the man they believed was Victor hissed. He clearly had a temper, and from the mess Brianna Lester's face had been, a violent temper.

"Then tell us what this is about, Victor," Paige said.

For a second, it was like time froze.

The boys looked at each other, as though they were surprised that they'd figured out their identities.

Then Victor shrugged and pulled off his balaclava. "I guess there's no need for these anymore," he said as he tossed it on the floor.

Dominick also removed his and fiddled with it, nervously staring around the room, deliberately refusing to look at either him or Paige.

If they were going to break either boy, it was Dominick. Victor loved every second of this. There was no way he was going to be persuaded to let them go. But Dominick was the one with the gun, so if they could convince him this was a bad idea, there wasn't really anything Victor could do about it.

"Dominick, thank you for letting Sophie live," he said, focusing on that brother for now.

"Y-you're welcome, D-Detective Xander," Dominick mumbled.

"Don't get any ideas of convincing my brother to let you two go," Victor grinned. "He used up his one 'get what he wants' card. He won't be getting another. And if he messes up again, he's going to find himself joining you." He shot his brother a warning glare.

"Why don't you just tell us what you want us to apologize for," Paige said.

"You don't remember us?" Victor asked, grin back in place.

Ryan honestly didn't.

From the look on Paige's face, she didn't either.

"You know this is a bad idea, Dom," Ryan said, ignoring

Victor. "Killing me is going to hurt Sophie, and I know you care about her." What was strange was that he actually did think that. As much as he hated to admit it, he'd been wrong about Dominick. The kid really did love Sophie, and if it weren't for him, his daughter would be dead right now.

"Don't waste your time, Detective, my brother wants to hurt you just as much as I do. Just because he went soft on your daughter doesn't mean that he doesn't want to watch you suffer. If he weren't as committed to this as me, then he would never have asked your daughter out just to drive you crazy."

So even *that* had been part of the plan.

Ryan had to admit for two eighteen-year-olds, they'd worked out a very detailed and well-executed plan.

"Enough chitchat. If you don't know who we are, then you will soon enough." Victor gestured at Paige and Dominick shot them both an apologetic glance then lifted his gun and pointed it at Paige's head.

As Victor dragged the tank over, Ryan weighed his options. He could try to knock the tank over and use his legs and free arm to get ahold of Victor and use him as a shield. But that would leave Paige unprotected. And as much as he believed that Dominick didn't really want to be doing this, he also knew that he would shoot Paige if he felt backed into a corner.

He didn't see any other options than to play this out the way Victor wanted until they could get through to Dominick and make their move.

Which meant he was going to have to let the bluebottle sting him.

Ryan tried to prepare himself, but the pain that launched through his body when Victor grabbed his hand and shoved it into the tank was off the charts.

* * * * *

11:02 A.M.

"Good morning, Mrs. Tremaine," Xavier said as the woman opened the front door. They were here to talk to Victor and Dominick's mother, and hopefully, find out where the Tremaine boys were hiding out.

Jodie Tremaine had lied to them the other day.

She'd told them that her boys had been at her store by a quarter to five the afternoon that Hayley and Sophie had been abducted, but that wasn't true. Instead, they'd grabbed the girls and taken them and stashed them someplace. They'd thought that it wasn't feasible time wise for the twins to get from the car where they'd been talking with Sophie and Hayley to the van, but it appeared they had. Perhaps they'd had it parked in the street ready to go so all they had to do was circle around and jump in it.

There was a BOLO out on the Tremaine brothers, but he and Jack were hoping that once Mrs. Tremaine realized just how much trouble her boys were in, she would do the right thing and turn them in.

It was a bit of a long shot.

He wasn't sure that he could turn either of his kids into the cops even if he knew that they had kidnapped and killed people. He liked to think that he'd know he was doing his kids a favor because staying on the run increased the chances that they were going to wind up getting shot or killed. But they were his children and he loved them, and he wanted to make everything in the world perfect for them. It was easy now, they were five, they thought he was like a superhero. But one day they would grow up, become teenagers, then adults with families of their own, even if to him, they would always be his babies.

"What are you doing back here?" the woman asked, looking distinctly displeased to see them. Because she knew what they were really doing here? Or just because no one liked a visit from two cops? He wasn't sure yet.

"We need to talk to you about your sons," Jack said.

"This really isn't a good time." Mrs. Tremaine tried to close the door on them.

"We can do this here or down at the station, but we *are* going to be speaking with you," Xavier warned her.

The woman stood there, obviously debating her options.

But she had none.

Ryan and Paige were like a brother and sister to him. He wasn't going to stop until they were home with their families.

Dominick and Victor had abducted them, were holding them—probably torturing them—at this very second. If their mother knew where they were, she would be telling them.

"Fine. Come in." Mrs. Tremaine held the door farther open and led them back into the living room.

The house smelled strongly of flowers.

He hated that smell.

Well, not *hated* it.

He sometimes brought flowers for Annabelle, but she was more of a chocolates kind of girl than a flowers girl. When they did have flowers in the house, it was never this many. There were vases full of them on pretty much every surface in this room, and by the strong floral smell that swamped you the second you walked into the house, he suspected there were just as many in all of the other rooms.

"What is this about?" Jodie Tremaine asked once they were all seated.

"Dominick and Victor abducted and killed three teenagers from their school," Jack said. "They also abducted and tortured Dominick's girlfriend, Sophie Xander, and her best friend, Hayley Hood. And now they are holding two police detectives, Sophie's father and Hayley's mother, prisoner."

"You're joking, right?" Mrs. Tremaine looked shocked, and yet at the same time, not that surprised to learn what they'd just told her.

"No, ma'am, we're not joking," Xavier said.

"How can you know that my boys are the killers you're looking for?"

"Because we have forensic evidence. DNA on one of the murder victims and on Hayley Hood," Jack told the mother. "We aren't here to find out if your sons are the men we're looking for. We already know that they are. We need you to tell us where you think they might be hiding out."

"They're my boys." Mrs. Tremaine's eyes filled with tears.

"We know that. And we know how hard this must be for you, especially given what happened with your husband, but your sons are in a lot of trouble, and the longer they're out there, the worse it gets. Help us bring them in safely."

"So you can throw them into prison and then throw away the key?" she glared at him.

"Prison is the choice that Victor and Dominick made for themselves," Jack reminded her.

"Not Dom." Jodie dropped her gaze to her lap and began to twirl her fingers.

"What?" he asked. It was interesting that she had singled out only one of her boys. Given that they believed Dominick was the submissive and Victor the dominant, he wasn't surprised.

"If—and I mean *if*—my boys really did what you say they did, then it was Victor's idea."

"Why do you say that?" Jack asked.

"Because Victor was so angry," she said softly.

"About his father?" Xavier asked.

Mrs. Tremaine nodded. "My husband claimed he was innocent …"

"But you thought otherwise?" Xavier asked.

"I-he-I-don't think it was the first time. There was a night, about a month before that girl's murder. I woke up, it was like two in the morning, and he wasn't in bed. There was a light on downstairs, and when I went to find out what he was doing, he was in the downstairs bathroom washing off blood. He claimed he had just been out in his shed because he couldn't sleep, and he'd cut himself. But there was no cut. Only blood."

"You let the boys believe that their father was innocent and had been falsely imprisoned?" Xavier asked. It was the only thing that made sense. If Victor and Dominick Tremaine believed that their father was innocent and that Paige and Ryan had arrested him anyway, that would be cause to want revenge on them.

Especially given that their father had been killed while in prison.

"I didn't want them to think badly of him. He was still their father. And I ..."

"You what, Mrs. Tremaine?" Jack asked when she didn't continue.

"I was embarrassed," she admitted quietly. "I didn't want to admit that the man I married was a murderer. So, I changed our names to my maiden name, and I told the boys that the cops set up their dad and that he was innocent."

Xavier shook his head.

That lie—while Jodie Tremaine could never have seen what the future held—had set in motion a series of events that had cost three girls their lives, irrevocably changed two other girls' lives, and could wind up costing Paige and Ryan theirs.

"What was life like after your husband's arrest?" Jack asked.

"We lost the house. I couldn't keep it up on just my wages. My parents ended up loaning me the money to buy a store. I built the business up over the last nine years to what it is now, but it was a lot of work. I would get up at five in the mornings, prepare dinner and get some laundry done, then drop the boys at school, work all day until well into the evenings, then come home, tuck them in, do more laundry, get a few hours' sleep, then get up the next day and do it all over. Those years were tough on the boys and me, but we made it through."

"You seemed to think that it was plausible that Victor might have done this but not Dominick. What is it about Victor that you could believe he would abduct and murder people?" Xavier asked.

"Dominick is a sweet boy, and he really loves your niece," Jodie said to Jack. "He means well, he's quiet and smart and hardworking. He would spend his weekends at the store helping me when he was younger. But Victor, he was ..."

"He was what?" Jack prompted.

"He was the opposite," she said like it explained everything.

"Was he ever violent?" Xavier asked.

"He used to hit his brother sometimes. I mean, more than just siblings fighting kind of stuff. He had a temper. A bad temper. Especially when he didn't get his way. He hated when anyone would cry. I was babysitting my two-year-old niece one day, and he completely lost it when she wouldn't stop crying. After that, I never had her over again. I didn't want to believe that he was like his father, but now, I guess I don't have a choice. I lost my husband, and now, thanks to Victor, I'm going to lose both my sons, because he's taken Dominick down with him. Dom always let his brother take charge. It was like he somehow sensed the darkness inside his twin and did what he had to, to protect himself from it."

"Mrs. Tremaine, do you know where they might be? We have to find them. They traded Sophie and Hayley for Ryan and Paige, the people they think falsely imprisoned their father, which led to his death. We need to find them before they kill them." If it wasn't already too late.

"I don't know. I'm sorry. If I knew, I would tell you. Despite what you think, there's still hope for Dominick. He's a good boy. He's a good boy." Jodie Tremaine started to cry softly.

"Your store," Xavier said thoughtfully. "It's an aquarium, right? You sell exotic fish and other sea creatures." The Number Nine Killer had used salt water to drown his victims. They hadn't known the significance of that, but maybe this was it.

"Yes," Jodie sniffed.

"Is there anywhere where they could hide a victim?" he asked.

"No. I would know if there was a kidnap victim somewhere in the store. But ..."

"But?" he asked feeling hopeful.

"There's another building at the back of the property behind the parking lot. It's where we keep most of the animals. Usually, the boys take care of feeding the animals out there so I can focus on running the store. That building also has a basement."

Perfect.

That had to be where Victor and Dominick had held their other victims and where they were holding Paige and Ryan right now.

Xavier just prayed that when they got there, they found their friends alive.

* * * * *

11:19 A.M.

"How much longer do you think it will be?" Paige asked her partner.

"Until they come back?"

"Yeah."

"If I had to guess, not long. Victor is having too much fun."

Unfortunately, she agreed.

Victor Tremaine loved every second of this.

Dominick Tremaine, on the other hand, did not.

Too bad they couldn't get Dominick on his own. She was sure if they could get him alone for five minutes, they'd convince him to let them go. He didn't want this. He was just going along with it because it was what his brother wanted, and he was afraid of his brother. She could see it in his eyes. He knew what Victor was capable of, and he knew his twin could turn on him in a heartbeat.

Paige was torn.

She wanted to know what was coming next so she could try to prepare herself, and yet, at the same time, she didn't want to know.

Her hand still ached horribly from the sea urchin sting. Besides the black and blue bruising where the spines had pierced her flesh, it was red and swollen, and she could see it was already infected. She had washed it with water from one of the few bottles they'd been given, but the wound really needed to be cleaned out properly.

As did Ryan's.

"Here," she said as she tossed him the last bottle of water. "You should use this on your arm."

After the bluebottle sting, Ryan had pulled off the tentacles and washed the wound, but she could see the red marks it had left behind, and if it was even half as painful as hers, she was sure he was suffering.

"No, you use it," he said, tossing it back. "The pain from mine is mostly gone. It only lasts around thirty minutes. Yours is already infected, and we don't know how much longer we're going to be stuck here or what else they have planned. You should wash yours out again."

"It's already infected. Cleaning it again isn't going to help. Maybe we should keep it for whatever is coming next," Paige suggested. "What other horrible sea creatures do you know about?" Ryan's trip to Australia a couple of years ago was coming in useful.

"There are a lot," he replied. "And I think I can guess what they're going to use to kill us."

She hated those words.

Kill us.

They were so final.

And she wasn't ready for final yet.

She had faced her own mortality before, been in situations where she had been sure she could never survive.

But this was different.

This time, her daughter had been physically and psychologically scarred. Hayley needed her; Ari too. They needed each other, and she hated that she couldn't guarantee she could be there for her girls because that was the promise she'd made to them when she and Elias had adopted them.

"Oh yeah? What?" she asked. She couldn't overthink about her daughters or her husband, or she was going to lose it. It was already a battle to not focus on the pain and let it consume her, but the pain of her injury plus the pain of knowing she wasn't going to make it home to her family were too much.

"Heard of the blue-ringed octopus?"

"No." She shuddered. She didn't really like swimming in the ocean. There were way too many scary things lurking about under the water.

"They're one of the most venomous animals in the sea. They're only small, five to eight inches, and pretty docile, but they're full of a poison that paralyses you."

"Oh," she said as that sank in.

So, they would be paralyzed and suffocate to death.

Great.

She'd been there and done that already, and if she hadn't been saved at the last minute, would have died before she even got a chance to become a mother.

"Try not to panic," Ryan said, reading her mind and exactly which direction it had taken.

"I *am* trying," she said as her breathing began to quicken.

"We don't know anything yet. And I could be wrong. Sophie had to have known that Dominick was one of the men who abducted her. She would have told Jack and Xavier, and they and every other cop in the city will be looking for us."

"Yeah, I know," she said shakily. Being trapped inside her body, unable to move, unable to breathe, was her biggest fear. She still sometimes had nightmares about it.

Before Ryan could say anything else to reassure her, they heard the familiar clunk of the key sliding into the lock.

"They're back," she said a little breathlessly.

It was her turn.

Whatever horrible sea creature they were going to use to torture her with was innocently swimming around in its tank, blissfully unaware of the sinister purpose it was going to be used for.

"Hello, detectives," Victor said cheerfully. "How are we feeling?"

Ignoring the smug teenager, Paige said, "If you want us to apologize for whatever you believe we did that was wrong, then tell us what we did." She didn't recognize either boy and as far as she could recall, she and Ryan had never worked a case with anyone with the last name Tremaine involved. But given the interest in the number nine, the case could be from years ago. The boys would only have been nine years old nine years ago, so it was no wonder they didn't recognize them.

"You sent our innocent father to prison where he was murdered," Victor snapped, smug smile gone. "You said he raped and killed a cheerleader, but you were wrong. Our mother said he was innocent. You framed him, and because of you, he was ripped away from his family, locked in a cage, and then murdered."

Paige exchanged glances with Ryan.

There was only one case she could think of that matched what Victor had just told them, and she believed it was about nine years ago.

"Steve Noonan?" Ryan asked.

Victor nodded. "You framed him, and because of you, he's dead now. And, because of that, soon you will be too."

Despite what their mother had told them, Steve Noonan was guilty. He had raped and viciously murdered that poor girl who had done nothing but forget her keys and gone back for them.

Paige still remembered the girl's naked body, cut almost in two. The killer had sat back and watched as she died a slow and painful death.

Like father like son. It seemed that Victor had inherited his father's vicious streak. They both liked to inflict pain, and just like his father before him, Victor would sit back and watch them die a slow and terrifying death.

"Do you know the pain that our father suffered being locked up, away from his wife and his sons? I wish we could make you feel every inch of it, but this will have to do." He held up a tank with a particularly disgusting looking fish in it. "This guy is a stonefish. It's the most venomous fish in the world, and its sting gives pain I can't even describe. At least, that's what I've heard." He paused and winked at her. "Maybe you can tell us if that's true."

Paige didn't want to touch that thing even if it wasn't poisonous.

But it wasn't like she had a choice.

She was handcuffed to the wall. Her free hand was swollen and infected and hurt when she just rested it in her lap, let alone if she tried to use it to fight back. And, as usual, Dominick was standing with a gun pointed at her partner. If she tried to fight Victor, he would shoot Ryan, and then most likely use the stonefish to hurt her anyway.

She hated being trapped like this.

Helpless.

Those years that her stalker had been in her life had been the most helpless of her life. And when he was finally arrested, she had promised herself that she would never feel that way again.

After how hard she'd fought to get her life back, now she was right back in that same position.

"Maybe we'll use your foot this time." Victor knelt in front of her and reached out to unzip her left boot. "Makes it seem more realistic."

The urge to kick him was strong, but she resisted.

He removed her boot, then her sock, and rolled up the leg of her jeans like her clothing getting wet was her biggest concern right now.

Then he brought the tank over.

She averted her gaze. She didn't want to look at the horrible fish.

"Your daughter is hot, you know. It's too bad that Dom interrupted me before I got a chance to have her," he said, then picked up her leg and shoved her foot into the water.

The pain when her foot touched the creature was immediate and off the charts.

Indescribable.

Bright red dots filled her vision, and although she didn't want to give him the satisfaction, she couldn't stop a scream being ripped out from inside her.

* * * * *

11:45 A.M.

"Hang in there, Paige," Ryan said to his partner, who was curled up on the floor. Her free arm clutched around her stomach while her other hand was hanging limply from the cuff above her head.

Victor and Dominick had taken the tank back upstairs and were probably planning which sea creature they were going to use next in their game of torture. He was starting to think that he and Paige weren't even going to make it to nightfall. Victor was having too much fun. He couldn't drag this out much longer. He wanted more, and once he killed them, he was likely to turn on his brother, and possibly his mother, and then embark on a killing spree that wouldn't end until he was caught or dead.

And Ryan wanted him dead.

For what he had done to Sophie and Hayley, he deserved to die.

Maybe that was wrong of him, but he didn't care. Sophie was his little girl and Hayley was her best friend and neither girl deserved what Victor had done to them.

If the kid blamed him and Paige, he should have taken up the issue with them and them alone. Not with all these innocent teenage girls.

Steve Noonan was a cruel, vicious, psychopath who deserved whatever he'd gotten in prison, and while he was sorry that Victor and Dominick had grown up without a father, it was probably a better life than they would have had growing up with a man like that in the house.

Paige moaned and retched. She had already thrown up twice, and her now empty stomach just kept dry heaving as the unbearable pain took its toll on her body.

Ryan was worried about her.

A sting from a stonefish could be fatal.

Especially, if left untreated.

Paige had basically been out of it ever since the toxin entered her body, and he hated that he couldn't reach her. He couldn't use their last remaining bottle of water to wash the wound, he couldn't even offer much comfort from over here.

"Arrgh," he groaned in frustration.

He wanted out of here.

Now.

He wanted to get Paige to a hospital; he wanted Dominick and Victor in custody; he wanted to see his daughter and hold her in his arms.

Right now, all he could do was monitor Paige's condition as best he could and pray that someone figured out where they were.

"Paige? Can you hear me?" he asked. He knew she was still conscious because she was crying, and her muscles kept spasming as pain coursed up and down her body.

"Yeah," she managed to get out through her labored breathing.

She was already experiencing muscle aches, probably headaches, breathing difficulties, nausea, vomiting, and, from the way she clutched her stomach, abdominal cramps. Abnormal heart rate and reduced blood pressure would be coming if they hadn't already. Then unconsciousness. And then death.

And there was nothing he could do to stop it.

Nothing.

She needed a hospital and proper medical care.

Soon he would too.

At best, he guessed he had maybe half an hour or so before the Tremaine twins came back, and whether he was right about the blue-ringed octopus or not, whatever they had planned next, would probably incapacitate him.

Then it was just a matter of time.

"Paige, just try to hold on, okay?" he said, because he had to do something, however miniscule, and right now, the best he could do was encourage her not to give up.

"Ryan," she sounded weak now. "If you get out of here, tell Hayley I love her, and I'm sorry."

"You can tell her that yourself," he said sharply. He wasn't ready to accept that Paige was going to die or that he would too.

"Please," she said, managing to lift her head a little off the ground to look at him.

How could he say no to that? "You know I will, but just hold on, okay? Fight. We still have a shot at getting out of here."

Paige said nothing.

Just laid her head back down and closed her eyes.

She was fading.

He didn't know how long she had, but even if the stonefish sting didn't kill her, whatever they did to her next, would take out her already weakened body.

Ryan clunked the handcuff against the metal pipe in pure impotent irritation.

Then he froze.

The door at the top of the stairs was shaking.

Were the boys back already?

It couldn't have been more than five or ten minutes tops since they'd left.

He was going to have to push Dominick when they came down. Make him see that this was wrong. The kid already knew it was; he just needed the confidence to stand up to his brother. Victor believed he had his twin under control because he was confident enough to give Dominick the gun. But he believed that if he could just convince Sophie's boyfriend to turn the gun on his brother and use it to keep Victor under control while they called for help, they could all walk out of this basement alive.

The door swung open, two sets of shoes appeared at the top of the steps, but no voice singsonged a mocking greeting.

It wasn't Victor and Dominick, so who was it?

A second later, he got his answer.

The two people descended the steps, and he saw his brother Jack and friend Xavier's faces.

"You found us," he said as relief nearly knocked him over.

"Are they here?" Jack asked, scanning the room.

"No, but I don't know when they'll be back," he replied. "You have to get Paige to the hospital. Now. Victor has this thing with sea animals. He poisoned her with a stonefish, she needs medical attention."

Xavier ran to Paige and crouched at her side, pressing his fingertips to her neck. "Yeah, she needs a hospital now," he said as he pulled out a key to the handcuffs and unlocked her.

Jack kept one eye on the stairs as he came over and unlocked his cuff. Ryan rubbed at his wrist as soon as it was free.

"Don't touch her foot," he said as Xavier moved to check the red and blistered injury. "The toxins could still be on the skin, and then they'll get on you. Who else is with you?" he asked his brother.

"No one. Xavier and I came alone. We knew that Victor wouldn't hesitate to kill you if he was backed into a corner, even if it meant he was killed too."

"We can't risk them getting away," he said, a plan already formulating.

"What are you thinking?" Jack asked.

"Xavier should take Paige to the hospital, and we wait here for them to come back. I can't let them get away. And if they didn't see you arrive, then they have no reason to believe that it's not just Paige and I down here. They know that Paige is already incapacitated, and they think I'm chained up. They only ever come with the one gun, and it's always Dominick who has it," he said.

"How badly are you hurt?" Jack asked, eyeing the red marks on his arm.

"Not that badly. I don't need a doctor right this second," he assured his often bossy and over-protective older brother.

"Why don't you take Paige, and Jack and I wait here for the Tremaine boys to return," Xavier suggested as he shrugged out of his jacket and spread it over Paige's now limp and unresponsive form.

"Because I'm not leaving here until I know that Victor Tremaine is never going to be able to hurt another person," he said. It wasn't up for debate. He wasn't leaving until the Tremaine boys were in custody.

"Ryan, I think—" Jack began.

"No." He cut his brother off. "We don't have time to argue. They could come back at any second. Victor is enjoying this way too much. He's not going to be able to wait long before he comes back with another innocent animal he plans to use to hurt us. Xavier, just grab Paige, get her out of here, lock the door so they won't be suspicious, then call it in and get Paige to the hospital. She needs to be seen by a doctor."

Xavier looked unconvinced, but he carefully picked Paige up

and carried her up the stairs. "Be careful," he called as he closed the door behind him.

"Here," Jack said once they were alone, handing over his backup weapon.

"You should go lie down over where Paige was. That way, he won't realize it's not her until it's too late. And I'll stay here, so everything looks the same when they open the door and come down the stairs. They won't realize we have them until it's too late," Ryan said, adrenalin flowing through his system and rejuvenating him now that he knew he was going home to his family.

His daughter was alive, his partner was alive, he was alive, and soon the Tremaine boys would be arrested.

That was what he called a win, win, win, win.

* * * * *

12:00 P.M.

"Victor—"

"Don't say it," Victor warned. "Not unless you want to end up handcuffed to the wall in the basement next to your girlfriend's father."

"Ex-girlfriend," Dominick muttered.

"Well, duh," Victor laughed. What had his brother been thinking? That after everything they'd done, Sophie would just understand and take him back? Was that why Dom had been so insistent that they not kill Sophie and Hayley?

His brother bristled but didn't say anything.

He knew better.

Victor had always been the dominant one, ever since they were small boys.

It hadn't taken much prodding to get his brother to ask out Sophie Xander. Dominick was good-looking and charming, but shy and quiet, and that combination seemed to be a magnet to girls. They flocked toward his brother, and Sophie had been no exception.

Hayley Hood, on the other hand, had been a tougher nut to crack.

The original plan had been for him to ask out Hayley and Dominick to ask out Sophie. Dom had succeeded, but he hadn't been able to make any progress with Hayley. It was like, on some level, she saw past his good-looking exterior to the evil that lurked just underneath.

It happened more often than it should.

While he never had an absence of girls wanting to go on dates with him, to kiss him, to sleep with him, it never lasted more than a couple of weeks, at the most. He couldn't seem to completely hide who he was, and once they started to get a feeling that he wasn't someone they should stay around, they left.

It was something he was going to have to work on.

He had no intention of going to prison.

He had only just found out how much he liked doing this; he wasn't going to give it up now.

He had so much to learn, so much to experience. He couldn't give it up now. He wouldn't.

Victor knew what he had to do to ensure his freedom. He just had to make sure his brother didn't find out what he was planning until it was too late for Dominick to do anything about it.

"We have to kill the cops. Now," Victor said to Dom.

"I thought you wanted to keep them alive for days, or even weeks," Dominick said, but Victor noted the relief in his eyes.

Sometimes it was hard to believe they were brothers.

Twins, no less.

Identical twins.

Shouldn't they be more … identical?

How could he find inflicting pain an exhilarating rush, while it made his brother throw up?

"The longer we keep them here, the greater the chance we get caught," he explained to his stupid brother. Didn't Dom get it? Didn't he know what they had to do? Didn't he sense it? Whatever had been imprinted on his DNA at conception certainly hadn't been imprinted on Dominick's. His brother was like everyone else. Boring, stupid, kind, no killer instinct. But it was the killer instinct that made you succeed in life. Without it, you were nothing.

"So, we're going to kill them and dump their bodies somewhere?"

"Something like that," he said, trying to hide his smirk. If his brother couldn't sense what he was thinking and what was going to happen next, then he wasn't going to tell him. Where was the fun in that?

"Then this is over?" Dominick asked hopefully. "No more killing?"

Well, not for you, he thought to himself. Out loud, he said, "I guess not."

"There isn't really any need to. The cops who are responsible for framing Dad will be dead. There's no one left to punish."

His brother was right about that.

The people who had stolen his father and his childhood would be dead.

Life after his father's arrest was hard.

His mom worked pretty much nonstop, and they were required to do more chores around the house than most other kids their age. They were also required to help her with the store.

Victor was smart, so keeping up with his schoolwork was easy enough, and he had emotionally blackmailed his mother into allowing him and Dominick to keep playing football. But that was all life consisted of—work, school, and football.

It wasn't like he felt empathy for his mother—he wasn't sure he was capable of that emotion—but he did feel protective of her. And she had lost as much as he and Dom had when his father had been arrested.

Now she could have peace, and they could have peace.

It was over.

Well, it would be soon.

"Once the cops are dead, there's only one thing left to do," he said to his brother.

"What?"

"You know what," he said, waiting for his brother to figure it out.

It took Dominick a moment, but Victor could tell the exact second it hit him because his brother paled. So much so that he thought Dom might actually pass out.

"Sophie?"

"Yes, Sophie. Hayley, too."

"But you promised," Dominick whined. "You said we could let them live."

Victor shrugged. "I changed my mind. It's safer for us if they're dead. We don't want to leave any loose ends."

"Sophie isn't a loose end," Dom snapped.

Whoa.

Was his brother actually growing a spine?

He was impressed.

Not impressed enough to let the girl live, but still, it was nice to see Dominick wasn't a complete wimp.

"She is, and she'll die. Hayley, too." Victor was disappointed that he hadn't had a chance to do her. She was a virgin, and he loved virgins, but there were plenty more fish in the sea. He snickered at his joke. He liked fish. They were small, but they could be so deadly.

He appreciated that.

It reminded him of how he'd felt when he was nine, and the cops had battered down their door in the middle of the night, slapped handcuffs on his father and dragged him away to prison. He'd been small and helpless, and he'd wished he was big and strong enough to punish those cops for what they'd done.

Back then, it hadn't been possible, but now, he was living the dream.

And nothing was going to end it.

Certainly not some stupid fifteen-year-old girl.

"As much as I find this side of you amusing and entertaining," he told his brother, "the girl dies. Once we finish up with the parents, we create a diversion by dumping the bodies someplace nice and visible. Then we go after the girls. Once we kill them, we split."

That was mostly true.

Once they were done with this, there would be some splitting; his brother just wouldn't be involved.

Dominick was going to make sure that the cops left him alone.

They'd have their killer, complete with confession and forensic evidence. There would be no need to look for anyone else. Which would leave him free to do as he pleased.

"Why does she have to die?" Dominick asked.

This assertive side of his twin brother was quickly getting tedious. "Because I say so."

"But—"

"No. No buts. If I say she dies, then she dies. And I don't see why you're getting all upset about it. It's over between you two. You abducted her, held her prisoner, cut off her finger, then kidnapped her father. She's not going to want to still go out with you. She probably hates you. So what difference does it make if she's alive or dead? Either way, she won't be yours."

Dominick frowned, but he didn't say anything else, probably because he had to admit that he was right.

Sophie hated him.

It was over.

"No more arguments?" he asked. He liked having his brother as his willing slave. He was going to miss Dominick when he was dead. His brother had always been there. Every single day of his life. They'd shared a room; they'd played together; they'd hidden under their covers, scared and confused, when their mother sent them back to their room the night their father was arrested. It had always been him and Dom, and now for the first time in his life, it would be just him. It was the end of an era and the beginning of a new one. A better one. One where he could be who he truly was inside without having to hide it.

"Are you sure you don't want to just let the detectives go and end this?" Dom asked.

"Positive." He had never been surer of anything in his life.

"Then I guess I don't have anymore arguments."

"Good. Now, what do you think about that van?" He pointed to a green one painted with flowers that belonged to a local florist. He couldn't use the one from the store anymore. He was concerned that the teacher from school who'd found Brianna Lester's body had seen it, but he needed something to transport the bodies.

"It looks fine," Dominick said dully.

"Then let's go take it, then back to the store to finish off those cops. Then, finally, we can move on."

* * * * *

12:22 P.M.

He was sick of being his brother's yes-man.

He was sick of being weak and spineless.

He was sick of letting someone else tell him what to do when he knew the thing that he was being told to do was wrong.

And he wasn't going to do it anymore.

Dominick knew he should never have allowed his brother to talk him into doing this. He had always known it was a bad idea. It was wrong. And he wasn't even one hundred percent certain that their father was innocent.

Now, it was too late.

He was in way over his head, and he didn't know how to get out.

Or if he even could get out.

Right now, he didn't see how it was possible. He might not have been the one who wrote the message on the bathroom mirrors or done the actual abductions. He wasn't the one who had drowned Talia, Ally, or Brianna. He wasn't the one who had done the tattoos, nor really understood their purpose. Victor had said it was to mark the girls as theirs, but he didn't see it. He hadn't hurt Sophie and Hayley, and he'd stopped his brother from raping Hayley. He hadn't tortured Detective Xander and Detective Hood.

But …

He had been complicit in everything.

He had known what his brother was doing and hadn't done anything to stop it from happening.

That meant he was headed straight to prison.

Dominick wasn't sure if his father was guilty or innocent, but if he went to prison, it would be because that was where he deserved to be.

There might be nothing he could do to save himself. He was never going to be a normal kid. He wasn't going to go to college, and he wasn't going to have a career as a football player like he'd dreamed about since he could run and kick a ball. He was never going to have the future with Sophie that they'd planned. There would be no wedding, no kids, no family, no growing old together.

But there was one thing he could do.

He could make sure that Sophie got all of those things.

He wasn't going to let his brother kill her.

Despite what her parents thought, he loved Sophie. At first, he had only asked her out because his brother told him to, but by the end of their first date, he had already fallen for her. He had known that she was the girl for him, and he had wanted to bail on the plan.

When he'd said that to Victor, the threats had begun.

They might be twins, but Dominick knew that his brother wouldn't hesitate to kill him if he became a liability.

So, he'd put himself before Sophie, and because of that, she had been kidnapped, terrorized, and tortured. He wasn't going to be selfish now. He was going to do whatever it took to make sure his twin brother didn't kill her.

He turned the truck they'd just stolen into the parking lot of their mother's store and parked it close to the building at the back where they kept a lot of the animals. He didn't want to walk in there. He hated that his brother had used those innocent animals to inflict pain on others. That wasn't what those creatures had been made to do. They had those spikes and toxins to protect themselves, not to inflict needless pain and suffering.

"Come on, hurry up," Victor snapped when he didn't get out of the van quickly enough.

He didn't want to have to choose between his twin brother and the girl he loved, but Victor had backed him into a corner. Eighteen years of threatening him into doing what he wanted had driven a wedge between them.

Victor might not know it, but he had just driven the final nail into his own coffin. He could have just stuck with killing the cops and then leaving town, but no, he had to go and insist on circling back and killing Sophie and Hayley first, after already agreeing to let the girls live.

All his life, it had been Victor's way or no way, but that was over now.

Now, for the first time, he was going to have his way.

And his way meant Sophie lived.

"What's wrong with you?" Victor asked as they headed inside.

"Nothing," he said distractedly.

"Then snap out of it. We have to get the blue-ringed octopus ready to go. Then we'll take it down and kill the detectives if the woman is even still alive. Then, as soon as it's dark, we'll load their bodies into the van. You can drive them to the police station, dump them out front. And while you're doing that, I'll go to the hospital. Sophie and Hayley are still there, and when the news breaks that Detective Xander and Detective Hood's bodies have been found, I'll go in, kill the girls, then we can meet up and leave."

Did his brother really think it was that simple?

Did Victor really think he was that stupid?

His brother was so arrogant and self-indulgent that he just thought that everything was going to go the way he wanted.

But Dominick wasn't an idiot, and he knew exactly what his brother had planned.

Victor was going to make him the fall guy.

He was going to kill him, then set it up to make it look like he had been the one who did all of this alone. Then his brother would ride off into the sunset where he would no doubt continue to abduct, torture, and kill people until he was either caught or he himself was killed.

Keeping his face neutral, Dominick nodded. "Okay."

The blue-ringed octopus was tiny and already in a tank of its own, so while Victor picked up the small aquarium, he grabbed the gun and unlocked the door. Victor thought he was so under his thumb that he never even worried about walking around unarmed while he held a gun. The idea that he would turn the gun on him, never even occurred to Victor.

Dominick was so lost in thought that he didn't even notice anything was wrong until the sound of shattering glass caught his attention.

Two guns were pointed at them.

Detective Hood was gone.

Detective Xander was free and one of the men holding a gun on them.

And another man, Detective Xander's brother, was standing beside him.

He wasn't sure what to do.

It was clear that he and his brother were only leaving this room one of two ways.

In handcuffs or in body bags.

As depressing as those options might be, he was relieved.

It was over.

And Sophie was safe.

There was only one thing left to do.

"Get down on your knees, hands on your heads," one of the detectives ordered. He wasn't really paying attention to which one; all his attention was focused on his brother.

"Don't do it, Dominick," Detective Xander said, apparently reading his mind.

"He hurt Sophie," he muttered, glaring at his brother.

"Oh, relax." Victor leaned against the wall as though they were friends standing around hanging out. "He's too soft to pull the trigger."

Anger surged through him.

At his brother, but mostly at himself.

It was his fault that Victor thought he was a pathetic, spineless, jellyfish.

He had never once in his life stood up for himself or what he believed in.

Well, not this time.

This time he wasn't backing down.

Victor had hurt the woman he loved, scarred her for life, and he deserved to die.

"Put the gun down, Dominick." Detective Xander took a step closer while his brother also kept a gun trained on Victor.

"He was going to kill you, then go and kill Sophie," Dominick growled.

Detective Xander paled, but his hand didn't shake, it continued to point the gun at his head. "And we're going to arrest him. He'll spend the rest of his life in prison."

That he would, too, didn't even enter Dominick's mind.

All he cared about was punishing Victor.

Sophie's screams as the pruning shears snapped her finger off echoed in his head. Her blood dripping down onto the floor. The pain on her face.

She was the sweetest, kindest girl he'd ever known.

She hadn't deserved that.

She deserved this.

She deserved to know that the man who had hurt her was dead.

Maybe that would help her move on.

"Arresting him isn't enough," he said.

Without hesitation, he fired.

The bullet seemed to fly through the air in slow motion.

It hit its target.

Piercing Victor right between the eyes.

Surprise filled his brother's face.

Memories seemed to pass between them.

Pushing each other on the swings, chasing each other around the garden, racing each other on their bikes up and down the street, walking into school together on their first day of kindergarten.

Dominick felt the exact moment his brother's life ended.

It felt like peace.

He was free.

He moved the gun, so it pointed at his own head.

"Don't do it, Dominick. Sophie will be devastated," Detective Xander said.

"She hates me," he contradicted. He had done the right thing by killing the man who'd hurt Sophie, but that didn't fix things. Victor had been right when he'd said that things were over with him and Sophie, and without her, he had nothing to live for.

"She loves you. I don't know if she can forgive you for what you did, but she wouldn't want you to kill yourself. Put the gun down, and put your hands on your head."

Was her father right?

Would Sophie not want him to kill himself?

Alive meant spending his life in prison, but it meant that there was always hope he could get Sophie back.

Slowly, he lowered his arm and let the gun fall from his fingers.

The second the gun was out of his hand, the cop pounced on him, yanking his hands behind his back and snapping on handcuffs.

But he didn't care.

Victor was dead, and maybe one day Sophie could be his again.

* * * * *

2:46 P.M.

"Why hasn't she woken up yet?"

"Because her body needs sleep to recover," her dad said, slipping an arm around her shoulders and pulling her closer.

"But it's been hours," Hayley said.

Hours.

Hours of sitting beside her mom's bed waiting for her to wake up so Hayley could tell her how sorry she was.

She should never have snuck out of the house that afternoon and left her ten-year-old sister and her friend home alone. She never should have let Sophie get so carried away and fall so hard and fast for a guy who was three years older than them. She never should have got herself into a situation where her mother had to trade herself so she would be set free.

This was all her fault.

"Mark said it might take a few hours," her dad reminded her.

Hayley knew that, but she thought the few hours would be up

by now.

Maybe something was wrong.

Maybe her mom was sicker than Mark had told them.

Everyone had been in her and Sophie's hospital room when Xavier had called to say that he and Jack had found her mom and Sophie's dad and that they were alive. But her mom had been hurt, and he was bringing her to the hospital.

Dad had wanted her to stay in bed, but she'd insisted that she had to see mom the second she arrived.

And she hadn't left her mother's side since.

She'd held her mom's hand while Mark pulled out the spines from some fish with a pair of tweezers. He'd washed out the wounds with soap and hot water and given her medication and oxygen.

Mark had said she was okay, but he could be wrong.

"Maybe you should go get Mark," she said to her dad.

He kissed the top of her head. "Mom will be okay, sweetheart; she just needs some more time to rest."

"I want her to wake up now."

"I know, baby." Her dad gave her another kiss, then reached out and stroked Mom's hair.

Hayley knew she was unfair. She knew that Dad was as worried about Mom as she was. She also knew that he loved her just as much as she did and that they both wanted her to wake up so they could convince themselves that she was okay.

"Maybe you should go and lie down for a while. I'll call you when she wakes up," Dad suggested.

"I don't need to sleep. I'm fine," she said. And it was true. Physically, at least. Her finger, or where her finger used to be, still hurt a little, but it was more a distant ache. It wasn't bad. And the drugs Victor and Dominick had given her had mostly worked their way out of her system. Now she was just tired. A weird kind of tired. It was like every single cell in her body was completely wiped out.

But there was time to sleep later.

After she knew that her Mom was okay.

"Daddy," she half sobbed. She didn't want to cry, but she had to know that Mom was okay. And to do that, Mom had to wake up. If she didn't wake up, Hayley didn't think she'd ever be able to cope with the guilt.

"Shh." Her dad pulled her into a hug, and the two of them just held onto each other and cried. She had never seen her dad cry before. It scared her almost as much as the thought of her mom never waking up.

She just wanted everything to go back to the way it had been before.

Only she knew that was impossible.

What had happened to her would change her.

There was no going back.

All she could do was try to find a way forward.

"I'm scared, Daddy," she whispered into her father's chest. When she'd first been adopted, she'd thought her new dad was the biggest, strongest man in the whole world. He'd been able to scare away all the monsters in her life. But now, she was old enough to know that there were monsters in the world her father couldn't protect her from.

"Hayley?"

She spun around at the sound of her name.

Her mother stirred on the bed and slowly opened her eyes.

"Mommy!" She practically threw herself at the bed.

"Are you okay?" Her mother struggled to sit up.

"Stay still." Dad pressed on Mom's shoulders, so she laid back against the pillow, then used the controls to elevate the bed.

"I'm fine, Mom," she assured her. "Are *you* okay?"

"I'm fine. Perfect." Her mom winced as she settled back onto the mattress, but the smile on her face said that her words were true.

"I'm so sorry, Mom," she said. Tears began to trickle down her cheeks.

"For what, sweetheart?" Mom reached out and brushed her tears away.

"I shouldn't have left the house that day. I shouldn't have left Ari and Rosie alone. I'm sorry. I'm sorry," she said again. Hayley wanted her mom to make her feel better, but she wasn't sure it was possible.

"Come here." Her mom held out her arms and Hayley folded into them. "It's my fault, sweetheart. It was me they were angry with. They just hurt you because of me. I'm so sorry, baby."

"It's not your fault, Mom. It's Victor's. He's the one who did this. He's the one who convinced Dominick to kidnap us. He's the one who hurt us, who hurt you. It was Victor. It wasn't you; it was all Victor."

Mom smiled, but Hayley could see in her eyes that she didn't believe it.

Hayley didn't either. She still felt partially responsible.

But maybe one day they would get to a place where they could place the blame on the only person it belonged and not on themselves.

"Mom." The door flew opened, and Arianna torpedoed the bed. Launching herself onto it and into Mom's arms.

Dad joined them, and the four of them held onto each other.

They were a family. The only way they were getting through this was together.

* * * * *

3:04 P.M.

What was taking so long?

Sophie hadn't felt this nervous in a long time.

She shouldn't.

She was only waiting to see her dad.

Waiting.

And waiting.

And waiting.

What was taking him so long?

She knew that he was okay. She knew that Victor was dead, and Dominick had been dragged off to prison. She knew that her dad only had minor injuries and that he was going to be okay.

She knew all of that, and yet, how could she believe it until she saw him with her own two eyes?

It didn't help that Paige had been brought in here unconscious after whatever Dom and his crazy brother had done to her.

What if everyone was lying to her?

What if her dad wasn't okay?

What if he was unconscious like Paige?

Or worse?

What if he was dead, and they were just scared to tell her because of what had happened to her?

"Mom?" She looked up at her mother who hadn't left her side since she'd woken up here. She liked that. It was comforting.

"Dad is fine, Soph. I spoke to him on the phone."

Right.

That was right.

Mom had asked if she wanted to speak to him, too, but she'd said no. She couldn't quite remember why.

"How did you know what I was going to ask?" she asked.

"Because I'm your mom."

Sophie smiled at that. "Yeah, you are."

Her mom smiled back.

Everything was going to be okay. Her boyfriend might have turned out to be a psychotic killer, but at least she had her family back. She just wished it hadn't been like this. She wished it hadn't taken something so dramatic to make her realize just how much she loved her family.

Family was life.

They were more important than the oxygen you breathed, the water you drank, the food you ate.

They were what kept you going when you didn't have any of those things.

Her family was the only reason she was alive now.

If it hadn't been for them, she wouldn't have had the strength to survive being chained up in that basement.

And without them, she would never have the strength she needed to survive the next few months, which she knew was going to be no small feat.

When she heard the door opening, her head snapped in that direction.

Her dad stood there.

Her eyes scanned him in search of any injuries. Other than a bandage peeking out under the cuff of his shirt, he seemed okay.

He was okay.

She was okay.

They had survived.

And now they had each other back.

"I'm so sorry, Daddy, Mom. I'm sorry for how I've acted for the last few months. I'm sorry for saying you weren't my parents and that I hated you. I'm sorry that I was ungrateful for the wonderful home you gave me. I'm sorry that I was so much trouble. I'm sorry that I let Dom come between us. I'm sorry." The words tumbled from her lips in a rush. Everything that she'd been thinking, while she was in the basement, and prayed she'd survive, so she got a chance to say them.

"We're sorry, too, sweetheart." Her dad came and sat on the bed beside her and took her bandaged hand gently in his. "We should have told you sooner."

"I understand why you didn't," she assured him.

"We didn't handle things very well even after we told you," Mom said.

"We wanted to give you space and time to adjust; we knew

what a big shock it was. We tried to make it better by letting you act out your anger anyway you wanted. But I think that made it worse. I think that by us doing that, it gave you the impression that we didn't care enough to discipline you, and that reinforced your feelings that we weren't your biological parents," her dad said.

"It wasn't that. I was scared," she admitted.

"Of what?" her mom asked.

"Of turning out like my biological parents."

"I felt the same way when I learned the truth about who my parents really were," her mom admitted.

"You did?" she asked hopefully. Maybe her mom really did understand.

"I was terrified. I was convinced that with their DNA inside me, I was going to turn out like them. But you know who helped me work through those feelings?"

"Who?"

"Your dad." Her mom smiled at her husband and reached for his hand, making them their own little family triangle.

"I should have let you and Dad help me too."

"I think it's safe to say we all made some mistakes," Dad said.

"I think my biggest was trusting Dom." She dropped her gaze. How was she ever going to be able to date again knowing that the first guy she'd ever fallen in love with had turned out to be a killer?

"I don't think so," her dad said.

"What?" she asked, surprised. Her dad had spent all these months hating her boyfriend, and now that they knew the truth about him, he'd changed his tune?

"He killed his brother for you."

"He did what?"

"Apparently Victor was going to come back and kill you and Hayley after he killed Paige and I, but Dominick wasn't going to let that happen. He finally found the strength to stand up for himself and break out from under his brother's thumb, and that was all because of you. Despite what he did and the mistakes that he made, I believe that he truly loved you."

Sophie absorbed that.

Dominick really *had* loved her.

Everything else had been a lie except for that.

At least, it was *some*thing to hold on to.

Maybe she wasn't completely terrible at falling in love.

Maybe she wasn't the world's worst daughter either.

"I love you, Mom and Dad, and even if my biological parents were still alive, they'd never be more of a mom and dad to me than you've been."

She was crying, Mom was crying, even her dad had tears in his eyes.

"You better go get Ned." Sophie smiled through her tears. "Then we can do the whole family hug at the end of a tragedy thing."

Jane has loved reading and writing since she can remember. She writes dark and disturbing crime/mystery/suspense with some romance thrown in because, well, who doesn't love romance?! She has several series including the complete Detective Parker Bell series, the Count to Ten series, the Christmas Romantic Suspense series, and the Flashes of Fate series of novelettes.

When she's not writing Jane loves to read, bake, go to the beach, ski, horse ride, and watch Disney movies. She has a black belt in Taekwondo, a 200+ collection of teddy bears, and her favorite color is pink. She has the world's two most sweet and pretty Dalmatians, Ivory and Pearl. Oh, and she also enjoys spending time with family and friends!

To connect and keep up to date please visit any of the following

Amazon – http://www.amazon.com/author/janeblythe
BookBub – https://www.bookbub.com/authors/jane-blythe
Email – mailto:janeblytheauthor@gmail.com
Facebook – http://www.facebook.com/janeblytheauthor
Goodreads – http://www.goodreads.com/author/show/6574160.Jane_Blythe
Instagram – http://www.instagram.com/jane_blythe_author
Reader Group – http://www.facebook.com/groups/janeskillersweethearts
Twitter – http://www.twitter.com/jblytheauthor
Website – http://www.janeblythe.com.au

sic enim dilexit Deus mundum ut Filium suum unigenitum daret ut omnis qui credit in eum habeat vitam aeternam

CPSIA information can be obtained
at www.ICGtesting.com
Printed in the USA
BVHW041044180523
664421BV00010B/23